MW01286636

BY AMY TAYLOR
*Search History*
*Ruins*

# RUINS

THE DIAL PRESS
NEW YORK

# RUINS

A NOVEL

## AMY TAYLOR

The Dial Press
An imprint of Random House
A division of Penguin Random House LLC
1745 Broadway, New York, NY 10019
randomhousebooks.com
penguinrandomhouse.com

Copyright © 2025 by Amy Taylor

Penguin Random House values and supports copyright. Copyright fuels creativity, encourages diverse voices, promotes free speech, and creates a vibrant culture. Thank you for buying an authorized edition of this book and for complying with copyright laws by not reproducing, scanning, or distributing any part of it in any form without permission. You are supporting writers and allowing Penguin Random House to continue to publish books for every reader. Please note that no part of this book may be used or reproduced in any manner for the purpose of training artificial intelligence technologies or systems.

THE DIAL PRESS is a registered trademark and the colophon is a trademark of Penguin Random House LLC.

Originally published in Australia in 2025 by Allen & Unwin.

LIBRARY OF CONGRESS CATALOGING-IN-PUBLICATION DATA
Names: Taylor, Amy, author.
Title: Ruins: a novel / Amy Taylor.
Description: First edition. | New York, NY: The Dial Press, 2025.
Identifiers: LCCN 2025014508 (print) | LCCN 2025014509 (ebook) |
ISBN 9780593595602 (hardcover; acid-free paper) |
ISBN 9780593595619 (ebook)
Subjects: LCGFT: Novels.
Classification: LCC PR9619.4.T34 R85 2025 (print) |
LCC PR9619.4.T34 (ebook) | DDC 823/.92—dc23/eng/20250414
LC record available at https://lccn.loc.gov/2025014508
LC ebook record available at https://lccn.loc.gov/2025014509

Printed in the United States of America on acid-free paper

2 4 6 8 9 7 5 3 1

First U.S. Edition

BOOK TEAM: Production editor: Cara DuBois • Managing editor: Rebecca Berlant • Production manager: Mark Maguire • Proofreaders: Liz Carbonell, Alissa Fitzgerald, Tess Rossi, Jennifer Sale

Book design by Elizabeth Rendfleisch

Title-page art: scaliger/Adobe Stock

The authorized representative in the EU for product safety and compliance is Penguin Random House Ireland, Morrison Chambers, 32 Nassau Street, Dublin D02 YH68, Ireland. https://eu-contact.penguin.ie

FOR CHRIS AND TEDDY

# RUINS

The passengers on the early evening flight from Athens to London Heathrow Airport were waiting impatiently. The plane, having landed half an hour before, was sitting idle on the tarmac while a delay of some kind kept the cabin doors closed. The sudden flurry of activity brought on by the landing—the unclicking of seatbelts, the retrieval of phones and bags—had subsided, and most of the passengers had now settled into a reluctant stillness, puncturing it only with the occasional sigh. In the middle of the plane, a man stood in the aisle, stooping as he attempted to entertain his restless and exhausted toddler. An older woman stood behind him, smiling at the red-faced child while her husband contorted himself in an effort to rummage through his belongings. The space the older couple took up prevented the woman in the window seat of their row from also standing in the aisle to stretch her legs. She glared ahead with annoyance. In the row behind her, a young couple remained seated, scrolling on their phones. For rows and rows behind them, more people fidgeted or sighed or stretched. The mood was melancholic. Their summer holidays were over and their optimistic, carefree attitudes had expired. The color the sun had imparted on their faces—ham pink, mostly—now looked peculiar, like a fancy-dress costume worn the day after the party. Frowns tugged at the corners of their mouths at the thought of the responsibilities they'd temporarily escaped, which now awaited them when they unlocked the doors to their flats. At this point, the joyful memories of their holiday were inaccessible. It would only be days later, when a colleague or friend inquired about their trip, that they would begin to recall the holiday in rosy, selective vignettes, a form of voluntary repression that enabled them to silence the creeping, regretful notion that perhaps they should have chosen to spend their yearly summer holiday in Sardinia or Majorca, instead of an island in Greece.

After forty minutes of waiting, an attendant's voice crackled over the intercom to announce the names of two passengers and request they report to the officer who was waiting for them after they disembarked. The announcement sent a surge of reenergized murmurs through the cabin.

"Did they just say a police officer is waiting for them?"

"I think so."

"Well, you don't hear that every day."

"Do you think they're in trouble?"

"Could be."

"Does sound like it, doesn't it?"

"I wonder why."

Heads swiveled to locate which passengers the announcement concerned. Catching the scent of a good story, the older woman turned her attention away from the child and back to her husband, who was patting his pants pocket to confirm the presence of their passports.

"I wonder what happened," she said, unable to conceal the excitement from her whisper.

"Not a clue," he answered, now searching his jacket pocket. "But it sure sounds like *their* holiday didn't go too well."

# ACT I

Marvelous things happen to one in Greece—marvelous good
things which can happen to one nowhere else on earth.

Henry Miller, *The Colossus of Maroussi*

# CHAPTER ONE

It was the sound of a child laughing, a sudden peal that pierced through the layers of sleep and delivered Emma back to the surface. She peered into the darkness of the inside of her sun hat and then slowly lifted it from her face, allowing her eyes to adjust to the blast of white sunlight. Julian's towel was empty next to her, his novel lying splayed and abandoned. She located him in the ocean directly ahead of her, where he floated serenely on his back.

The child squealed again, and Emma turned in the direction of the sound. A family was setting themselves up on two of the deck chairs nearby. The mother had long blond hair arranged over one shoulder, and she wore an elegant red one-piece bathing suit and a large pair of tortoiseshell sunglasses. A sleeping newborn was slung from a piece of beige fabric fastened around her torso. Emma watched the woman as she moved in a businesslike manner, unpacking a tote of toys, snacks, and water bottles, before battling with the umbrella to adjust the shade covering the chairs. Meanwhile, the father walked their giggling toddler across the sand, growling theatrically, before grabbing the child and inciting another shriek of laughter. The mother, now spreading towels over the two chairs, had taken her sunglasses off, and even with the distance, Emma could see the deep, dark rings of total exhaustion underneath her eyes.

"It's beautiful in there." Julian sighed, collecting his book before dropping onto his towel. Emma could feel the lingering cool of the water radiating off him the way heat would. "Are you going back in?"

She nodded. "I think I'll have one more dip."

He located his sunglasses before lying on his back and closing his eyes. The heat was already drying the salty water into chalky lines on his skin.

They'd arrived in Palaiokastritsa, on the island of Corfu, four days before, and already Julian's brown hair had been bleached under the sun, resembling the kind of sought-after balayage that would cost hundreds of pounds in a salon back in London. To add insult to injury, he'd also developed a deep, consistent tan, which made him look younger and healthier—carefree, even. Emma's own pale skin did not take to the sun so willingly; it was provoked and antagonized, and in response, it spread brown freckles across her chest, face, and arms as if in defense, the numbers increasing daily. Her cheeks were perpetually florid. She'd taken to applying bright red lipstick when they went out for dinner in the hope that, by comparison, the color of her cheeks would appear more like an innocent, peachy flush.

On their first day, as they followed the sloping streets down to Agia Triada beach, Emma realized she'd left her hat in the room. The price of that mistake was a burnt scalp that hurt whenever she brushed her hair. It had begun to peel too. Just that morning she'd extracted a disturbingly large scale of skin and held it between two fingers, staring at the tiny pinpricks through which her hair had once grown. "Look at this," she'd said to Julian, who was reading an article on his phone in bed. "I just pulled this off my scalp." She walked over to him and held the piece of skin close to his face. He narrowed his eyes as he looked, and when the realization dawned, he recoiled. "Oh, gross," he groaned. She laughed and threw it at him.

The mother called out to her husband in a language that sounded like German, and Emma saw Julian turn to look over at the family. She watched his lips unconsciously pull into a small smile as the father hoisted the child over his shoulder and returned to the deck chairs with his squirming, giggling captive. Emma felt a small, hard rock of dread in her stomach, like the pit of an apricot. The dread wasn't new; Julian's smile had just reminded her of its constant presence.

Before they discovered that Emma was pregnant, they'd had no desire to have children of their own, a mutual agreement they'd established early on. The matter was closed and never reopened for discussion, not even as they progressed into the first half of their thirties—Emma trailing two years behind Julian—and watched the couples around them introduce children to the world. Even then, they would smile and embrace these new members of their life, feeling a love for them that was immediate and intense, as if they were simply an extension of the people they loved already.

It was a shock then when the test was positive. Slowly, as they contemplated a new and different future, Emma watched Julian realize that, yes, actually, he did want this for himself. He took charge, walking excitedly ahead into this new territory as Emma apprehensively followed behind, unable to feel the same certainty that they were going in the right direction.

Glancing back now at the family, she saw the woman was breastfeeding the newborn, grimacing as she did so while attempting to entertain the restless toddler who, at that inconvenient moment, was demanding to sit on her lap and was growing increasingly hostile against her redirections. Meanwhile, the father was looking at his phone. Emma stood and walked toward the water, not stopping when she reached it, nor when the cool water hit her knees, and then her thighs, and eventually her stomach. She dived and reemerged, pushing her hair out of her face and allowing the shock to bring her firmly back into her body. She mimicked Julian and floated on her back for a moment, feeling the strange sensations of muted sound and warm sunlight as the water covered her ears and the sun shone down on her face. She tried to remain firmly present in the corporeal sensations, but in her mind, she saw the hopeful yearning on Julian's face as he watched the young family.

When, at eleven weeks, Emma had a miscarriage, she and Julian were left adjusting their image of the future back to its original vista. It was then that she realized Julian was struggling to return. Of course she could sympathize with him; it was as if their names had been called out, and they had been ushered into a new room, only to be informed of the mistake and told to return. She suspected that, for him, the room they returned to, and had never previously been dissatisfied with, suddenly felt small and stifled, lacking in mystery and in a depth of feeling he'd only glimpsed and yet now missed. From that moment, he understood that he wanted to have children, and he'd simply assumed that Emma felt the same. He seemed to take for granted that they would try again, mentioning it here and there and watching young families with an open longing. Unsure of how to delicately approach this discussion,

Emma had passively allowed his belief to grow. Soon, she surprised herself by wondering if having a child with Julian would actually be easier than ripping the root of his hope from the ground.

Seeking some other thread of thought, she opened her eyes and began to tread water, tracing the shelf of land that ran along the left of the Agios Spiridon beach and curved around to shelter it. Where the cliffs met the water, a group of people were taking turns leaping from the edge. Their laughs and shouts were carried to her by the breeze. She watched as the small figures of their bodies dropped into the water, some controlled, others flailing, and all of them, she thought, landing far too close to the rocks below. She recalled the grim story of a boy she'd attended sixth form with who'd gone cliff jumping in Malta. On one descent, he failed to break the water's surface tension with his feet, landing instead on his coccyx and shattering his spine. His vertebrae, so the story went, had been like a line of fast-moving traffic, and it was as if the car at the front of the line had slammed on the brakes.

Emma watched as one jumper seemed to almost tumble from the cliff, waving their arms and legs as they fell. When they connected with the water, a sharp slapping sound ricocheted around the bay. Emma gasped, unable to stomach the moments before they either did or didn't surface, and turned away.

Later, when the sun crept lower in the sky, and the bass from the surrounding bars and restaurants began to hum, they packed up their things and followed the dusty path that traced the bends of the road back to the small family-run hotel where they were staying.

To get to their room, they first had to walk up a steep driveway, past the pool and the poolside bar where Nico, the owner's son, could often be seen watching something on his phone when he wasn't being ordered around by the elderly couples who spent all day camped on the pool chairs drinking beer and eating peanuts. They waved to him as they passed, receiving a smile in response.

"Spiridon today? Or Triada?" he called out, tapping his phone screen and removing his headphones. They'd asked him for advice on where to swim on the second day, and since then, he'd taken to inquiring about their beach experiences each day.

"Spiridon," Julian replied.

"Busy?"

"It was pretty quiet, actually."

"Good." He beamed. "Going out for dinner tonight?"

"We're going to that taverna you recommended."

Nico's phone vibrated in his hands, drawing away his attention. Emma imagined some other Greek teenager sending Nico flirty messages and provocative photos from another island where they would be spending the summer holidays with their own family.

"Enjoy your dinner," he said without taking his eyes from his phone.

Back in their room, they showered together, taking turns holding the showerhead up, which was attached to the wall by a rubber cable and had nowhere to be hung from.

After they changed, they returned once more to the driveway and made their way back to the gravel path, tracing through the olive groves toward the beach and restaurants. Emma followed behind Julian as they walked. He wore a white linen shirt and brown pants. His hair, still damp, was slicked back, and his face gleamed. It was now golden hour and the sun's slow departure had relieved them of the day's harsh and dry heat, allowing them to float comfortably through the thick air and to admire the soft, pastel colors the sun left in its wake. It seemed to Emma that she and Julian transformed into the best versions of themselves when they were free to swim in the ocean, siesta whenever they desired, and reach for each other's bodies upon waking in the morning and sometimes again in the afternoon, after the sun had sapped any energy for anxiety and blunted their minds into contentment. She wondered whether it was possible for them to exist like this permanently, or whether the charm of the circumstances only existed because of its novelty.

They found the taverna Nico had recommended: a lively, homey place with paper tablecloths and photos on the walls of smartly dressed people who Emma assumed owned the place. Their arms were over each other's shoulders in the photos and they were standing in front of the bar at the back of the room. It was a shinier, more vibrant restaurant than the version they sat in now, the passage of time having stripped the space of its youthful glamour but still left it warm and inviting. They ordered octopus, swordfish, and some sort of stuffed tomato dish paired with a jug of wine. The wine was called *retsina* and was infused with a form of pine resin. It was a pale, translucent yellow color and often tasted as though it could probably be used to remove nail polish, but the ambience of the soft light reflected on shimmering water and the unassertive breeze that surrounded them made enough astringent mouthfuls surmountable until they acclimatized.

The food arrived and Emma squeezed the juice from a lemon wedge over it all. Back in London, she would buy a lemon if a recipe demanded it, only to use a quarter of it before leaving the rest to shrivel in the fridge. She had never truly appreciated the sharp, acidic cut, but now, on the rare occasion a lemon wedge didn't arrive on the plate, she missed it, each lemon-less mouthful playing out like a song stopped just before its chorus.

"Alistair emailed to explain where the key is," Julian said, placing his glass back down on the table. The echo of a grimace caused by the wine was still present on his face. "He's left it with the staff at the pharmacy near the apartment building."

Alistair was an old friend of theirs. They were leaving Corfu the day after tomorrow and would be house-sitting his apartment in Athens for three months while Julian worked on his research paper. Emma had met Alistair a few times when he'd come to stay on the couch of their London flat. He was a short and solid man with wispy, receding dark hair. When Emma thought of him, she remembered his habit of biting his thumbnail when he thought no one was looking or the gesture of him running a finger back and forth over his top lip as he pondered what someone was saying around their dinner table.

He was currently writing a text on Gorgias, the ancient Greek sophist, and had been invited to spend a few months in Lentini, Sicily—the native home of the philosopher—to work on it.

"Is he excited about Sicily?"

Julian brought his eyebrows together and frowned thoughtfully.

"He is. It will be good for his work, but he admitted to me that the move was partly motivated because Andre is back in Athens."

"Is he the married man Alistair was in love with?" Emma asked.

"Yes, well, arguably *still* in love with."

Emma pictured Alistair in her mind; he was not a conventionally handsome man, but he had a sort of intellectual energy, a deepness of thought, that Emma could see someone desiring. He was exactly the type of man who was only capable of desiring someone if he could not easily have them.

The waiters began to clear space close to the bar; those seated nearby were politely requested to stand and help move their tables out of the way. The music was turned up and some of the diners began to dance in the space that had been cleared. The two waiters then brought trays covered with small glasses of ouzo around, dispensing them to everyone. Emma and Julian accepted theirs, smiling at each other before tipping the liquor back and wincing as the aniseed taste burned away the taste of the wine.

"No, no." The waiter returned to the table. "To drink slowly—to enjoy," he explained, pointing to their empty glasses.

"Oh." They laughed. The waiter tutted and served them two more. This time, they sipped them.

More and more patrons were recruited to the floor. An experienced older couple twirled each other around with their eyes trained on each other. Some sort of colorful disco light was set up and the waiters continued to hand out small glasses of ouzo. Emma appreciated the business intelligence of the transformation. Rather than the patrons paying their bills and the restaurant closing its doors until tomorrow night, some would now stay, buying more and more drinks and doubling, even tripling their bill. And the whole scene would entice more people walking by on the street to join in the fun.

Julian looked at Emma with a smile on his face. "Want to dance?"

The second glass of ouzo encouraged her, and she observed the other tourist couples who were laughing as they attempted to join in the dancing. "Yes." She grinned.

They had no idea what they were doing, but they managed to fall into some sort of stumbling, swaying rhythm, accompanied by the occasional twirl and broken in parts as they laughed into each other's ears.

After the song finished and another began, a woman approached them. Emma had noticed the woman greeting people in the taverna earlier with the air of welcoming them into her home. Now she stood before them, holding her hand out to Julian and proposing a dance. Julian laughed, suddenly shy, and looked to Emma as if for permission or perhaps rescuing. She nodded to him in encouragement, and after the woman dragged him away, she moved from the dance floor to stand by the bar and watch. The woman, possibly in her fifties, had a thick, strong-looking body. She took hold of Julian, and Emma laughed at the sight of him being led through the dance like an obligated teenager at a wedding. He was blushing, leaning his body away from hers as she pulled him tighter against her. She appeared to know the song well, moving her body expertly in time. Emma almost felt as if she should look away to give them some privacy, but she couldn't. The woman's face was calm; a knowing smile was held on her lips, and her eyes were locked on Julian's. Emma could envision the younger version of the woman, her long dark hair, her handsome features, a beautiful siren luring men to the dance floor, mesmerizing them with the control she held over her body and the pleasure she derived from moving it. Rather than feeling jealous of the sight of Julian being flirted with, Emma felt envious of the connection the woman had to her body, of the way she remained so present. It seemed to give her a certain power. The woman moved Julian's hand, placing it on her lower back and drawing him closer still. It was then that Emma was surprised to find herself slightly aroused. She laughed to hide her embarrassment. If she were not standing in a restaurant filled with people, she felt she would have been free to use herself for the singular and selfish act of her own pleasure. She enjoyed the idea of being present yet invisible. She liked the idea of not being the focus for once.

When the song ended, Julian disentangled himself, thanking the woman and making his way back to Emma.

"Wow," he said, flustered. "What just happened?"

Emma laughed and kissed him, his lips still tasting of aniseed.

"Let's get the bill," she said, and pulled him by the hand.

They laughed and leaned into each other as they wound their way back along the side of the road to the hotel. They passed the pool, where the moonlight was casting abstract silver shapes across the dark water. Early the next morning, the older guests would spread their towels over the pool chairs, cordoning them off for the whole day while they roasted their dark red skin in the sun, but for now, the space was quiet and peaceful. Julian took a seat on the edge of a chair, pulling Emma by the hand to sit with him. "Let's stay for a moment," he said.

Emma knew what was coming: some form of sentimental, earnest soliloquy about how lucky they were, how they should cherish these moments. It was a habit of Julian's that Emma found both endearing and exasperating. Sometimes, she wished to just enjoy the moment without acknowledging the grim reality that it would pass by and become a memory that she would long to return to later. It made her feel that, without constant conscious appreciation, life was never truly lived, only anti-cipated and then remembered.

She found some irony in the way Julian wanted to retreat from the moment and view it objectively from a distance in the hope of getting closer to it. She understood that he desired these moments of conscious gratitude because he spent so much of his life yearning: yearning to finish his paper, yearn-ing for an indifferent and distracted world to sit up and pay attention to his ideas, yearning for recognition. Emma be-lieved she inhabited the present more frequently than he did, and so thinking about the present this way, as a transient mo-ment that never really existed before it became the past, made her feel like her whole life was slipping away. It made her chest begin to tighten, and her breath become shallow.

"Look at this exciting life we live," Julian began, placing an arm around her shoulders. "We're so lucky."

Emma leaned her head against his shoulder, and they stared beyond the pool at the dark shapes of the hills in the distance and, further still, the stars in the sky above.

"Yes, very lucky," she replied before letting the silence hang so that Julian could enjoy his moment.

When she felt she'd looked at her life for long enough and wished now to return to feeling it, she stood, reaching for his hands and pulling him up off the chair.

She began to dance against him coyly, copying the move-ments of the woman at the taverna.

"I much prefer it when you do that." He laughed. She smiled at him, swaying her hips and trying to remember how it felt to watch. Then she turned around, pressing her back against his body. As she moved, his energy shifted to some-thing more serious, more hungry. She lifted her arms above her head, slinging them around his neck, and he breathed into her hair.

She turned back around and they kissed. Emma used her body to guide him back to the pool chair and climbed on top of him. She removed his glasses, placing them carefully on the table next to them. The simple act of taking off Julian's glasses had, through repetition over the years, become an aphrodisiac to them both, and every time she performed this ritual, she moved slowly and theatrically to draw out the effect. They kissed again. Emma desperately wanted Julian to lift her dress and touch her, but he seemed to be awaiting a signal from her. This was a new pattern that had developed over the last couple of months. One that frustrated Emma. It seemed that Julian was overly conscious of some newly formed boundaries, places where he stopped and waited for permission to proceed. He was cautious with her, as if there were something broken within her and he was being careful not to damage her further. She lifted the hem of her dress up to her thighs, taking his hand and placing it on her. With each movement of her body, Emma imagined what they would look like right now: Julian's loafers still on, his pants now undone and bunched around his ankles. He untied her dress, which wrapped around her body and fastened on the left of her waist, so that it now hung open like a coat, exposing her chest and body to him. It was the thought of what they looked like that led to another, the thought of what Julian would look like with another woman on top of him, and it was that image that sent a tremor of pleasure through Emma. She closed her eyes, imagining the woman from the taverna in her place. Her body moving with the same certainty and control she had on the dance floor. Emma moaned, and when she opened her eyes again, she saw a flicker of movement in the corner of her eye. She turned her head and glimpsed the skinny ankles and scuffed white sneakers of Nico as he quickly stepped out of the light and into the darkness at the top of the stairs.

"Was that the pool boy?" Julian asked. They stopped moving.

"I think so."

"He saw us?"

"I think he did."

"Uh-oh."

They laughed guiltily and looked at each other for a moment before laughing again.

"Maybe we should go to our room," Julian said. Emma began to tie her dress back up.

Afterward, Emma lay in bed, her mind hovering in the realm just above sleep. There was an enjoyable, peaceful silence in between the sound of the wind passing through the olive trees by the room and waves cresting in the distance. Julian was breathing softly beside her, and though he was silent, she knew he was not yet entirely asleep.

Her body had surprised her this evening. She hadn't felt that level of intense arousal in a long time; it recalled the visceral, pleading desire that had consumed her when she and Julian had let their urges—over the course of their first four dates—reach boiling point before they finally relented to them.

The genesis had been watching the woman in the taverna dancing with Julian, the inspiration that Emma had taken and fashioned into the idea of another woman being with Julian. Why? She wondered. Or at least, why now? And where did the limits lie? She imagined Julian with an older woman, then with a younger woman, then with a woman she knew—an ex-colleague. She flashed images across her mind: an endless stream of scenarios and women. Her body responded, the urge returning surprisingly quickly and intensely. She reached her hand across the bed and found Julian again, imagining once more that it wasn't her hand but another woman's. Julian reacted immediately, crawling under the sheet and pressing his mouth against her wordlessly. When she cried out, she was imagining herself floating above their bed, hovering and watching.

# CHAPTER TWO

Julian ran, his breath moving his lungs rhythmically like a pair of bellows. The path was not ideal, loose and dusty. It was mostly downhill as it wound its way to the beach, and the sun, although only just beginning to exert itself, was providing an uncomfortable blanket of warmth. Still, the act of running was doing what Julian had intended it to, and he was happy he'd committed himself to the task. He hadn't run in over a week, not since they'd arrived in Corfu. This was unusual for him. For years, he'd committed to running in the morning a few times a week, a habit formed during his time at Cambridge years before, where he would trace his way alongside the River Cam, detouring through meadows and commons, as his mind wound its own path through thoughts as green and serene as the meadows themselves. It was a necessary reminder of his physicality, a moment spent in the corporeal realm, which was needed ahead of many hours spent struggling to understand his coursework. He'd since grown to rely on the repetitive nature of running to adjust his measurement of time down from days, weeks, and years to minutes and seconds. It was that sudden attention to the minutiae that made him feel as if he had full control over time. If he could be aware of the seconds passing, then he had the opportunity to push every moment to its fullest realization. In this way, he could believe that life simply came down to a series of micro-decisions, like the decision to not slow down despite the cries of his lungs and legs, and every time he committed to the more difficult path, he felt like he was achieving his full potential. It was ironic, he thought, that when his body moved fast, time slowed down. Whenever he returned to a walking pace, he was usually quickly reminded that life was not so easily simplified. Multiple decisions often swamped any given moment, layering upon one another, entangling their consequences and creating a maelstrom of options so that the correct choice was rarely clear.

His route took him to the beach and then past the row of cafés and restaurants. Workers carried crates of produce into the restaurants, while others enjoyed a cigarette or a coffee on a stone step. Julian enjoyed his inclusion in this quiet time of preparation. It made him feel like less of a tourist, a detached observer or disruptive force, and more like a thread within the fabric of the moment. When he reached the end of the path, he turned and retraced his steps, faced with the inclines he had enjoyed as descents just minutes before.

At the foot of the steep driveway that led up to the hotel pool, he began to walk. Thoughts made quiet in the noise of his exertion reemerged, and he regarded with apprehension, as he had come to do frequently, Emma.

Her behavior had been erratic for months now, culminating with the more recent unceremonious decision to quit her job—a job that Julian had believed she genuinely enjoyed. He could trace the beginning of the shift to the miscarriage, and he felt sure that symptoms of her unresolved grief were breaking through the surface in an unexpected way. He caught her staring blankly at the pan as the eggs she was frying turned into a blackened mess, or stepping out of the shower and leaving the water running, or mixing up dates and days and generally losing her usually tight grip on time. Emma had always been so organized, so reliable. She had two hands on the wheel at all times, but recently, she seemed to have released whatever it was that had, at her core, made her truly care about such details.

He recalled the day before when he'd seen Emma watching the mother seated nearby them at the beach. It had hurt him to glimpse an expression of longing on her face. But every time he tried to reach beyond her detached facade, she claimed she was fine. He felt helpless to ease her suffering.

Emma had always had a habit of falling deeply into thought. He recalled the moment when he first saw her: she was standing in line at a sandwich shop he visited frequently, a cheese and pickle baguette in her hand to match the one he held in his. She wore a knitted beige scarf, and her tawny red hair was gathered and held in a clip. Her face held a vacant expression that implied her attention was fully engaged in some other internal world. Just below her hair and above the scarf, Julian could see a glimpse of her pale, lightly freckled neck. He was compelled by the image of her, by a sudden and inexplicable desire to speak to her. He found himself envious of whatever it was that was arresting her. He wanted to feel what it was like to be the object of her full attention. It was then that he noticed a small sticker, the kind usually attached to the skin of an apple, caught in the fabric of her scarf. He watched and waited as she paid for her sandwich. When she then turned and walked past him toward the door, he said, "Excuse me." He intended to inform her of the sticker and use that as a segue to begin a conversation. He'd imagined her blushing and lifting the sticker from her scarf. He'd imagined her smiling at him, laughing at the hilarity of their matching sandwiches and growing more interested in him with each second spent in his company. He'd even imagined her boldly asking for *his* number and suggesting a drink, saving him the guesswork of whether the interest was mutual. What he had not imagined was that she would continue walking, showing no sign that she had heard or even noticed him. In a matter of seconds, she was gone, replaced by a draft of cold air as the door swung shut behind her. He stood dumbfounded for a moment before a smile, partly embarrassed and partly pleased, spread across his face and remained there until he reached the cashier.

In the early days of their relationship, he'd been delighted by Emma's dry, dark sense of humor. Her existentialism seemed at first intellectual, sexy even. He liked that she was always probing for meaning and maintaining a wide lens on life. It helped him keep perspective when his own goals and challenges threatened to consume him. He loved the way her dark humor often surprised others, inciting eruptions of shocked laughter and having the pleasantly contradictory effect of lightening the mood, which was especially appreciated whenever one of his academic friends became stuck laboring a point. It was only later that he was forced to tend to the roots from which a sense of humor like that could grow. Her bouts of despondency didn't fit neatly into the idea of depression; she didn't stay in bed for days, forget to shower, or abandon her work. She appeared to function as normal, responding appropriately to social cues, meeting deadlines, and buying

groceries. But there were subtler signs that she'd retreated somewhere mentally. He would catch her staring off into space when
she thought no one was watching. It was as if she were a computer running in sleep mode, activated only when prompted
by someone else. Even though there were no stereotypical
lows, there were no highs either. Things she usually enjoyed
were not able to move the needle. There was no pulling her
out of her mood—Julian had tried. It was easier for him to
endure the season than it was for him to attempt to change the
weather. He'd come to learn that, after a few weeks, she would
complete some necessary internal journey and awaken. Her
full presence would return to their conversations, and she
would be renewed, appearing to be able to feel her emotions
once again.

After the miscarriage, one of these moods had arrived,
only this time it had lingered for longer than ever before. That
was, until last night when they returned from dinner, and
she'd approached him as he sat on the pool lounge. Something
had changed; her presence seemed distilled. It had felt to Julian like she was truly, in body and mind, right there in the
moment with him. She'd been incredibly responsive to his
touch; they'd held eye contact and murmured words to each
other throughout. The deep and consistent acknowledgment
of his presence and his—specifically *his*—clear and vital role
in her pleasure had made him immeasurably happy. Only now
he wished to know what had brought on this change. He
wanted to know how they might experience it again.

When he reached the stone steps that led to their room, he
saw her sitting with her legs pulled up to her chest, her hair
wet and an open book resting against her knees. She looked
small, and as he always did, he felt a duty to protect her. He
knew she'd hate to know that he saw her like that: fragile and

in need of anything from anyone. "That's sexist and infan-
tilizing," she'd probably say while pulling a face so serious
and so inadvertently petulant that it would only serve to make
her look younger.

Emma glanced up from her novel to see Julian climbing the
steps and looking entirely spent from his run. When she had
woken to find that he was not in the bed next to her, she assumed he must be out running, and so while he worked
through the miles, she showered, dressed, and made an instant
coffee. She then took her mug of coffee, along with a jar of
olives, and sat at the little table by the front door of their
room. She drew her knees to her chest and read her book as
she ate the olives, tossing their pits into the grove that ran ad-
jacent to the room. Her hair was still damp. Occasionally, it
dripped onto her shoulders in a pleasant way. Their room was
situated up an incline at the back of the property, a position
that allowed a thin view of the ocean and horizon in the distance, as well as a view of every other hotel, road, and olive
grove that separated them from it. The temperature was rising
quickly, and even though it wasn't yet 9 A.M., she could see the
leathery elderly couples already setting themselves up for a
long day by the pool.

When Julian reached Emma, he leaned over and kissed her
before dropping into the seat across from her.

"Good run?" she asked.

"A tough one—it's mostly uphill on the way back."

"Do you want some coffee?"

"Please." He pulled his shirt off, sighing as he slouched
back in the chair.

Emma returned to their kitchenette and made him a coffee, bringing it back with her to the table and handing it to him. He thanked her before selecting an olive, placing it in his mouth, and looking out toward the ocean. A moment passed, a particular kind of silence that Emma was acquainted with, not uncomfortable to bear but still heavy with presentiment. Such moments usually preceded an invitation to join a discussion that was already well underway in Julian's mind.

"Last night was fun," he said, tossing the olive pit into the grove.

"It was."

"You seemed"—he paused as if to locate the right words—"very present."

"I felt very present."

"Was it something we did?" He glanced at her. "Something different?"

Emma remained silent. The visceral pleasure she'd felt at the thought of someone else being with Julian couldn't be easily communicated. She watched as Julian took another olive, placing it in his mouth and once again tossing the pit. She wondered whether the journey of the conversation could be shortened, smoothed of unnecessary obstacles if she simply got straight to the point and said the shocking thing so that they might recover from it faster.

"How would you feel if I told you I wanted to watch you sleep with someone else?"

Julian raised his eyebrows and laughed in surprise. "Is this one of those 'If I decided to join a Mars expedition, would you come too?' type of questions?"

Emma observed her feet, the gesture speaking into the silence on her behalf. When she looked back up, the smile had fallen from his face. "It's more like an 'If I order dessert, will you share it with me?' type of question."

Confusion, maybe hurt, flickered across his face. "Do you mean that?"

"I think so."

" 'I think so' doesn't sound so sure."

"I'm about as sure as I can be until I'm actually in the situation experiencing it."

He looked away from her and out into the grove. His forehead creased in demonstration of his incomprehension. "Where is this coming from?" he then asked.

"Last night, when you were dancing with that woman, I had a sort of reaction to seeing you with someone else. It was like I could imagine you with someone else, and then the thought of that turned me on."

"I see." He frowned. "But wouldn't it hurt you to see me with someone else? It would hurt me to see you doing that. In fact, I think it would be torture."

She considered the question, attempting to determine how best to explain the feelings she didn't even fully understand herself.

"I think it would shock me initially, but maybe part of me wants to feel that." She could see Julian's confusion plainly on his face and decided to change tack and move forward more cautiously. "Mostly, it would turn me on."

"How would it turn you on?"

Emma drew a breath.

"It has something to do with seeing another woman desire you." She paused. "I think I'd be able to see myself in her position. I don't know if that makes sense. I could witness, but I wouldn't have to be involved. I could just observe it entirely for my own pleasure."

Concern had now arrived on Julian's face. He deliberated over his next words. She knew immediately what was coming.

She wondered how much time would need to pass before her moods and behaviors could be attributed to something else or, ideally, to nothing in particular.

"Has this got something to do with the miscarriage? Do you think maybe it . . ."

"No, I don't think they are related at all." Emma knew that if she just admitted to him the startling and intensely guilty sense of relief that had crept up on her in the days following the miscarriage, he was sure to stop thinking that grief was the source of her frequently baffling behaviors. But she didn't know how to even begin to explain that or how to then admit that, just as the experience had revealed to Julian a newly discovered and emphatic desire to be a father, it had shown her the opposite.

Julian was silent, and she felt that he didn't believe her.

"Well, then," he began, "are you unsatisfied with us? With our—"

"No, no, of course not." She reached under the table and squeezed his leg. "It's not that I'm unsatisfied. I just think—shouldn't we try to enjoy ourselves? You said that— remember?"

She registered a vague guilt at taking Julian's words out of context and fashioning them for use against him. "When we decided on moving to Athens for the summer, you said we should take this situation"—she hesitated very briefly on the word, wondering if it was too crude—"and embrace our freedom to explore what brings us pleasure in life. To have fun."

Julian nodded at her, a mute gesture of burgeoning understanding.

"I love our life," he said. "I guess I'm concerned that an experience like that could complicate things. I don't want anything to ruin what we have right now."

"I would never let that happen," she said, leaning across and taking his hand.

He sighed, retrieving his hand and standing. "I'm going to need some time to think about it."

Emma nodded. "Of course."

Julian walked back inside the room, and Emma remained where she was for a moment, watching as an elderly couple by the pool lovelessly rubbed oil into each other's backs in brisk, slapping movements.

# CHAPTER THREE

Early the next morning, they checked out of the hotel. Nico refused to meet their eyes as he carried Emma's backpack down the steep, dusty driveway. When he placed the bag down beside the road, Julian gave him a generous tip, which only seemed to make him more uncomfortable. He murmured a quick thanks and sprinted back up the drive.

A car took them from Palaiokastritsa to a port, where a ferry took them to the mainland, where a bus would finally take them to Athens. When traveling, Julian often preferred to take a bus or train so he could immerse himself in a place, even if it meant a significant increase in the length of the journey. Emma didn't mind this. She could watch the passing scenery for hours, her eyes panning side to side as her attention seemed to sink deeper and deeper inward. It often felt as if a long road journey allowed her to access some part of her brain, perhaps her subconscious, that remained unreachable otherwise.

At first, the small houses the bus passed were piled to-

gether, but soon, the space between them increased until the
houses were spread few and far between across the sloping
olive groves. Then they were driving through tunnels and freeways that cut right through hills covered with pine and cypress
trees. Emma spent most of the time listening to an audiobook.
She experienced motion sickness whenever she tried to read,
and although she'd never before been a fan of listening to a
novel, she had found herself appreciating the comfort of someone reading to her. It was suggestive of childhood, when someone else was responsible for her well-being, and she had no
other responsibility but to exist. Julian stared out of the window for a while before eventually resting his head back against
the seat and, despite the jerking, rattling motions, effortlessly
fell asleep. Emma had always envied this ability of his. During
their six-year relationship, she had memories like this from all
over the world: Julian asleep on a train, a bus, a plane, while
she sat and stared out the window, lingering somewhere between awake and asleep, unable to commit to either.

Just past the midway point of the journey, Emma pulled
out some bread, cheese, and salami they'd bought by the port
in Corfu and made sandwiches. The sandwiches were dry, but
that didn't bother her—if anything, it added further depth to
her feeling of regressing to childhood comforts. Her mother
had always made her ham sandwiches when she was in primary school. Back then, Emma had liked the type of ham that
was imprinted with a smiley face, but her mother would slice
it up to fit within the bread, and so Emma would sometimes
peel back the top layer of the sandwich to reveal a severed eye
splattered with blood-like tomato sauce. Julian awoke and accepted a sandwich, which he ate before promptly falling back
asleep. She watched as his head bounced gently against the
glass of the window. She'd always been proud of how they

met—not through a dating app but rather through the act of frequently finding themselves at the same sandwich shop, an event they could easily claim as being orchestrated by fate. Their story began when, on one otherwise insignificant Tuesday, she went to the sandwich shop near her office only to find that the sandwich she usually bought—cheese and pickle—had sold out. Instead, she could have prawn or egg. She stood at the fridge, trying to assess which was least likely to make her unwell, when a voice interrupted her deliberations to say, "Here, take mine."

She'd turned to see a man holding out a cheese and pickle baguette. She was startled into speechlessness for a moment, partly because he was handsome but mostly because he somehow knew which sandwich she usually chose.

"Sorry," he said. "That probably seemed really creepy. I'm not a weirdo—I just noticed you always choose the same as me, and today I took the last one. I feel terrible."

"Oh." She laughed awkwardly. "No, you keep it. I'll have"—she looked back at the options grimly—"prawn."

"At least choose the egg—trust me."

She looked at the egg sandwich mournfully.

"No, honestly, take this." He held the baguette out to her again. "I couldn't live with myself if I took it. I wouldn't even enjoy it."

"At least let me pay for your sandwich then?" she offered.

"Absolutely not," he said, selecting the egg sandwich from the fridge. She observed how pleasant it was to view the profile of his face. "But maybe if you wanted to, we could eat them in the park together?"

At that point, she might have considered the whole situation to be frankly disturbing if not for the fact that she was immediately attracted to him. Her attraction seemed to muffle any instinctive alarm bells, recasting creepiness into something that resembled romance.

"Okay." She smiled.

The city of Athens was like a bowl, the edges of which were the hills that bordered it on one side and the vast Aegean Sea on the other. Its contents were a sprawl of buildings flocking upward to the center of the bowl, where the Acropolis stood elevated. Emma noticed the overwhelming presence of awnings, beige or green, which cast protective shade over the balconies and windows of the sun-beaten buildings. She paused her audiobook and watched from the window. She'd never been to Athens before—like Julian had—and although she felt no connection to the place the way he did, she could understand why he was drawn to it. It was a place of accessible history and measured grandeur. A fertile ground that had supported the growth of many of the minds Julian most admired.

Julian's paper, he'd explained many times—though each time he did, Emma was suspicious he was defining it differently just to confuse her—had something to do with phenomenology. Even the term "phenomenology" was slippery to her. Once she'd finally grasped its meaning, it eluded being held for long and if she managed to hold it once again, it would look blankly back at her without recognition. Purely from repetition, she knew that phenomenology was the study of phenomena—the appearance of something as understood by our experience of its appearance, conscious experience as experienced through the subjective lens of our own experience, or something like that. The fact was, being in Athens brought Julian closer to these thoughts and ideas, closer to the lingering energy of those who took the first steps down the path

Julian had been walking for all of his adult life. What Athens offered her, on the other hand, was yet to be determined.

By the time they arrived at Kifissos bus station, they were tired and impatient, speaking monosyllabically but occasionally squeezing each other's hand to remind themselves that they were allies against the common enemy of the journey. They disembarked into a giant garage where buses lined up diagonally. It was dark and hot, and the air was choked with petrol fumes, the combination of which seemed to bring into question whether the vast azure of the sky and sea they had grown accustomed to had ever actually existed.

On the metro, they took their backpacks off and placed them on the ground in front of them, squeezing themselves into a corner to be as inconspicuous as possible. It was now early evening, and the metro was busy with the final wave of suit-wearing workers making their way home. Emma leaned against the wall and gently swayed with the movement of the train. It always fascinated her the way a completely foreign place could be rendered so immediately recognizable by something relatable like a metro system. She felt the same way about airports. They were a comforting common language, like a smile or a nod.

At the third stop, a commotion echoed up from further down the carriage. It was the sound of a man yelling. A few people turned their heads in the direction of the sound, but for the most part no one seemed particularly interested. The noise grew louder, and soon the source of the sound was revealed as a man carrying numerous plastic bags. He was dressed in a stained pair of tracksuit pants and a white tank top. He approached their carriage, occasionally shouting something in Greek. His disgruntled monologue was aimed at no one in particular until he locked eyes on Emma, who hadn't looked away quickly enough and had been caught watching him. He then began to direct his shouting toward her specifically. She dropped her eyes to the floor. When he reached her, he stopped, now pointing and openly addressing her. Emma kept her eyes on the floor, hoping he would tire and move off. When he came closer and kicked her backpack, Emma flinched, and Julian stepped forward.

"Hey, move back," he said sternly.

The man then became furious, his pupils like islands in the bloodshot whites of his eyes. Spit flew from his mouth as he shouted.

"Back off," Julian said, holding his arm out. Another passenger, a man in a suit, stood and held a hand palm up to Julian as if to say *Stop*, as if it were Julian who was being aggressive. The man in the suit then spoke calmly in Greek to the shouting man, somehow defusing the escalation. Eventually, the angry man said something, some final point, and continued on his journey down the train.

Julian thanked the man in the suit, but the man simply shrugged as if to declare he'd been left with no choice and sat back down.

"Are you okay?" Julian asked Emma.

She nodded, though, truthfully, her hands were shaking. She gripped her bag to steady them.


Alistair's apartment was located in Monastiraki on the fifth floor of a *polykatoikia,* the uniform, tiered apartment buildings erected in the 1950s to replace many of the older neoclassical buildings that weren't able to accommodate the rapidly growing population of Athens. It was dark by the time they arrived, entering Alistair's building through a narrow lobby with white marble floors and wood-paneled walls. At the end of the room was a thin staircase with a black railing, which curved around and up through the floors. Between the second and fifth floors, the staircase had no windows or lights, meaning it became so dark that it was impossible to navigate the thin steps without using the light of a phone. Instead, Julian and Emma used the elevator: a coffin laminated in a faux wood print, which had a spring floor that would drop unpleasantly an inch or two underneath the feet of whoever stepped in first.

The apartment itself was small but regal, with worn parquet floors and old, mismatched mahogany furniture. Alistair, unsurprisingly a collector of books, had built crudely constructed shelves wherever he could fit them—slotted in thin, awkward spaces of the wall or precariously positioned above doorways. They risked a head injury courtesy of Proust every time they passed from the hallway into the living and dining room. Behind the dining table, more shelves covered the entire wall, all of them filled to the creaking brink of collapse.

The apartment had a balcony, as every apartment in Athens appeared to. In the foreground, the view was mostly of other balconies all stacked tightly above and below one another. In the background, beyond the surrounding buildings, Julian could see the Acropolis reposing indifferently, wise and ancient, and seemingly unreachable upon its limestone pedestal. Floodlights were arranged along its outer wall to illuminate it at night, though Julian felt this made the site look as if it were attempting to be menacing, like a child holding a flashlight under their chin. He also found it strange that the ruins should be so visible, as if its constant availability dispelled some of its mystique. It reminded him of a trip he and Emma went on to Agra years ago when Emma had returned laughing from the bathroom to tell him that the Taj Mahal was visible from the toilet.

As they moved around Alistair's apartment, unpacking their belongings into cupboards and drawers, Julian watched Emma's reaction carefully. She was silent, not unhappily, but not with any air of contentment either.

Sometimes, Julian longed to return to the uncomplicated earlier years of their relationship. Occasionally, he found himself revisiting the first time they met, guiltily meeting with that younger version of Emma in his mind as if he were meeting with a mistress. He could recall her sitting next to him on a bench in Cartwright Gardens the day he'd given her the last cheese and pickle sandwich and asked her to eat lunch with him. A meeting they now agreed upon as their first date. He remembered them enjoying the still, chilly air of early spring and the sunlight that made its way through the gaps in the trees. A dull *thwack* emanating from the tennis courts to their left consistently punctured the air around them in an almost soothing way.

"I don't do this often enough," she'd admitted to him. She was wearing a dark gray coat and the same beige scarf she had worn the first time he saw her. Her face was pale, and her nose and ears were slightly pink.

"Do what?" he asked. "Have lunch with strange men who accost you in sandwich shops?"

She laughed. "Oh, no, I do that all the time." She pointed across the park to a man in a suit who was pacing in front of a bench while taking a call. "He's tomorrow."

"Right." Julian made a show of pretend jealousy. The man was now holding the phone away from his ear and shouting directly into it. "Definitely a prawn guy."

"Definitely." Emma laughed. "No, I meant, I don't eat

lunch outside enough. I seem to just gravitate back to my desk. This is so nice."

She closed her eyes, taking a deep breath in and angling her face upward to catch the sun.

Julian smiled at her as she did this. With her eyes closed, he was free to observe her, to travel the journey of her face until his eyes rested on the dark freckle at the top of her lip. When her eyelids flickered, he shifted his line of sight back to the park in front of them.

"It's pathetic, really," she resumed, "how infrequently I spend time outside. I bet you're a real outdoorsy type."

He laughed.

"I'm right, aren't I?" she pressed. "What is it? Camping? Swimming at the lido? Are you one of those people who climb walls?"

He laughed again and shook his head. "I stare at a screen all day, every day."

She sighed sympathetically. "Do you ever wonder what that's doing to us?"

"Do you mean 'us' as in each other specifically, or 'us' as in society?"

"Both."

He looked down at his shoes and considered the question.

"I mean, do you think we will all look back with regret one day? Are we wasting our lives?" She was looking directly at him now, and he lifted his eyes to meet hers, pleased to witness her cheeks color slightly in response.

"Sorry," she said, looking away. "I'm drab company. I bet you regret giving me that last pickle and cheese."

"Not at all," he countered sincerely.

She smiled at the ground, her cheeks darkening. "I can be fun, I promise. There's just something about lunch breaks that inspire nihilism, don't you think? Sitting around eating a factory-made sandwich, trying to enjoy thirty minutes of free thought."

He laughed then, enjoying being included so much that he refrained from admitting that, after lunch, he was going to return to a desk in the Humanities reading rooms at the British Library to continue to work on his PhD thesis rather than an office and that, unlike her, he didn't have a boss, and could take lunch whenever and for however long he wished. He definitely didn't feel the need to admit that, before he saw her for the first time in the sandwich shop a fortnight ago, he'd only very rarely used the library's reading rooms.

"Free thought?" He held out his phone. "I usually use the time to scroll on a smaller screen."

She laughed genuinely. Her freckled nose crinkled on the sides, and he had a sudden urge to kiss it.

Then she sighed, a disappointingly conclusive tone in her voice. "I should get back." She stood, brushing crumbs from her jacket before checking the time on her phone. "Thank you for inviting me to join you—I really mean that. Thank you for reminding me of the outside world."

Julian stood, and they began to retrace their steps to the entrance of the park.

When they reached the gate, she turned to him. A beam of sunlight shone across her face, and she squinted as she looked up at him, the light intensifying the pale green of her eyes.

"Same time next week?" she asked.

Even though it was far too early, ridiculously early, for such strong feelings, Julian knew then that he was already in love with her.

"Same time next week." He nodded, feigning professionalism.

When he turned up to the sandwich shop the following week, unsure of whether she'd be there, and found her waiting for him with a cheese and pickle baguette in each hand, his heart had soared.

Julian left Emma to finish unpacking their bags and ventured out to the closest mini-mart to buy eggs, parsley, chives, tarragon, and feta. As he wound back and forth through the unfamiliar aisles, he continued his thoughts of Emma. This time, circling on more immediate events: the request. It was ironic that, inwardly, he'd celebrated Emma's sudden shift toward presence, only for her to explain that she wanted to essentially create further space between them. The request was baffling to him. Baffling and, despite his confusion and prudence, exciting. Shortly after meeting Emma, Julian had determined that he wished to spend the rest of his life with her. He wanted to live forever in the place they created in each other's company. Never in the presence of someone else had he felt so excited, so intellectually and physically stimulated, and yet so calm, so sure.

He'd assumed that his decision to choose Emma as a life partner also required him to accept that he would never sleep with other women ever again. He'd felt a small amount of grief over this—related less to his desire to sleep with another woman and more to the reminder that the passage of time had a way of solidifying a path in life and removing all other options, which made him reluctantly think of his own mortality. Still, the sacrifice felt noble and necessary, and the intensity of his attraction to Emma was helpfully distracting. Only now he was being told that he could have both: the continuation of his relationship with Emma and the ability to sleep with a stranger. Taken at the surface level, it would seem like a lucky glitch, yet he couldn't consider it so simply. The first concern he had was that after Emma experienced this distance between them and watched as he slept with another woman, she might decide that she never wished to close the distance again. Second was the concern that it could be a test; Emma might be hoping he would refuse. Or it could be a trap, some kind of self-sabotaging technique on her behalf. He knew she was capable of such convoluted methods; she'd once told him the story of how she'd fabricated a story of infidelity purely so her boyfriend at university would break up with her and save her the trouble of breaking up with him. What if she was harboring some secret and desperate urge to end things? Would he agree to the request only to be accused of cheating after the fact? It seemed that none of these questions could be answered until after they had committed the act. To refuse posed its dangers too. Emma might resent him, condemning their relationship to a slow disintegration. Or he'd have to live with the uncomfortable knowledge that he was denying her something she had bravely declared desiring. And what did he want? He hadn't yet determined that, but any version of any reality he desired always contained Emma.

Julian returned to the apartment and made them both an omelet, which they ate in silence, too tired to even speak to each other.

After they showered and made the bed using linens they'd found in the cupboard, they crawled under the sheet and clung to each other, falling asleep quickly and heavily even as the sound of traffic and sirens rang out from the streets below.

# CHAPTER FOUR

Most mornings around 8 A.M., Julian went to work in the reading room at the Vallianeio Megaron, leaving behind a half-full French press and the smell of toast mixed with the scent of his cologne. In her mornings of solitude, Emma allowed herself the luxury of moving slowly. She made a piece of toast, poured the rest of the coffee, and took them both out onto the balcony.

The view from the balcony fascinated her. She loved to catch glimpses of the lives that surrounded them: the elderly couple who maintained a whole garden on their meager balcony, lining up rows and rows of potted plants in every available space; the young woman whose clean laundry—a constant presence on her balcony—was almost exclusively dainty lace lingerie, which somehow managed to hang provocatively despite lacking the crucial element of flesh; the large, hairy man reading his newspaper every morning—Emma knew if she missed the brief window of time, she would see the newspaper folded and left upon the plastic table.

The Acropolis looked down on them all, and even though it was more likely to be described as imposing or formidable, she found the sight of the ruins comforting. It was a direct reminder of history, and like the glimpses of other people's balconies, it reminded her of just how many lives had been lived as richly as her own, of how many were yet to be lived. In this way, Emma enjoyed being reminded of her insignificance. In a similar way, she would often rattle off facts about the incomprehensible size of the universe, enjoying the jarring sense of perspective. Julian didn't share her desire to be reduced in importance. In response, he would blanch and eventually ask her to stop. He'd once explained that this reminder didn't put all his worries into perspective, as it did for her, but rather highlighted that the power he had over his life had significant limitations. It reminded him that there were things he could never fully understand and, therefore, could never control.

After she ate, Emma would usually shower, dress, and then leave the apartment. Although it had been nearly a fortnight since they'd moved in, she had still not met any of the other occupants in the building. After a few days, she'd begun to try to purposefully cross paths with them, but she only ever encountered vague evidence of their existence: the echo of heels rapping against the stone stairs below, the sound of a door closing and the deadbolt clicking into place, or the lingering phantom of perfume or cigarette smoke in the empty elevator. Sometimes notices would appear pinned to the board in the lobby, often eliciting an ongoing dialogue scrawled in pen underneath. What information the notices concerned remained a mystery to her because they were always written in Greek.

Emma's morning walks had become essential to her, and she treated them with the same respect she would give an occupation. At first she purposefully meandered for a couple of hours, but she soon noticed that she had begun to carve a route. It seemed that unless she intervened, her body would mindlessly follow the path it already knew. She stubbornly began to detour, forcing herself to take hard rights or lefts, crossing through unknown squares and down unfamiliar streets. Through this, she came to know the neighborhood's particular flow: the busy, tourist-flocked streets of Plaka where the restaurants' tables and chairs were piled along the path and where the stone underfoot was polished completely smooth by all of the steps it had endured over its long life. The rows of stores and stalls selling alabaster busts of scholars or ancient Greek gods, or plastic talismans adorned with the blue evil eye, which promised to protect the wearer from curses. It was the sort of tourist loot that only appeared charming or interesting after it was stripped of its context and taken thousands of miles away. The stores continued on and on down these streets, selling linen clothing, sandals, olive oil, and herbs. Even though these areas of Plaka did not fully come to life until nighttime, after the sun ceased its tyranny, Emma still avoided them. Instead, like one of the old street cats, she chose the quieter streets where she could move freely and be ignored. The sun in Athens felt harsher than it had on Corfu, where it seemed to extend an invitation to linger. On the beach in Corfu, they had lain prone under the comforting blanket of warmth; here, the direct sunlight was domineering, slightly sinister, as if it intended to slowly boil them.

In the afternoon, after her walk, Emma would read. She'd taken a copy of Euripides' *Medea* from Alistair's shelf, drawn by the image on the cover of a woman screaming in rage, her dark hair spread out behind her, Medusa-like, as she rode through the sky upon a chariot steered by dragons. It was a formidable image that fit the tumultuous and dark story of infidelity and infanticide. She would read slowly and carefully, pausing and rereading if at any point her lethargic afternoon brain failed to grip the meaning. This was one opportunity not working afforded her: the ability to bestow any recreational task with great importance and attention.

As publicity manager for a prestigious advertising agency, unironically called The Agency, Emma had been excellent at her job, and for many years she derived consistent satisfaction from that fact. Her events and product launches were so exclusive and well attended that she occasionally had requests for invitations come through from the publicists of celebrities. Her emails to media contacts were never ignored. It gave her a thrill to watch as newly launched brands took off and went viral, reaching the tipping point at which she no longer had to try to incite interest from the world and instead had to control the flow of interest directed her way.

The miscarriage had begun when she was on the tube one morning on her way to the office. Not ideal. It was preceded by the sudden disappearance of her nausea, a relief rather than a cause for concern given she was approaching the second trimester, but as she sat there swaying with the other passengers in the stuffy, warm air of the carriage, she began to feel unusual twinges in her abdomen. She had an important meeting first thing that morning. The final meeting with a prospective client, a prestigious luxury brand, one that would bring in the largest contract the company had ever had. Emma had been working on this client for the last eight months, stalking, courting, and delighting them at every turn. They were going to be hers. The monumental potential of this achievement had loomed over her, seeming to grow after she found out she was pregnant, as if some strange desire, some need to prove her unequivocal usefulness to the company to compensate for the inconvenience of her pregnancy, had cast itself in the shape of this deal. By the time she arrived at the office, she was experiencing cramps. It was not a foreign feeling, but the timing signaled something was wrong. Still, she presented to the client, locked in the contract, and shook their hands, praying they wouldn't feel how damp and clammy hers were. In the bathroom afterward, there was blood. She called Julian and asked him to meet her at the hospital.

The part that Emma struggled to reconcile with was the fact that she knew something wasn't right as she sat on the tube. She knew she should probably have taken action. She imagined anyone remotely maternal would have called their doctor, gone to the hospital, or done anything necessary if there was a chance to prevent what was happening. Instead, she'd decided to go to her meeting. In that moment, in some dark corner of her mind, she'd concluded that maybe the miscarriage was for the best.

The thought had given her clarity, revealing an empty space where her desire for motherhood should have resided. Another question then proposed itself and began to follow her: if you won't be a mother, what will you be?

At first she'd offered up her career at The Agency in response to the question, but when she imagined dedicating her life to the role and thought about the rewards—potentially being made partner one day, collecting clients who were even more prestigious or famous, running campaigns on a larger, global scale—she felt utterly hollow. She was left having to acknowledge a truth she had never before made so explicit: her career at The Agency did not give her any real sense of purpose.

The damage was done. Her motivation for achievement and upward progression disappeared, and the sudden lack of propulsion left her struggling to keep the elements of her life in order. She knew Julian had picked up on a shift in her mood, but only vaguely, as if he felt the vibrations in the ground but had incorrectly assumed their point of origin. He was tending to the wrong wound, but she didn't have the heart to tell him.

About a month after Emma's miscarriage, Melanie arrived. Hot off the back of filming the first-ever season of *Muscle Match*—a new reality TV show dubbed as *The Bachelorette* meets *Gladiator*—Melanie and her manager planned to maximize the public interest that would soon be directed her way by launching a swimwear brand.

Emma knew that if a soon-to-be reality TV star wanted to monetize the brief moment in time when the public had any interest in them by hastily launching a halfhearted swimwear label in time for summer, it was not her job to say: Don't you think we'd all get along just fine if this brand never existed? Don't you think we have quite enough? It wasn't her job to think of the islands of junk floating in the ocean, the mountains of unwanted, poorly constructed, plastic clothing accumulating in Ghana or Senegal or the Atacama Desert of Chile.

Her job was to act excited, to pitch The Agency's services and win the account; to plan a lavish launch party, to inform all her media connections; to create a story, a message—preferably a social message, *a purpose*—and infuse it into every specifically chosen word. It was her job to create a hunger. It was her job to compel people to buy more things they truly didn't need.

Instead, Emma walked out in the middle of the meeting. In the very middle of the sentence Melanie was speaking, Emma stood and, without a word, left the room.

She left the office, turned off her phone, and wandered the

streets until the rain ushered her into a café, where she sat for three hours watching commuters rush by, grim-faced and hunched under their umbrellas. She wondered then if she was having some sort of mental breakdown, but still, she sat. If it was a mental breakdown, then she had to admit she was enjoying it. The next day, as predicted, she was called into a meeting. Philip, the director of The Agency, probed gently, aware of Emma's recent miscarriage and only too willing to believe that there would be logic and reasoning—or at least transience—behind her bizarre actions. When it was apparent that Emma had no reasoning and was unapologetic, Philip listed some other complaints he'd had about her recent performance. Emma could see no way backward, and there was only one way forward. She handed in her resignation.

In the early evening, when Julian returned to the apartment, they would have a glass of wine on the balcony and discuss their day. Even though it was Emma who technically spent her day idle, it was quickly apparent to them both that her daily recounts contained the most interesting aspects. Julian's were limited to the same few scenes and mostly consisted of a musty, quiet room and the cool light of his laptop screen. Without any pressure on Emma's time, it seemed that she had become more observant, more fundamentally curious.

"Did you look into courses?" he asked one evening as they ate the risotto they'd somewhat successfully made and drank white wine. When it had been established that Emma would not return to her job, Julian—conditioned to believe that the lack of a job would leave her bored and rudderless—had brought up the idea of her studying something new. He'd suggested she could channel her energy into retraining for a different career. Emma knew that Julian didn't understand how she could comfortably exist in the undefined, liminal place of goal-less unemployment, and so she had agreed to his suggestion at the time, but only so the conversation would move on to another subject.

She was a little suspicious at the timing of this question now, after she'd just finished recounting another interesting and leisurely day. She hadn't told Julian that, two days ago, she'd received an email from Anika, a journalist she'd befriended years before:

Hi Emma,

I heard you left The Agency and was wondering if you'd be interested in finishing an exclusive for me? Something time-sensitive has come up, and I can't meet the deadline, but I'm so confident you're the right person for this. I've always thought your writing talents were wasted over there . . .

I've attached the interview recordings and a bit of background info I've gathered. I have a feeling you'll find it very interesting—let me know what you think.

P.S. The Agency must be devastated to have lost you. What have you moved on to? I'm back in London next month, let's catch up.

For a few years, before she moved on from fashion and lifestyle reporting, Anika had taken almost every press release Emma had sent her. Now she mostly did accountability reporting, investigating unethical practices and fact-checking politicians. Emma followed her career, looking her up online every so often to find her latest article. She inspired Emma, and her belief in Emma's ability was flattering.

Although their relationship had been professional in origin, they'd met for drinks a few times before Anika began to travel more. The last time they met, Emma had left feeling ashamed that she might have got carried away. After learning that Anika was not overly familiar with the topic, Emma had become preoccupied with ranting about click farms. She recalled herself describing the factories of low-wage workers who spent all day churning through the world's precious resources just to artificially bolster the fake, paid-for "fame" of attention-seeking, engagement-addicted individuals. She remembered concluding it was frankly sickening—*dystopian, even*—in her opinion.

But a week later, Anika emailed her to thank her for the article pitch idea. She'd secured access to a click farm in the Philippines and would be writing an exclusive for *The Guardian*. Maybe it was then that Anika had identified potential in Emma.

The article Anika wanted her to write was to be an exclusive detailing multiple whistleblower claims that UK water providers were knowingly dumping raw sewage into rivers and seas instead of treating the water as they are legally required to do. The evidence was damning, and the environmental consequences sounded significant. After receiving the email, Emma had decided to dip her toe in by playing the interview recordings while brushing her teeth, only to find herself listening to the whole audio file, riveted and outraged, toothpaste dripping from the corners of her mouth. She sat with the opportunity for another twenty-four hours, and just that morning, she responded and took on the article.

Despite her excitement, she was procrastinating the task of telling Julian about it. Even though a report was very different from a research paper, she knew that he was sensitive even to the word "published." If he could have had it his way, he would have finished and published his paper years ago. Because of this, the success of his colleagues often tormented him, throwing him into a dark, moody spiral of insecurity, even if he did ultimately want the best for them. She decided to wait for a better moment.

"No, I haven't found any courses I like the sound of yet," she replied. "Actually, I've been reading *Medea* by Euripides. Have you read it?"

"That's the play about the woman who goes insane and kills her children as revenge against her cheating husband, right?"

"Well—" She paused, feeling a sudden desire to defend Medea and wondering why or how she might, before resigning and simply saying, "Yes."

"Dark stuff," Julian said, eyeing the tea light that burned in a dark blue glass on the table in between them.

"Why do you think the ancient Greeks were so compelled by tragedy?" Emma asked. Her head was newly filled with these sorts of inquiries. The spare time had encouraged a desire to probe deeper and to pull at the cords of things to better understand how they were made. She also knew that Julian enjoyed these sorts of discussions, and if she directed his attention in this way, he would forget that seconds before they were talking about her career.

"Some would argue that Greek tragedy was likely born from the tragic nature of everyday life in classical Athens— plagues and wars, grief and loss. But they often found resolution that wasn't possible in real life, which some people, including Aristotle, didn't like." Julian then launched into an explanation of deus ex machina and the criticisms Aristotle made in *Poetics*, his arguments that the device—by carting a god onto the stage to fix the tangled plotlines the playwright had created—stripped the characters of their autonomy and was seen as narrative weakness.

"But I guess that if you lived in classical Athens, it would be preferable to believe in intervening gods and fate," he continued. "Because otherwise, you just lived in an inexplicably mad and violent world." He made this statement from a distance, as if he were trying to understand someone with very different beliefs from him, but Emma found herself comforted by the idea.

"I think the hand of god intervention is pretty realistic, actually," she admitted. "Not explicitly the figure of god, but the idea that strange and random things happen and that not every resolution—negative or positive—is engineered by us. Don't you find it comforting to think that for all our striving and desperate grasping for control, our fates are still largely tied to some dispassionate and ambivalent force far greater than us?"

"That's quite fatalistic of you." Julian laughed, reaching for his glass. "You don't believe in free will?"

Emma let her eyes drop down to her plate.

"Let's say . . ." Julian ran a hand over his jaw as he searched for an analogy. "Let's say you're unwell. Do you go to the doctor? Or do you sit back and accept that whatever happens to you is fate?"

She thought about the decision she'd made to ignore her miscarriage as she sat on the tube.

"Do I have health insurance? Can I afford the doctor's bills?" she asked, aware that in an effort to deflect from her more personal feelings she was being elusive and combative.

He laughed. "For the purpose of this specific scenario, yes."

"Hang on—so you're saying free will is mastery of fate, and therefore mastery of fate is possible, but only accessible to those who have the resources?"

Julian considered the statement. "I mean, that's a pretty broad stroke, but there is some truth there," he concluded. He was calm—accustomed to debating without his feelings being involved. Emma, on the other hand, was not; unnecessary frustration circulated in her body.

"I think that's unfair," she concluded, draining the last of her glass.

It was 8:41 P.M., and the sun had almost dropped behind the hills in the distance, setting them ablaze in orange. The sound of the cicadas created a thick humming in the background.

Julian stood and wandered, glass in hand, over to the balcony railing. "The sunsets here are incredible," he said, not for the first time, as he stared out past the buildings.

Emma made a noise of agreement as she swallowed a mouthful of risotto.

Julian was leaning his forearms on the metal railing and pitching himself forward to see further when the railing wobbled underneath him. He stepped back, frowning as he gave the railing a shake, and watched as it moved a couple of inches forward and back.

"I forgot to say," he said, returning to the table. "Alistair offered to introduce us to some of his colleagues. I was thinking of inviting them over for dinner. Would you be okay with that?"

"Sure, that'd be fun," Emma agreed, not entirely truthfully.

She often found Julian's academic colleagues difficult to talk to, trained as they were to talk as if they were analyzing everything rather than feeling any emotion. When they spoke to her, they seemed to do so from the heights of their education, as if they were looking down upon her. On top of this, the conversations were almost always limited to their specific spheres of interest. Any generalizations or hyperbolic statements, which Emma often made in sacrifice to the cause of conversation, were treated uncharitably and scrutinized at length for their ambiguity or lack of evidence. The conversations often lacked humor, which felt to Emma as if the room were lacking in oxygen.

"When?" she asked.

"I was thinking this weekend. Friday?"

"Sure, okay."

"Great." He smiled at her, and she smiled back.

The sky was now rapidly dimming around them. Julian stood again and began to collect their plates, pausing when he reached Emma to bend down and kiss her on the top of the head. He moved inside and left her there. She sat for a moment, surrounded by the sounds of music and voices that floated up from the busy streets below. When Julian turned the lamps on in the living room behind her, she stood, blowing out the tea light, and went to join him.

# CHAPTER FIVE

"You have lipstick on your teeth," Julian said, as he frantically paced past Emma in the hallway on his way to the dining room. Emma turned, baring her teeth to the mirror that hung on the wall and rubbed the mark away.

"Can you light the candles on the table?" he asked, storming past her once more and turning sideways to slide by the upright piano Alistair inexplicably kept in the hallway. "They'll be here soon."

Julian often behaved this way when entertaining guests. He would play one particular jazz playlist, something he never did otherwise, and dwell extensively over insignificant decisions like which wine to serve. He would pick at Emma, becoming unfairly critical of her, and she knew it was best to remove herself from sight and provide him with one less variable to control. A sadly tinkling piano began to emanate from the dining room as Emma collected the matches from the kitchen. When she returned, she found Julian concealing their small Bluetooth speaker behind a stack of Alistair's books, as if the sight of something so modern was too crude. She lit three candles and arranged them on the dining table, before retreating to the bedroom, where she lay down on the bed and drew a deep breath.

Emma could never understand this transformation. To her, Julian was intelligent and impressive; he could hold his own in a conversation with anyone about anything. He was affable too, and well attuned to the particular needs of the ego that was often present in those who dedicated their lives to exploring the full depth of one, often obscure and intangible, topic. But some insecurity of his always broke through to the surface. He was undone by the self-inflicted pressure of impressing others—a pressure Emma did not feel.

There was also the fact that Julian made considered efforts to conceal his wealthy upbringing from other academics, and inviting a group of them into such a casual setting opened him up to the risk of exposure. The academic social circles Julian moved in back in London often prided themselves on their lack of money. Emma felt that, in most cases, this was a reflexive reaction to the fact that permanent and well-paid positions were not going to be a reality for many of them; there was a sense of empowerment that could be gained by viewing their passive acceptance of the circumstances as more of a determined and moral decision. Emma had also observed that there was a certain aesthetic that came with this declarative rejection of wealth; it was not true financial hardship, but rather a romanticized version. It was the rejection of designer brand clothing, but the acceptance of overpriced mid-century or neoclassic vintage furniture, extensive record collections, and art. It was declarative disgust for showy, expensive cars or excessive land ownership, but unblinking acceptance of constant travel and stylish food and wine. Still, the lack of funding and scarcity of stable positions remained a constant source of complaint among Julian's peers and Emma knew he didn't want to reveal himself to be exempt from the common struggle.

The guests arrived, introductions were made, and conversations were lumbered through until everyone had finished a glass of wine. While they ate, Emma sat at the end of the table next to Frederik, a tall Norwegian scholar with a blond mustache and a permanently furrowed brow, who had a tendency to hook his finger and rub his nose vigorously with his knuckle.

"Human geography," he replied when Emma asked what he studied.

"Oh, interesting, I've never heard of that before," she admitted, excited by the idea. "It sounds like it could be a form of medicine."

Frederik looked back at her in open confusion, and she leaped to clarify, "I just meant, it sounds a little like you could be studying the terrain of the human body."

"It's nothing like that. It's about observing the relationship between human societies and the geography they occupy," he explained. "There's a lot of spatial analysis of population distribution and cultural consequences. I say 'consequences' because I'm particularly interested in the management of crises. My thesis is about the historical and economical geography of Ottoman Greece in the eighteenth century."

"That's fascinating," Emma said politely. She hunted for a follow-up question but found nothing.

"And what do you study?" he asked in return.

"I don't study. Actually, at the moment I'm in between jobs."

He blinked at her expectantly and she felt compelled to continue.

"I had a job in London. A good job, actually. I was head of publicity at an advertising agency. Our client list was mostly heritage luxury brands." She watched his top lip involuntarily curl. "But I left that job."

"Why did you leave?" he asked.

Emma observed her wineglass. "Alistair said he was going away and asked if Julian and I wanted to come to Athens to housesit for the summer," she answered, heavily summarizing. "So I suppose I do nothing now, technically. Although I don't feel like I do nothing. I feel like I have this whole life within my own brain—if that makes sense."

Frederik made no charitable motion to affirm that anything she'd said did indeed make sense and after a pause she continued.

"I mean, I'm never bored, and my brain still feels very occupied. I'm starting to realize that it's a myth, this idea that we *need* a consuming occupation or a passion, or even children, to feel fulfillment, you know?"

Frederik's eyes narrowed almost imperceptibly. She realized she was making grand generalizations and could almost feel him tallying them up against her.

"I don't mean to say that everyone should give up their jobs or academic pursuits," she went on, attempting to gracefully backstep. "But I guess for me I've felt my brain expand rather than contract. So anyway, I'm really enjoying it."

When she stopped talking, Frederik frowned and nodded at the same time, a confusing mix of expressions. Then he reached for his wineglass and took a slow, deliberate sip, using the interlude to direct his attention to another conversation further down the table, performing his migration casually as if he were moving from the outskirts of one lively group discussion to another at a cocktail party. In reality, Emma felt more like they'd been rowing a canoe together and he'd suddenly thrown his oar away and jumped into the water. She reached for her own glass and drank to soften the rejection.

After they finished eating, the group halved in size, some taking the transition to the living room as an excuse to leave. Those who remained, sprawled on the couch and carpet, began to discuss Guy Debord's *The Society of the Spectacle,* a conversation sparked by someone sharing their opinion of the text after finding a worn copy on Alistair's shelf.

"I think it's never been more relevant. Here, this quote: 'Where the real world changes into simple images, the simple images become real beings and effective motivations of hypnotic behavior.' It's almost prognosticated the advent of social media," Elias, a short and energetic scholar of Greek poetry, declared.

"Well, yes, but you must admit that's a gross simplification of its original points," Frederik argued, "and the advent of social media wasn't the birth of manipulation via simple images. Are we going to ignore propaganda and print advertising? I just don't think the text is as vital as it's heralded to be."

Elias made a face of disbelief, and Frederik went on, "No, truly, Elias, you could interpret almost any meaning you wish from a quote so vague."

"Okay, what about: 'Separated from his product, man himself produces all the details of his world with ever increasing power, and thus finds himself ever more separated from his world. The more his life is now his product, the more he is separated from his life.'"

"I've got to say I agree with Elias," Angeliki added. Frederik rolled his eyes, as she continued, "I reread it when I was in Vienna, and I think it's never been more—"

"Yes, but," Frederik cut in, "I just don't think it's that insightful. It's a banal series of disconnected and amorphous passages and you're all assigning it more meaning than I think it deserves."

Elias, Angeliki, and Julian all leaped to the text's defense and a clamor of indistinct arguments erupted between them all. Emma felt herself shrinking away from the sound of their voices, unable to perform even the simple task of nodding and smiling. The conversation seemed to be racing ahead without her, and she found herself sipping her wine more frequently than the others, who paused and placed their glasses down while they contributed some comment or reacted to another's. She had the sudden urge to leave the room on the rare chance that somebody decided to ask her a question, at which point it would become obvious just how far behind they had left her. As she stood up from where she'd been seated on the carpet, the ground lurched and she realized she was a little drunk. She left the living room, feeling the familiar sensation of Julian's eyes following her.

In the kitchen she emptied the full ice tray into the sink and ran the hot water. Then she poked her head back through the doorway into the living room and announced to the party that they'd run out of ice.

"I'll go get some," she called, feigning dutiful cheeriness for no reason as the party was carrying on entirely uninhibited by her absence.

.  .  .

As Emma stepped into the elevator the floor jolted under her feet. She flinched in surprise and then sighed in frustration, rubbing her hand over her face, before remembering that she was wearing lipstick and mascara. Sighing again, she leaned closer to the worn metal plating that encased the elevator buttons and attempted to use the scratched and distorted reflection to assess the smudging.

Out on the street, she walked aimlessly. After walking every day for over a fortnight now, she was easily able to keep track of where she was; still it continued to surprise her how different the neighborhood was at night. Strings of lights dangled across narrow streets, and tables and chairs populated unlikely spaces: arranged up thin rows of uneven stone steps or spilling onto the road. Swarms of people moved slowly in all directions, navigating around one another blindly in their distracted search for somewhere to stop, the warm, still night encouraging them all to linger outside. Emma swerved away from the arm of another tourist just in time to avoid wearing the melting gelato they held in their hand. She stopped by a mini-mart and purchased a pack of cigarettes and a lighter. The occasional act of smoking was a sort of communion with a younger version of herself who she didn't want to lose contact with entirely: the version of Emma in her early twenties, who smudged her eyeliner carefully, deliberately ripped ladders in her stockings, and wore a faux leopard-print fur coat everywhere. The version of herself who was broke and reckless, but freer than she'd ever be again.

As she stood across the road from the mini-mart, not yet ready to buy ice and return to the dinner party, a door to her left opened and a couple spilled out of it, illuminated by the warm light that shone from behind them. Music leaked out too, crooning and lyrical. The woman lit a cigarette and handed the man her lighter as the door shut behind them.

"Is that a bar?" Emma found herself asking the couple.

They turned to look at her blankly. Then the man tilted his head forward almost imperceptibly. Emma took that to mean yes. The couple turned back to each other and moved off down the street, smoke disappearing above their heads.

Inside was a small but lively space, with a dark wood bar that ran along the right-hand side of the room. Tables and stools were organized all the way up to the back wall, which was occupied by a doorway concealed behind a red curtain.

Emma took a seat at the bar and looked around as she waited to be served. The walls of the room were painted an off-white color, which aged to yellow under the warm lighting, and seemingly random selections of photos and prints covered the walls in heavy, mismatched frames. Emma was holding eye contact with the seductive glare of a photo of a Greek screen siren, when a voice interrupted her.

"What would you like?" the woman behind the bar asked, leaning her forearms on the counter.

"A negroni, please," she replied.

Emma watched the woman move back down the bar. She had long, dark wavy hair, half of which was tied up; a rogue strand had freed itself and curled around her face, which was slightly flushed, symmetrical and pretty. Emma registered vaguely that she must be in her early twenties. There was something overtly sexual about the way she carried and held her body, like a woman who had learned that she held a certain power. Julian had always found women with darker features attractive. He liked boldness: a strong nose below a pair of sharp, brown eyes, and long, dark hair. His most recent ex was from Seville, and the woman before her was Lebanese—both of them strikingly beautiful. In the past, during the early days of their relationship, Emma had brought this up with him. "So then . . . why me?" she'd joked. She couldn't be fairer. She was practically translucent. Her features were small and plain and even her eyes, which were green—apparently the rarest of all eye colors—looked entirely expected and unsurprising as part of her overall image. In response to Emma's question Julian had laughed and shaken his head. "Because you're perfect," he'd replied vaguely.

The woman placed Emma's drink in front of her, accepted her cash, and returned the change wordlessly, before moving off to serve a man further down the bar.

As the man ordered his drink, he glanced artlessly at the woman's chest. It appeared that the woman was aware of the man's eyes and in response her body language grew more playful. The attention seemed to please her, rather than disturb her. As Emma judged the man, she realized that she was observing the woman in a way that was not so different from him; she was also sexualizing her and being prurient.

After she finished her drink, Emma stepped out into the alleyway next to the bar to have a cigarette. As she stood there, smoking and considering her inevitable return to the dinner party, a young man appeared at the entrance of the laneway. He stooped against the wall, his neck bent over his phone, as if he was waiting for someone. A moment later, the woman from the bar appeared and called out to him. He stowed his phone away in his pocket and kissed her. Emma averted her eyes instinctively, before glancing back. The woman laughed and pulled the man further down the alleyway past Emma. They kissed again, passionately this time as if they were alone, not seeming to mind that Emma was standing right there, an audience to their intimate moment. The man's mouth was moving fast, clumsily. His hands touched the woman's face and neck, moving quickly—too quickly—down her body. He slid his hand to where her denim shorts met her thigh and hooked a finger up underneath the cuff. She pulled away, laughing and swatting his hand. Emma shifted her gaze down, unsure if she should leave. She observed her own shoes, as she listened to them speaking in hushed voices to each other. Something final was said and the man walked off, passing Emma with his hands in his pockets, most likely pulling his shorts so his erection was not so obvious. Emma watched the back of him as he left.

"Do you mind if I stand with you?" The woman was suddenly next to Emma, vaping and releasing toxic, artificial watermelon fumes into the air around them.

"No, not at all."

"You still smoke cigarettes," she observed.

"It's nostalgic for me," Emma answered, glancing at the woman's pleasingly symmetrical face.

"It's a little nostalgic for me too," she admitted. "I prefer the smell of this now though."

"Was that your boyfriend?" Emma asked to change the subject.

The woman laughed, releasing another cloud of vapor. "No, I don't want to date a boy my age."

"Why not?"

"They know nothing about how women experience pleasure. He"—she nodded toward the street—"is just obsessed with pussy."

Her crude comment was surprising. It took the conversation to a jarringly intimate depth, but it didn't displease

Emma. Already she was more engaged than she'd been the entire evening while entertaining Alistair's friends.

"I see. How old are you?" Emma asked.

"Twenty-two."

Emma smiled knowingly as she exhaled. "They get better with age," she said.

"Good to know," the woman responded, now looking back at Emma. "How old are you?"

"Thirty-four," Emma said, and then because the woman said nothing in response, she added, "That probably seems ancient to you."

The woman frowned. "No, I can't wait to be older."

Emma laughed then. "I used to say the exact same thing at your age, and to be honest you couldn't pay me to go back to being twenty-two."

The woman smiled.

"So why do you do this then?" Emma ventured, buoyed by the woman's apparent openness. "If it doesn't bring you pleasure?"

She shrugged and pondered the question as she exhaled. "I like that he thinks he's in control, but really he's powerless. That is what brings me pleasure."

Her statement didn't ring true to Emma. She didn't think the man had looked powerless. She imagined him using all of his strength against the woman. It was easy to imagine her helpless.

"Is he really powerless though?" Emma asked. "I mean, he could overpower you if he really wanted to."

"No, he couldn't," the woman rebuked, offering no further explanation. She pulled her phone out of the back pocket of her shorts.

As Emma watched the woman look at her phone, she tried

to pinpoint why she was drawn to her, why she was finding it hard to look away.

"I have to go back," the woman said suddenly. "Are you coming back in for another drink?"

"No, I should get going," Emma admitted. "I left a dinner party to get some ice and now they're probably wondering where I am."

"Why did you leave?"

"I was bored."

The woman smirked as she slid her phone back into her pocket. "And was this more fun?"

"Definitely."

"I'm Lena by the way."

"Emma," she replied.

They smiled at each other briefly, before Lena turned and left. Emma retrieved her phone from her pocket to see she had a missed call and a message from Julian. He'd sent the message twenty minutes ago:

*Ice?*

Another followed as she was reading the first:

*Are you OK?*

She wrote back: *On my way. Sorry!*


"What took you so long?" Julian asked Emma as he dried his face with a towel. She was brushing her teeth over the sink and he waited as she completed the task before she answered him. She'd arrived back at the apartment in time to see the last of the guests off. Julian had watched her say goodbye with a bag of ice clutched uselessly in her hands. An hour after her departure, the party had registered her absence and from then on

Julian felt an excruciating awkwardness hanging in between the words everyone spoke, as if Emma and he had openly fought in front of the group and they were all trying to pretend they hadn't witnessed it.

She spat into the sink. "I was just trying to find ice and I forgot where the mini-mart was."

"Right," he said, declaring skepticism.

"Okay, honestly, I just needed a break. I went and had a drink at a bar."

Julian stopped drying his face and looked at her. He couldn't circumvent the question anymore; it had been weeks since he'd asked plainly and it was time to ask again.

"Emma, are you really okay?" He tried to make meaningful eye contact with her, but her eyes fled his.

"I'm fine. We don't need to have this conversation again."

"I don't mean to keep pressing, but you walked out in the middle of our dinner party."

Emma said nothing, her eyes trained on the sink as she washed her toothbrush.

"You told me you want me to sleep with someone else," he continued. "I don't know what to make of—"

"Those two things are not at all related, I promise. These aren't all symptoms of some deeper issue. Really, I mean it."

"You haven't really seemed yourself lately. Part of me wonders whether this idea of you wanting me to sleep with someone else is more of a temporary interest brought on by a mood."

She turned to face him.

"The issue being," he continued, "if we do it, we can't undo it."

"What are you afraid of?" she asked.

He sighed, returning the towel to its hook and putting his

glasses back on. "I guess I'm afraid you'll regret it and that maybe I'll be too closely linked to the regret. Then the only way to dispel it will be to get rid of me too."

"There is absolutely no way that could ever happen." She smiled at him through the mirror. "And I'm fine, really."

He gave her a small smile and she resumed rinsing her toothbrush.

"How was the rest of the party?" she asked after a moment.

"Well," Julian said, "Frederik eventually managed to insult everyone enough that they all decided to leave. I thought Elias might actually throw a book at his head at one point."

She laughed, putting her toothbrush away and turning to him once again. Still smiling, she slowly lifted his glasses back off his face and he felt—like he always did whenever this gesture was performed—that he was happy to forget everything else.

# CHAPTER SIX

Julian stared at the words before him, his neck bent at an inadvisable angle. Blue light beamed onto him from the screen, casting shadows that exaggerated his frown lines and the furrows between his brows. He checked his notes and tentatively typed out a sentence before checking his notes once again. Then he reread the words he'd written and deleted them. This had become a familiar dance and as he pushed and pushed, attempting to use brute force against something intangible, he found that he seemed to only be making the situation worse.

For years Julian's research paper had provided him with a feverish source of energy. It had given him a sense of hope, which he'd hung upon its unknown—and therefore unlimited—potential. He woke in the early mornings and worked hard at it, convinced that his ideas were crucial and timely. Then, one morning, about a week after Emma's miscarriage, he'd opened the document and found it was missing something. It was as if the vital connection he'd had to the central argument of the

text had simply disappeared, leaving behind a structure ana-
tomically correct but devoid of soul. Now he couldn't feel any
emotion as he read back his own words. Recently, he'd even
stopped reading the chapters he'd already written because,
whenever he did, he could only see all the fallacies he'd poorly
concealed like a bad card trick. Julian had given so much of
his time—his precious youth!—to the endeavor that he felt
obliged to return uselessly to the battlefield day after day and
continue waging a war against himself. He'd tentatively held a
hope that living in a different city might be the kind of shift
needed to begin a conversation once again with whatever
spirit had once resided in his mind and handed him words.
Instead, the problem persisted. It was becoming clear that
he'd packed up the issue between his books and shirts and
brought it along with him. Now he was beginning to panic,
far more than he'd let on to Emma, who assumed he was deal-
ing with a series of small hitches in the road, not unlike the
many he'd encountered and overcome in the past while completing his PhD thesis. She would often ask him, in a well-
meaning way, how the paper was coming along, and he would
lie to her, like a man amid an affair, fabricating milestones
along a convoluted timeline. He hoped these developments
would satisfy, or at least bore, her enough that eventually the
topic of his paper would be visited only in passing, as if
through a bus window.

He picked up his phone and opened an app, one that promised to show him endless images of other people's perfect
lives. He was in the mood to punish himself, to find some salt
to rub into his wound. Such was the nature of the app that he
found something almost immediately. Another academic he
knew—a woman he'd studied at Cambridge with, who he'd
long ago dismissively concluded was not capable of original

ideas—had once again proven him wrong. The first time was when she'd published a paper the year after they graduated; though admittedly he was not overly impressed with it, it had been well-received and had gone on to be applauded by nearly all of Julian's current academic heroes. At the time he'd been optimistically working on his own research paper and the outcome of hers aided in making him feel confident that if *she* could publish, then perhaps he was not so foolish for thinking he could too.

Then, last year, she'd done something unexpected and published a book: a genre-redefining fictional biography of the world's first great female philosopher. The novel sought to show a vision of an alternative present-day, in which our foundational understanding of philosophy had developed differently by not being formed in a patriarchal, xenophobic, and imperialist society like classical Athens. The book did something Julian would never have expected: it released itself from the echo chamber of academia and managed to find a broader appreciation. She had woven an engrossing narrative into the story of the life of this fictional philosopher, and as a result, everyday people, laymen to philosophy, were enthusiastically buying and reading it. It was a monumental and exceedingly rare achievement and a great shock to Julian.

He was clear with himself that it was not because she was a woman that Julian had estimated her potential to be lower than it had since revealed itself to be. It was more that he'd felt, during many discussions in the course of their studies, that everything she said and wrote was relentlessly forced through the lens of her oppressed gender. Julian most often enjoyed when the discussions, in the musty rooms at Cambridge, took flight beyond the subjects of class and gender and approached the broader human experience. But whenever she was involved, she would force the discussion back down to the ground, where it would begin to shrink timidly in the shadow of its own privilege. It had been Julian's opinion that she would need to learn to lay those grievances of hers aside; otherwise, she might find their professors would quickly grow tired of her limited perspective. They had not, it turned out. And neither had the rest of the world.

The image Julian was now looking at was an announcement that her book was in the running for an extremely prestigious international fiction award. She'd been short-listed. She might *win*. Julian's stomach lurched with envy. He'd never had the desire to write fiction, and he'd certainly never fantasized about winning a fiction award, but he did allow himself to envision publishing a nonfiction book one day—a pragmatic vision in which he was well into his fifties with many published papers under his belt. Certainly, he fantasized about a roomful of people clapping in awe of his talent, his indisputable accomplishment. Now that he questioned whether he'd even be able to finish his paper, let alone be published, this announcement cut him deeper than he even thought possible.

He looked to excuse himself from the self-inflicted competition. He wondered whether, if he were a woman, he would have been considered to have a more urgent and desirable view. He then wondered whether, if he had grown up poorer, people would be more excited to hear his thoughts. But even amid his paroxysm of insecurity, he stopped short of lamenting his lifelong proximity to wealth. He stared at the image, feeling self-pity grow from his envy, and despair grow from his self-pity. Finally, he felt deep despondency grow from his despair. What was the use of having goals like this, arbitrary and vain goals, which were almost entirely out of one's control? Why did he torture himself?

Growing up, he'd always been applauded for his intelligence—the only available form of affection from his mostly aloof and distracted parents. His father was a world-renowned cardiothoracic surgeon, who expanded his wealth exponentially in the late 1980s by being an early investor in the angioplasty balloon catheter; his mother was an operating theater nurse who, upon marriage to his father, took off her scrubs and became a philanthropist and well-respected figure within their local community in Surrey. There was a special place in his parents' hearts for those who worked and worked until they reached the ankle-deep waters at the upper end of the bell curve. He could recall the moment he bluffed his eye examination at age eleven in the hope of acquiring a pair of reading glasses, which he believed were a requirement for entry into the academic elite because every guest his parents had over for dinner at their estate wore a pair. What poetic symbolism that memory contained, such desperate striving— a clear indication of his maladjustment and self-consciousness, even at such an early age. He felt sorry for his younger self. He wanted to hold him, stroke his hair, take the book out of his hands, remove the falsely acquired glasses from his face, and tell him: this pursuit will only make you suffer.

After having his fill of all the repetitive congratulations and compliments in the comment section below the photo, he put his phone down and looked around the reading room of the Vallianeio Megaron. In his despair, he ignored the grand and historical spectacle of it: the walls covered in ancient age-worn books, the row of impressive ionic columns that lined the whole room. Instead, he observed the others, all of them frowning at books and screens. He knew that his particular affliction was not unique; many others had dealt with, and even eloquently documented, the strange sense of grief that came from discovering that whatever life a project had once harbored was now gone. Even though it was most likely true that the world did not need Julian's paper, even though it was also statistically probable that any paper he ever wrote would at best amount to nothing more than a published sermon read only by the mostly sympathetic choir of his colleagues—its completion and publication were still important to him, not least because of the common saying among his peers: *Publish or perish.* He didn't want his career to perish; he simply didn't know how to regain control over the situation. He snapped his laptop shut and packed up the small stack of books that he brought along for both research and supportive totemic purposes.

He left the library, emerging back into the startling heat of the day and walking down the curved stone staircase with care. The stone was treacherously smooth. Occasionally, if he was too distracted, his foot would glide, jolting him back to attention. He walked past buildings, all of which were either gray, beige, or yellow, until he arrived at the Old Royal Palace, an austere neoclassical building that housed the Hellenic Parliament. Every day when Julian passed this building, he watched the *evzones*. These were soldiers that historically belonged to an elite light infantry of the Greek army, a ceremonial unit of which guarded a war monument out in front of the parliament building. They wore kilt-like skirts, and each carried an M1 that rested heavily on their shoulders. Julian knew that the changing of the guard happened every hour, and in between, the *evzones* were not allowed to speak or even move, they could only stand and sweat in their uniforms. One morning, he'd walked past a family of tourists who were conducting a photo shoot with the guard unfortunate enough to be stationed close to the footpath. Julian had watched as the soldier stared straight ahead, refusing to break character, until the small child touched his uniform, at which point he let out a loud shout, sending the child running terrified back to its mother.

After Julian reached the parliament building, he crossed through Syntagma Square, passing the fountain and the groups of people sprawled on the grass under the shade of the trees. Alistair had warned Julian that summer in Athens was brutal. Families who had the means often left the city to rejoin their extended family on the islands or smaller towns where they originally came from. When Julian and Emma had arrived in Athens in the second week of June, the city seemed full, but Alistair had explained that by the time August arrived, they would see the difference. Already, the heat was oppressive, and he knew that the temperatures would continue to climb until the end of August. Alistair had no air conditioner in his apartment, and even though the maximum temperatures of summer were not yet being reached, Julian and Emma were using multiple fans arranged strategically to sleep at night. Was staying here necessary, he wondered, now that he'd established the issue he was having with his paper was unlikely to be shaken off by the change of scenery?

He thought of Emma. She appeared to be drawing something from these new surroundings, as if from a well, and it seemed to be changing and renewing her. Her request to watch him sleep with someone else seemed to be a direct example of the freedom she felt in being here, and her desire to explore life was heartening to him, even if it had manifested surprisingly. Julian had always suspected that Emma lacked an inherent driving force, a burning ambition that kept her directed, as he did. After she abruptly quit The Agency—an uncharacteristic decision—he felt this suspicion to be confirmed. Now, however, he found himself envious of her. Every day, she ventured out into Athens and experienced life firsthand. Every day, he ventured to the library and experienced life via the thoughts, accounts, and theories of others. Perhaps he was wrong to pity her, as he occasionally had. Perhaps he should follow her lead a little more, dilute his focus, spread his interest, and expand his experiences. It would be good timing, given that, after they returned from Athens, he assumed they would resume their plans to enter into a new phase: parenthood. That phase would come with its own new experiences, but it would also render others practically impossible. Maybe Emma had already had all of these thoughts, and he was merely plodding along the path behind her. Maybe she was waiting patiently for him to catch up. Unconsciously, he picked up his pace, turning left and right through the winding streets of Plaka.

A few streets away, Emma walked quickly. Her mind and her body were severed from each other, her body performing the simple repetitive act of retracing steps while her mind circled in the same spot, fixated. Her thoughts had traveled back to Lena countless times since she'd met her at the bar and spoken to her in the alleyway days before. She continued to seek an explanation for why Lena had captivated her so entirely. For one, it was the way that Lena had said the word "pussy." She'd never met anyone who would say something so crass to a stranger and pull it off with the style that Lena had. Emma herself could not even say the word unironically. She could say "cock" or "dick," no problem, but "pussy" was too loaded. There was a memory she had from primary school; she'd been

eight years old, sitting in one of the library aisles attempting
to decide between two books, when a boy from her class urgently approached her, thrusting a note into her hand before
running away. She'd opened the note to see it only contained a
single word, scrawled in a way that seemed to show the author
had been in a heightened emotional state: *pussy*.

During sex, Emma would say "me," "in me," "on me,"
"touch me." She took lengths to circumvent the need to refer
too directly to herself. She'd once told Julian how she felt, and
together they'd repeated all the names they thought might be
right for the setting, grimacing as if testing all the different
pitches and finding them all off-key. But Lena had said the
word so that it sounded both authentic and dignified in a way
that added dimension and removed any ties to the flat screech-
ing of bad porn. Emma could imagine her saying it in bed; the
effect would be galvanic. It would push a man right over the
edge.

It was these thoughts that sent Emma wandering back to
the bar, which she knew, after searching online, opened to
serve coffee during the day. She wanted to see Lena again. She
was not attracted to her, but she kept imagining how Lena
would have sex, how she would move, how she would sound.
At first, she pictured her with the young man from the
alleyway—their youthful, messy, inexperienced fervidness.
She imagined Lena toying with the man's uncontrolled excitement, but the vision had only one note—the pleading desperation of the man—and Emma bored quickly of him. It was
then that she replaced him with Julian, leveling the field between them so that sometimes Lena pleaded with Julian, and
he would look at Emma for permission, and in response, she
would nod.

She reached the bar and was about to cross the road toward it when she saw that it appeared to be open only halfheartedly. There were no tables laid out on the footpath and no signage inviting people in for coffee. Emma stopped, unsure of how to proceed. It was then that Lena appeared as if summoned, walking out of the bar with a chair in her arms and laughing over her shoulder at someone inside. Emma turned, feigning interest elsewhere, as Lena placed the chair down. A man emerged through the door after her. An older man in a button-up shirt and business slacks holding an espresso glass and a small tumbler of water. He sat down on the chair Lena had set up, and she leaned against the nearby wall, pulling out her vape and chatting with the man. Emma, suddenly conscious that she was simply standing on the street and staring, entered the mini-mart next to her and hovered over the produce section so she could continue watching through the window without being noticed. Lena was wearing denim shorts again and a white tank top that was cropped at her waist. On her feet, she wore a pair of combat boots. Emma recalled the glimpse she'd seen in the alleyway, the man's finger reaching up under the cuff of her shorts.

The man continued talking to Lena as she exhaled another cloud and scratched her arm absentmindedly. Eventually, Lena stood and squeezed the man's shoulder as she passed him on her way back into the bar.

Although she hadn't been sure of exactly what she was looking for, Emma felt she had found it. She would ask Julian to come to the bar and orchestrate a meeting between him and Lena to see what would happen. She imagined the meeting, and all the ways it could go well, until an older woman bumped her aggressively, mumbling something in Greek, and Emma realized she was standing in the way of the tomatoes.

"Oh, sorry," she said, blushing furiously as if the woman had caught her watching porn.

They sat on the balcony that evening and ate a salad Julian had made, which resembled Greek salad and fattoush. Julian had seemed occupied all afternoon, arriving home from the library with groceries and immediately disappearing into the kitchen, only to emerge to announce dinner was ready. Emma had not pressed him into conversation, knowing it was better not to get in the way of whatever knots he was tying or untying in his mind. His distracted mood had suited Emma and she'd used the time to consider how to talk to him about Lena. When he eventually sighed conclusively, as if mentally closing a book, and turned his attention back to the present, Emma refilled his glass and began. "The other night when I went out for a drink, I found a bar that I think we should go back to."

"Okay, sure," he replied lightly.

"Maybe on Friday night?"

"That sounds fun," he said, lifting his glass to his lips.

She could easily leave the conversation there, bringing Julian unwittingly into her plan, but it felt dishonest not to be clearer about her intention. She also knew that it was never a good idea to ambush Julian. If an ulterior motive was revealed when they were already at the bar, he was liable to respond defensively.

"There's a reason I want to go to this particular bar," she admitted.

Julian put his glass down and looked back at her.

"I saw a woman there who I think you might find attractive, and if she was interested in you too then . . . I mean, she's very . . ."

He looked confused for a moment before realization dawned. "You really want to pursue this?"

"I do," Emma replied. "But I know you needed some time to think about it."

He studied the stem of his wineglass.

"Have you thought about it?" she pressed.

"Yes."

She waited for him to continue.

"I suppose I still don't fully understand why it appeals to you." He paused as if to give her time to explain, but she remained silent. "But if you're sure." He looked at her meaningfully. "Then, okay, we could explore it."

She smiled at him, and he returned the smile with a weaker version of his own, his joy clouded with apprehension.

"I don't think I can explain why it appeals to me," Emma admitted. "I can't intellectualize it—it's a physical desire."

Julian nodded, doing his best to comprehend. "There will need to be rules," he said, the smile sliding away. "We'll have to consider a few things and set boundaries."

Emma nodded. "I completely agree."

"I think we need to be clear that either of us can stop what's happening at any point."

She continued nodding enthusiastically, only too willing to accommodate these conditions. She was half in disbelief that they'd arrived at this stage of the conversation.

"We need to be in complete control of the situation," Julian added.

"Absolutely."

They looked at each other for a moment.

"And you need to let me know what you're thinking and feeling, Emma," he went on, his tone now grave. "We need to communicate."

"I promise I will."

"Okay."

"Thank you," she then said, reaching for his hand, "for being so open to this."

Already, she felt a thrill of excitement, an energy that coursed through her in a way she hadn't been able to summon for a long time, as if she were now in communion with some part of herself that had been ignored or misunderstood for too long.

# CHAPTER SEVEN

By memory, Emma led them to the bar, but upon seeing the familiar door, she was disappointed to find it looked pokier than when she recalled it in her mind. This was partly because she had taken on the responsibility for managing Julian's experience and was now viewing everything through his eyes.

The plain, dull look of the bar gave her a feeling of presentiment. Perhaps all of her memories of meeting Lena were filtered flatteringly through the lens of her fantasy, maybe she'd inferred too much about Lena and the interaction was doomed to fall drastically short of her goal.

She felt some relief when she opened the door and immediately saw Lena—the first large hurdle of the evening successfully cleared. Lena was pouring two glasses of wine, wearing a long black skirt and a faded blue T-shirt. Her hair was arranged in two plaits that bounced against her collarbones as she moved. Emma led Julian to the bar and they took a seat. There were other immediate requirements for her desired objective to stand a chance and one of them was for Lena to remember Emma.

When Lena eventually turned and approached them, she smiled at Emma in recognition and said, "Hello again." Emma felt relief at having passed over another hurdle, a feeling that shifted quickly into a rising sense of anticipation.

"Hello," she replied, matching Lena's tone.

Emma introduced Julian and watched as Lena blushed slightly in response to Julian's greeting. He had this effect on some people. He was handsome and well-dressed, but it was more than that. It wasn't that he flirted or encouraged such responses, it was more that his comfortable and confident demeanor occasionally seemed to throw into question the confidence of those around him. He had a way of holding eye contact and smiling that seemed to imply a shared inside joke. Strangers would sometimes stutter or grow flustered in his company; in one instance a barista knocked over the coffee they'd just made. It was almost cruel, but given Julian was simply being polite, he could not be held responsible for the thoughts, feelings, or reactions of others. Emma knew what the disorienting experience of receiving his full attention was like, having been caught off guard by it when she first met him. She could recall the way her own cheeks had burned under his gaze as he stood in front of her in the sandwich shop. After their first few dates, she found herself increasingly immune to it. Instead of feeling the exhilaration of his attention, or the frantic rush of her attraction to him—those transient, electric sensations—she soon felt something calm and solid: definitive love.

They ordered two negronis and Lena moved down the bar to make them, casting side-eyed glances every so often.

"What do you think?" Emma asked, leaning in toward Julian.

Julian glanced at Lena, rubbing a hand over his chin and jaw.

"She's beautiful, no?" Emma pressed.

Julian let out a small, almost embarrassed laugh. "She is," he agreed. His words stabbed Emma sharply with both pain and pleasure.

When Lena returned with their drinks, she placed them down and leaned her forearms on the counter. "You're back," she said. "Escaping another boring party?"

Emma felt Julian's eyes on her. "No, we wanted a good negroni and I knew I could trust you."

Lena smiled at the compliment. "So, are you here on holiday?" she asked.

"Yes," Julian replied. "Well, kind of—we're housesitting for a friend."

"You're English. From . . ."

"London."

Lena gave a single nod, tilting her head slightly as she did, a gesture Emma had seen many times since arriving in Greece.

"You aren't going to any islands? Most tourists don't hang around in Athens for long."

"We went to Corfu a few weeks ago," Emma explained. "But we're happy spending time in Athens."

Lena raised her eyebrows. "Many people leave Athens in the summer—it gets very hot."

At that point another customer arrived at the bar, pulling Lena's attention away. After she finished serving, Lena moved around the bar collecting used glasses, and as the distance between them stretched, Emma began to lose confidence. The assumption that Lena would have time to speak to Emma and

Julian was proving to be a significant fault in her plan. The bar was busier than it had been when Emma first visited it and, even though it was edging toward midnight, patrons came and went frequently. Every time the door swung open, she felt an irrational annoyance.

Julian was talking about a recent email from Alistair. He'd met someone and was now considering a permanent move. This kind of impulsivity was typical of Alistair. He was always chasing something or someone, always moving at high speed. Julian read the email out loud as Emma scanned the room past Julian's shoulders. Further up the bar, Lena was pouring beer from a glass bottle into smaller glasses, tilting each of the glasses carefully. As if she felt Emma watching her, she glanced over and met Emma's gaze. They held eye contact for a brief moment, Lena's smile shifting into a smirk. Fearing Lena's stare would cause her to blush, Emma reciprocated for as long as she could before turning back to Julian.

After serving the beer, Lena returned, standing before them and gesturing to their empty glasses. "Two more?"

Emma knew some daring move was required to demonstrate her and Julian's intentions. She leaned across the bar, further than necessary to hand Lena her credit card, and asked, "What time do you finish?"

To her relief, Lena seemed pleased by the question. Her eyes narrowed slightly as if she were amused, and the corner of her mouth twitched into a small smile. "In half an hour," she replied. The machine beeped, drawing her eyes. She removed the card and tore the receipt.

"We wanted to invite you to come back to our apartment for a drink," Emma said.

Julian stiffened slightly beside her, astonished perhaps by how boldly she'd stated the question.

Lena handed Emma back her card. "Okay," she replied without hesitation.

"Who are you?" Julian whispered into Emma's ear.

The idea of being someone else sent a surge of excitement through her.

Emma and Julian waited on the street outside while Lena and the other two bartenders finished closing up. They'd changed the music to some sort of house music. Bass thrummed through the walls, and Emma could hear the sound of their laughter and voices rising occasionally above the music as they cleaned. Then Lena appeared, a tote bag slung over her shoulder. She said goodbye to the others, kissing them on the cheek and waving as they disappeared down the street. She had a set of keys in her hand; Emma and Julian stood idly as she locked the bar's door, before pulling down a metal security shutter and crouching down to lock that as well. Then she stood, dusting off her knees.

"So," she said. "Should we go?"

Despite the fact it was midnight, the streets of Plaka were still busy. Families remained at restaurant tables settled among the detritus of their meals. Young children slept in their chairs, or in the arms of their parents, too young to have formed the endurance necessary to remain awake.

"Are you staying around here?" Lena asked as they walked.

"Yes—not far," Julian answered.

"Where do you live?" Emma asked.

"With my family in Colonus." Sensing correctly that they would not be familiar with the suburbs of Athens, Lena clarified, "It's much further out from here."

The conversation continued to carry itself with surprising ease. It seemed to be mutually understood that constant motion was required, and all three of them took turns helping to keep the conversation afloat.

When they arrived at the apartment, Emma watched as Lena wandered around touching and complimenting Alistair's belongings.

"This apartment is beautiful," she said, running a hand along a bookshelf. "I want to live in a place like this one day."

She turned to Julian, accepting the glass of wine he handed to her. "Where is your friend?"

"He's in Sicily for a couple of months."

"He lets you stay here for free?"

"Yes, well," Julian answered, seeming to hover before the option of giving further information before deciding against it. "Yes."

"I want to live in my own apartment," she said, picking up the previous thread of conversation. "I want to decorate it like this, with books and old furniture."

She selected a book from the shelf and turned it over in her hand, before putting it back.

"Do you have your own place in London?" she asked, facing them once again.

"We do," Julian answered.

"Do you have to share it with anyone?"

"No," he said, pausing briefly. "We own it."

Emma saw Lena's eyebrows momentarily rise before she smoothed them back down. Emma was surprised Julian had divulged this information. He usually didn't like to discuss money or assets, especially not the flat his parents had given him. She wondered if he was trying to impress Lena.

There was a moment of silence, which lingered slightly too long.

"Can I put some music on?" Lena asked.

"Of course," Julian said, reaching for the speaker and turning it on.

He handed Lena his phone, before taking a seat on an armchair nearby. Lena scrolled in search of some particular music, the lull in conversation threatening to lower the energy in the room. Emma knew that, given the strangeness of the situation, it was crucial they were all moving in the same direction and at the same pace. She finished her glass in a few mouthfuls and poured herself another, before crossing the room and taking a seat on the couch in the hope that Lena might follow her lead.

A song was selected and bass began to drone as a woman's voice alternated between rapping and singing sedately. Lena remained standing and browsing, subtly moving her hips in a slow, swaying motion to the music. Julian's eyes were drawn to Lena. He watched her with a still but intense expression that Emma felt conveyed both his attraction to what he saw and some conflicting feeling as a result. The music took up the space of conversation. Lena placed the phone down next to the speaker and made her way over to the couch where Emma was sitting.

"Dance with me," she said, holding a hand out.

Emma laughed and shook her head. "I like watching you dance."

Lena smirked, seemingly pleased with the spotlight. She danced, winding her hips around as she drank from her glass and performing a couple of graceful turns before laughing and dropping softly onto the couch next to Emma.

She leaned over and touched Emma's hair. "Your hair is such a beautiful color."

Her face was so close that Emma could feel her warm breath.

"It's natural, isn't it?" Lena asked, holding a piece of Emma's hair on her palm and observing it closely.

Emma turned to meet Lena's eyes, momentarily adjusting to the image of her face so close: the clumps of eyeliner that had collected in the corners of her opaque eyes; the small dark hairs just above the corners of her top lip. They were hovering right on the edge of something, the strength of the pull increasing like the moment just before two magnets snapped together. Emma opened her mouth to answer the question, but the words were unable to form before Lena's lips were on hers.

This was not exactly the plan, but it was a leap in the right direction. She kissed Lena back. Her lips were soft and tasted pleasantly of wine. It was not the first time Emma had kissed a woman. Although she didn't sexually desire women, kissing strange women was on the whole a more pleasant experience than kissing strange men: the size of their mouths being better matched, their intuitive sense of give and take. She met Lena's lips harder, performing for a moment, before pulling away. She looked over at Julian, who was staring back at them—his expression stranded somewhere between surprise and arousal.

She brought her face close to Lena's ear and whispered, "I want you to seduce him."

Emma saw a combination of relief and excitement briefly pass across Lena's face. She stood, making her way over to Julian. Emma's heart accelerated as she watched Lena hitch her skirt up around her thighs and climb on top of him. For a moment Julian seemed frozen. Emma willed him to touch Lena, to engage in what was happening and not stand in the way of the momentum that was building. When he placed his hands on either side of Lena's waist, she was relieved. Lena swung a rope of plaited hair over her shoulder, brought her face down to meet Julian's. Then they were kissing.

Emma felt an explosion of feeling: hurt, jealousy, and humiliation arriving suddenly and intensely. She looked away to shield herself. She had anticipated feeling like this. She was aware that there would be some initial shock at the sight of seeing Julian kiss another woman. She was not naïve enough to think that she would feel only desire and arousal from beginning to end, but she was also sure that the shock would soon give way to other sensations, and that this would all happen faster if she allowed herself to desensitize. She took a deep breath and looked at them again. Julian was looking back at Emma with concern, while Lena kissed his neck, oblivious to the intense exchange occurring around her. He pulled away from Lena and everything stopped. They both looked at Emma—Lena blank-faced, and Julian concerned, confused.

"No, keep going," Emma said.

"Are you sure?" Julian asked.

"Completely," she lied.

"You don't want to join us?" Lena asked.

Emma shook her head. "I want to watch."

She picked up her wineglass as they began to kiss again. She felt herself relaxing, acclimatizing. After a moment, she was able to enjoy Lena's enthusiasm, her attraction to Julian given full rein. Julian seemed more restrained, but Emma could tell that his resistance—sourced from his conflicting feelings—was proving weak against the visceral sensation of Lena on top of him. He was slowly leaving Emma behind and that was exactly what she wanted him to do. Lena pulled off her top and Julian began to kiss her chest without even a glance at Emma. That was the signal she was looking for, the sign that Julian was capable of becoming entirely immersed in what he was doing. Emma slid a hand down the waistband of her trousers and felt her body respond. When Julian glanced at her and saw what she was doing, he crept a hand under Lena's skirt. Lena moaned, but Julian stared at Emma, their eye contact remaining unbroken as his hand continued to move underneath Lena's skirt. Lena pleaded into his neck, asking for more, but Julian hovered there, looking at Emma, perhaps awaiting another signal to move forward. Emma nodded, and Julian shifted Lena down his legs so he could unbutton his pants. He didn't look at Emma again after that point, and in her privacy, Emma watched, and when she was ready she gave herself over to the rushing pleasure.

Julian woke before Emma, who appeared to be sleeping with a grimace on her face as she did whenever she drank more than three glasses of wine. Julian knew this meant she had a headache and that it had managed to make its presence known even in her dreams.

He crept quietly into the living room, where Lena was sleeping on the couch. The sight caused visions to return to him: Lena's eyes rolling skyward with pleasure, and the pink, wet inside of her mouth. A pulse shot through him. He thought of Emma, of the way he watched her touch herself while he touched someone else. It had felt as if his movements were linked to her pleasure and so when he touched Lena, he was by extension touching Emma too. He was free to observe her pleasure from a distance; it was like what she had said to him, something about observing without being involved. He understood it better now.

Replaying the events back to himself was like watching a scene from a movie, rather than his own life, but seeing Lena asleep on the couch opened the door allowing reality to step back in. Instead of being softened by sleep, her face appeared older. She was frowning, wearing a stoic expression that appeared wrought out of hardship and suffering beyond her twenty-something years. He could picture her expression rendered in oil paint on the inured face of a subject in a Gentileschi painting. The image was intimate and uncomfortable. He hurried past her and into the kitchen.

He began to make coffee as loudly as possible, harboring the hope that if he woke everyone else up he would not need to wait alone for much longer in this strange liminal space. He'd just slammed a cupboard with unnecessary force when he turned to see Lena standing in the doorway, her sudden apparition causing him to jump

"Sorry," she said. "I scared you."

She was dressed in her clothing from the night before, her boots on and her tote bag slung over her shoulder. She looked tired, her hair messier and her eye makeup slightly smudged.

"No, it's okay," Julian said, glancing back at the French press to avoid her gaze. "I hope I didn't wake you."

"It's okay. I have to go anyway."

Julian had the sense that she wasn't being genuine. Most likely she had picked up on his desire for the day to move forward and for the whole event to transition into memory where it could be enjoyed more simply. Perhaps she knew that couldn't happen while she was still present in the apartment.

"You didn't want some coffee?" he asked.

"No, thank you." She smiled, a knowing smirk that confirmed Julian's suspicion.

She turned and he followed her down the hallway to the

door. When they reached it, she stood back awkwardly to allow him to open the door for her, their bodies once again close.

"Bye," she said, turning to him and standing on her toes to kiss him on the cheek. More memories, invoked by the smell of her hair, flashed through his mind: her warm breath against his ear; the weight of her hips anchoring down hard against his body; her pleading moans. She turned away from him and stepped into the hallway.

"Bye," he said to the back of her head. She half-turned, giving him one last quick smile. He shut the door and stared at it.

"Julian?" Emma called from the bedroom, her voice small and strained. "Can you please bring me some painkillers? I have a headache."

# CHAPTER EIGHT

The Monastiraki Flea Market opened at 10 A.M. Emma arrived as the stall owners were still setting up. Not wishing to loom impatiently over the scene, she decided to go for a walk. Across the road, the street was lined with restaurants, all of them preparing for the tourists who would arrive over the next few hours and occupy tables with a languor that carried well into the afternoon. Emma watched as a young woman set a chair down on the footpath and returned to the restaurant to collect another. The woman looked like Lena, or, rather, Emma's mind had begun transforming any young woman with long dark hair into Lena. It had been days since Lena had stayed over, but the memory of how explosively her body had responded to seeing Julian with someone else could still send a charge through her.

It had felt strangely liberating. She had been able to remain so present within herself that the experience had expanded her perception. Being herself no longer felt so restrictive. She now viewed the world differently, seeing it filled with endless opportunities for new experiences. It was as if she had pierced some facade and glimpsed behind a curtain that most people never bothered to notice.

She imagined that her and Julian's life could go on like this forever, the two of them traveling and throwing themselves into new experiences one after another.

It wasn't hard to imagine. Sure, Julian had his own goals and dreams, and Emma was respectful of their importance to him, but she also knew that he could write from practically anywhere. They had the money to support themselves, some of which she had earned and saved but most of which resided in Julian's trust. Julian insisted on referring to the money in his trust as *theirs* rather than *his*. Emma had argued against this phrasing, relenting eventually on the condition that he was never to refer to his trust as *theirs* in front of his parents. She imagined her face burning as Julian's mother, Eleanor, stared at her through narrowed eyes across the table in the formal dining room at Gramercy, recasting her opinion of Emma now that she'd finally exposed her exploitative intentions. For a long time, Emma could only view the figure that sat at Julian's disposal as theoretical, as if it were not really money but something else, a feeling compounded by the fact that Julian managed his money in such a way that it seemed to regenerate itself, losing a limb and growing it back. If they chose to live stringently, the money they had and the interest it accrued could potentially stretch on indefinitely. They could live only for themselves and their own pleasure. But there was an obstacle that needed to be overcome: Julian's sudden desire to become a father.

Emma could recall the first time she and Julian had discussed children. It was a Sunday morning, and after dragging themselves out of bed, they had emerged, mortally hungover but in high spirits, into the sunshine to take a walk along Regent's Canal. At the time, Emma was sharing a small flat with three other women in Dalston, and they were forced onto the street in part to escape the communal fug of the house with its dirty dishes, clotted wineglasses, and painted-over window frames that could not be opened. She and Julian had been dating for only a couple of months; Emma was twenty-eight, and Julian was thirty. Because of this, it was not unexpected that Julian would want to have the discussion, but it was surprising that he had approached it so soon. Without any apologetic self-consciousness, he'd simply asked, "Do you see yourself having children one day?"

It was early, both in the day and in terms of their relationship, but Emma could appreciate that the conversation often did not arise early enough. She knew that many couples waited until their lives were inextricably intertwined before they thought to check whether their life goals aligned.

"Do you want the radically honest answer?" she asked him.

"Preferably," he replied, grimacing in the sunlight.

"Well," she spoke slowly, gathering her thoughts, "I've never felt the desire to have children."

A child, she felt, was something she should probably *want* to care for if she was going to bring it into existence. When she reflected on her own upbringing, she was never entirely sure that her mother had truly wanted children. Her parents were married by twenty-one, and Emma was born just over a year later. Although she had felt loved and wanted as she grew up, later, after she reached adulthood, she identified a passivity in her mother, a preference for being carried along, for fitting in quietly, rather than taking on the difficulty of forging a different path. She wondered if her existence was owed to this passivity rather than to any deep, genuine desire. It would have taken a lot of strength for her mother to identify and choose an alternate path, and Emma was under no illusions that the expectations she faced in her own life were not nearly as strong. Still, she felt that the endless choice of paths her life could follow came with the obligation to be deliberate, and that having children, despite not truly desiring them, was not deliberate.

"I feel the same way," Julian responded. "I've never really wanted children for myself."

Emma had looked at him then. He was smiling, though he looked tired and slightly unwell.

She smiled back at him. "That's good news for us."

He took a deep breath, his smile replaced by a look of concern. "Excuse me."

He swerved across the path to the canal's edge, pitching forward and retching straight into the swampy water as murmurs of disapproval and disgust rose from a busy café nearby. Emma crossed the path to stand by him, placing a hand on his bent back and rubbing it supportively. Despite her youthful distaste for such earnest conversations, she knew this was a big moment for them. The future now extended out visibly before them as if a bank of fog had cleared and revealed a path ahead. She'd never previously attempted to peer too far into the future, mostly because the weather never permitted it, but now that it was possible, she realized that she could imagine a life with Julian. As she stared into the murky canal and rubbed his back, she smiled.

How simple their love was back then! It was the time before they were required to begin making decisions that would shape their relationship into its final form. Children, marriage, and a permanent home were like vessels into which a

relationship was poured so that it became tangible and identifiable to others. Only afterward would it be discovered that
the relationship could no longer exist without the vessels that
held it.

She needed to remind Julian of the compelling vision for
the future they'd shared back when they were unified in their
decision not to have children. She felt, if she conveyed it correctly, he would eventually share the vision again. Still, she
was apprehensive. Already, her sense of excitement was beginning to dull.

When Emma returned to the flea market, she saw it had
come to life. She wanted to trawl through the antiques and old
furniture located at one end, but to get there, she needed to
walk through a stretch where the stalls sold most of the same
things they did elsewhere in Athens: Tevas and Birkenstocks,
linen pants, phone chargers, and olive oil. She continued
through until the stalls began to take on the look of a garage
sale, with people spreading blankets out on the ground and
covering them with dusty glassware, rusted cutlery, and
chipped picture frames.

She found a stand selling boxes of pirated DVDs. Hu-
mored, she stood next to an elderly man and flicked through
the titles until she quickly realized that she was not looking at
pirated films but rather a box of porn. The cover of the DVD
she held in her hand seemed to imply a woman was about to
have sex with a horse; she posed bare-chested next to the
horse's limb-like erection. Instantly sickened, Emma dropped
the DVD back into the box and glanced at the man next to her,
who was intently reading the description on a sleeve depicting
two adult women wearing schoolgirl-inspired outfits. She
frowned and quickly moved on.

The tapering path toward the end of the market revealed

rows of narrow antique stores, which were filled to the ceiling with old furniture. Emma began to stroll more slowly, stopping to peek into a long, thin store where chandeliers hung from the ceiling in glittering crowds. She admired a dark mahogany chair, the seat of which had been upholstered in a pink-striped fabric. Nearby, a moody oil painting in a gilded frame depicted a stormy sea with a small, helpless-looking wooden ship being knocked around in the waves. It was an unsettling scene to have hung on a wall.

She'd been right in thinking that this market would not impress Julian. He spent his childhood and school years in grand old buildings filled with grand old furniture. She often thought about Julian's childhood, attempting to imagine what it would have been like to grow up on an estate with a name like Gramercy, to have a housekeeper, and to go to boarding school. He spoke of his childhood with restraint, never appearing to feel particularly nostalgic about any specifics, unlike Emma, who could be transported into the past by small, insignificant things, like the smell of vinegar on hot chips or a particular brand of deodorant with a sickly vanilla scent. The shrieking laughter of a group of teenage girls at the back of a bus or on a bench out front of a supermarket would turn her head, and she would half-expect to see her younger self, hair tied in a ponytail on the side of her head, chewing gum and staring back petulantly. She'd grown up in a nondescript English village in the West Midlands where it seemed nothing ever happened. Her father, a painter of walls not canvases, would often go to the pub after knocking off and return home just before dinnertime. Her mother, an elder-care worker, would cook dinner, and then together, her mother and father would sit transfixed in front of the television late into the night.

She felt envy when Julian spoke of his teenage years. All
the family holidays he went on during school break: the weeks
spent lounging poolside at their villa in Majorca; the months
they spent in Somaliland while his mother and father volun-
teered at a hospital; or the year of school he spent on exchange
in Rolle, Switzerland, where he'd lost his virginity to his host
family's beautiful daughter, who would later become a model
and then, later still, an actress. Julian had admitted that digi-
tal love letters from her, long-winded and earnest, had arrived
in his inbox for years afterward. Emma had never received a
love letter. At sixteen, she'd lost her virginity to a boy inside
the red plastic tunnel of a playground slide. The next week at
school, he called her a "mousy minger," a cruel nickname that
would be used to taunt her all the way through to graduation.

Emma could see that Julian's life was broken up into acts,
which were often marked by a change of scenery and some
resulting epoch. When she compared this to her own adoles-
cence, she was seized by the disturbing notion that there were
few truly distinguishable experiences to mark that passage of
time. All she saw was a monotonous, desert-bordered road
that extended into the past until it reached the horizon, at
which point it wobbled like a mirage with the even vaguer details of her early childhood. The evening with Lena had
burned a permanent mark on her memory, and that was what
she wanted: a signpost along the landscape of her life. She
wanted to have experiences so vivid that when she one day
looked back, she would see a Vegas Strip of memories, undeniable evidence of a life *lived*.

She wanted to watch Julian sleep with Lena again. She
wanted to remain close to this feeling of aliveness, to the sensations that had elevated not just her physical pleasure but her
outlook on life.

Soon, having tired of looking at the old furniture, she began to retrace her steps back through the market, which was now bustling and full of crowds that flowed in all directions. She set course to call by a mini-mart on the way home to pick up ingredients for dinner. She planned to make gazpacho without a blender. It would be chunky gazpacho, rustic.

When Emma returned to the apartment, Julian was on the phone. He'd answered the call as she walked in, giving her an apologetic wave and slipping through the balcony doors.

"Desmond!" he said into the phone, using his nickname for his sister.

Emma could hear Desi respond, "Julie! How is Athens?" as he shut the balcony door behind him. He began to absent-mindedly tap his cheek in a gentle, tic-like slapping motion as he paced back and forth.

Emma removed the grocery-filled bag she wore slung over her body and sat down heavily on the couch. She intuited that Julian's conversation had reached the subject of his paper when his cheek-slapping motions grew more vigorous.

"Yeah, it's going well—really well." His voice was strained.

Emma knew he was finding writing difficult at the moment, but she was also aware that, for whatever reason, he was attempting to conceal this from her. Julian's family was incapable of declaring struggle. Only death, or at least grave illness when it occasionally entered their lives, was allowed to be difficult. She had decided to let him have his privacy for now. Eventually, she would draw it out of him. Though, frankly, she was a little offended that he didn't think she would notice the change in him. This was a man who would emerge from his laptop practically breathless with excitement on days when his work was going well.

Emma noticed her own computer on the coffee table and

opened it. An unread email from Anika's editor was waiting for her:

> This is great, Emma. Your writing is very strong. I'll have a proof sent through to you next week.
>
> Have you got any other ideas you'd like to pitch? I'd love to take a look at anything you have.

She pulled her laptop onto her lap, leaned back into the couch, and reread the message. A smile tugged at the corners of her lips.

Writing the article had been a surprisingly enjoyable and straightforward experience. It felt natural, like she intrinsically knew how to organize the information, how to build a narrative that pulled the reader's eyes along word after word. It had been so enjoyable that Emma had begun to grow concerned that she hadn't done a good job—surely it wasn't meant to be this pleasurable? Perhaps Anika had been right that her writing talents had been wasted until now; perhaps she was just discovering a talent she never knew she had. Now that it seemed the article was going to be published, she would need to find a way to tell Julian.

"Yes, yes. Brilliant," Julian said, opening the balcony door. "Okay, I'll speak to you soon. Yes, bye, bye."

He continued to repeat the word "bye" as he took the phone away from his ear and tapped to end the call.

Emma shut her laptop. "Desi?"

He closed the balcony door behind him. "She's got the dates for when she'll visit."

"Oh, great."

"She's going to come over soon—just to stay the weekend."

"Did she want to stay with us?"

"No, she's going to get a hotel room."

"Okay. That'll be nice." As much as Emma loved Desi and enjoyed her company, she had a way of regressing Julian, pulling him back into personal jokes and drawing out old behaviors. Desi dominated Julian in a way that was common of older sisters, and Emma had for a while been intimidated by her. Truthfully, though, Emma's biggest complaint was that whenever they got together, she felt a little excluded.

Later that evening, they ate dinner on the balcony quietly. Emma's gazpacho had been a failure, a sort of pulpy tomato juice, leaving the bread to shoulder the burden of the meal. Julian, so occupied by scattered thoughts of his paper, barely registered the soggy bread as he chewed. Emma was equally lost in thought. The pensive silence between them was so complete that when Emma finally spoke it almost startled Julian. "I was thinking," she said, "I'd like to see Lena again."

"Oh?" he responded, still in the process of trading his thoughts for hers.

"We have her number. We could text her and invite her over again?"

Julian observed his soup, trying to figure out his feelings.

"If you want to, of course," she added.

"Well, I did suppose it would be a one-time thing, so I guess I am a little surprised."

"It doesn't have to be a one-time thing."

He rested his elbow on the table and his chin on his closed fist. "I only wonder whether there will be consequences if we keep this up. What if someone gets hurt? I mean, it's unusual behavior. It's not exactly normal—"

"No, it's not normal," she said, the word seeming to spark her defenses. "It's exciting and fun precisely because it's not normal behavior. Didn't you find it exhilarating?"

It was true that he had found it exhilarating. It was also true that the event had altered the material of his fantasies immediately. Now, when he masturbated, he found himself fashioning visions out of his memories of Lena and combining them with memories of Emma, shifting the images around like letters in an anagram so that it seemed as if their bodies and the sounds they made could morph and change into each other's. He'd never been one to fantasize about the idea of a threesome; something about the responsibility of ensuring a pleasurable experience for two women was intimidating to him. Despite this, he'd almost had a threesome while on exchange in Switzerland. The three of them had locked themselves in a bathroom at a house party, but the two girls merely giggled and kissed each other as he watched on, unsure of how to proceed. Eventually, he ran out of beer and lost his nerve. This was different. Emma was not performing her pleasure, nor was the situation orchestrated for him. All of which made it even more exhilarating. Still, Julian remained sure that the situation could only be repeated so many times before someone went off-script and spoiled it for everyone. He knew a line existed and that if it was crossed, it would result in someone's feelings being hurt. He was uncomfortable only because he didn't know where the line was.

"What if it gets messy?" he asked.

"It won't. We're in control. We can stop at any point. I just think that if we enjoyed ourselves, why wouldn't we do it again?"

Julian tore another chunk of bread off the loaf. It was surreal, he thought, to have your partner sit across from you and

argue the merits of you sleeping with someone else, especially
if they were not angling for the same privileges. He knew some
people would not have as many reservations as he did. He
wondered how Lena would feel about the proposition. He assumed he was a decade older than her, maybe more—all of his
experience would amount to a significant difference between
him and the younger men he assumed she usually slept with.
Lena had behaved as if her participation, her enthusiasm, was
a rebellion against something, and although he didn't know
what exactly, he'd been more than happy to be a tool she used
for this purpose.

"Okay," he agreed as Emma reached for the wine bottle.
"If Lena is okay with it, then why not?"

She smiled at him then, emitting such a radiant beam of
affection that he knew he'd made the right decision.

Together they drafted a message on Julian's phone.

*We'd really like to see you again. Come over for a drink
after work sometime soon?*

"I think that's good," Emma said, eyeing it as she drank
from her wineglass.

Julian read the message one more time before he took a
deep breath and hit send, feeling a thrill of anticipation pass
through his body. He placed his phone down on the table.

"God, this is such a strange feeling." He laughed. "It's sort
of like we're dating someone together."

"It's fun," Emma said.

Her happiness once again made him question what would
happen when this arrangement inevitably ran its course. He
didn't want her to retreat again.

"But say we do see her again, where do we go from there?"
he asked, voicing his concern. "Will you want to see her again
after that? Obviously, it has to end at some point."

"Of course," Emma said, "in a couple of months, we'll leave Athens, and that'll be it. On to the next adventure."

The words "next adventure" made Julian pause. They'd made few plans beyond Athens. Most likely, they would return to London. Where he would continue working on his paper. Conjuring his work, which lay like a buried corpse on his laptop, caused a sinking apprehension to drag once more at his thoughts. He fell silent, aware that Emma was watching him. Mercifully, the vibration of his phone distracted them both.

*OK,* Lena had responded.

Julian and Emma looked at each other.

"What—" Julian began to say, confused by her blunt answer. Another text arrived:

*Thursday night?*

"Oh," he said, looking back at Emma with eyebrows raised.

Another thrum of anticipation moved through him. He stood, walking around the table and standing before Emma. He took the glass out of her hand and pulled her from her chair, placing her arms over his shoulders. "You're coming with me," he said.

"Is that an order?" she replied innocently, staring up at him with widened eyes. She was following his lead, but as always, she was doing a better job. A flare of arousal shot through his stomach. When he kissed her, he was surprised that, for a moment, he imagined she was Lena.

# CHAPTER NINE

A few evenings later, Lena arrived after her shift, the intercom rattling violently and startling Julian's already heightened nerves. Emma answered the call and invited Lena up, and Julian walked into the hallway just as Emma was opening the front door. Perhaps because of the angle and the distance from where he stood, he saw a residual look of apprehension on Lena's face flicker away before she smiled and greeted Emma, like the transformation a performer underwent the moment before they walked out onto the stage.

"Come in," Emma said, stepping to the side to let her enter. Lena kissed her on the cheek as she passed and did the same when she reached him, standing on her toes and drawing him into a cloud of the sweet perfume she wore. Emma offered Lena a glass of wine, and Julian slipped out of the hallway and into the kitchen to fill the glasses, his heart beating faster. When he joined them in the living room, Lena was complaining about her boss, the owner of the bar—a moody and suspicious man who had a pattern of temporarily favoring one of his employees before turning on them randomly and targeting them with unexplained punishment. Julian gave Lena a glass and took a seat on the chair opposite them. Emma was nodding, laughing, and commiserating, and he could tell she was succeeding in making Lena feel comfortable. When Emma wanted to be, she was highly skilled at operating a conversation. She could walk into any room, sidle up to anyone—from senior executives to entitled influencers—and have them laughing within minutes. The first time Emma had invited him to one of her work events, she'd been apologetic, promising him that they would not need to stay long and could go for dinner afterward. They had only been dating for a couple of months at that point, but Julian already thought he knew everything about Emma. The event was being held in Selfridges for the launch of a celebrity chef's cast-iron pan collection. Julian arrived in time to catch the end of the speech, in which the chef was declaring with teary eyes that creating a cast-iron pan collection was a labor of love and a dream realized. Julian took a glass of champagne that was offered and smiled to himself, knowing the truth from Emma about the complete disinterest the man had shown toward the collaboration. But, as Julian stood in the homewares and kitchen section and watched Emma moving from group to group, inciting warm greetings, air kisses, and tinkling laughter, he realized just how talented she was at her job. He'd felt a flare of attraction to her at that moment.

Now, watching her freckled nose crinkle with laughter and her eyes widen with enthusiasm in response to Lena's stories, he was reminded of the strength of his love for her, which never went away but often lay beneath the surface of his thoughts until he was startlingly reminded of it. He took a sip of wine, rejoining the conversation and laughing along with them.

When the first bottle was finished and Emma returned from the kitchen with another, Lena proposed a game. She leaned forward in her seat, casting her dark eyes over them both as she explained the rules. "We answer questions about each other. Every time we get one wrong, we have to remove a piece of clothing."

Julian was impressed by the proposal. It was such an adept strategy that, for a moment, he entertained himself with the remote theory that Lena might have a history of these sorts of interactions.

"Okay," he agreed, looking over at Emma.

"Why not?" She shrugged, amused.

Lena sat up straight. "I think we should start with you, Julian." She turned to face him, smiling coyly. "What year was I born?"

"Oh, I see." Julian laughed. He didn't know Lena's exact age and was realizing now just how quickly their clothing would be removed. He ran a hand through his hair as he considered the question and completed some rudimentary math in his mind.

"Nineteen ninety-nine."

Lena tilted her head and raised her eyebrows at them both, prolonging the anticipation. "Close, but no."

"You both have to take something off," she added, pointing a finger at them both.

Emma laughed and looked down at her clothes. By wearing a linen dress and slipping her shoes off before the game even began, she was at a disadvantage. Julian unbuttoned his shirt and removed it while Emma pulled her dress over her head, revealing her black bra and underwear.

"Okay then," Julian said. "What's my favorite color?"

Lena considered him for a moment.

"Green," she said finally. Julian's favorite color was in fact green, but he knew the true objective of the game should not be hindered. He frowned and shook his head. "Blue."

Lena laughed, pulling the elastic waistband of her skirt down over her hips. She was wearing white cotton underwear printed with the face of a grumpy cat, bewilderingly suggestive of a consciously made decision. Her exposed legs and the dark pubic hairs that he could see behind the white fabric of her underwear made Julian realize in that moment that he was equally attracted to them both: Emma, the known, solid, and enduring depth of his feelings for her, meeting the novelty of experiencing her in a new situation; and Lena, the perplexing, yet exciting, representation of everything else—everything unknown and unpredictable.

"Does that mean it's my turn now?" Emma asked.

"Sure," Lena said, kicking her skirt off her foot so that it fell away in a heap.

"What's the full square root of pi?"

Lena laughed without bothering to attempt an answer and pulled off her T-shirt before falling back against the couch in defeat.

"How many miles is the moon from the Earth?" she then asked Julian.

He began unbuttoning his pants, watching as Emma removed her bra before reaching for her glass of wine. She took a sip, leaning back against the chair and smiling at him. The image of her sitting there, so at ease with herself, made Julian want to launch himself across the room at her. It conjured memories of the days and weeks when they hadn't yet slept together when his whole body pined—*ached* almost—for her, as she sat across from him, unreachable beyond a threshold they were yet to cross.

"How about a dare this time?" Emma suggested, looking over at Lena.

"Okay." Lena smirked.

Emma leaned over to her and began to whisper in her ear. Julian sat stunned by the image of them, by the intensity of his arousal.

They broke apart and Emma sat back with an air of satisfaction. Lena now turned her attention to Julian. He returned her gaze, watching as she stood, and moved toward him. She stood before him, holding her hands out. He placed his own in hers, and she tugged at them, signaling she wanted him to stand. When he did, she closed the space between them, joining her lips to his and urging him onward. His attention was then entirely directed to her, the smell of her hair and her skin, the still lingering scent of her perfume. She pulled her bra over her head, exposing her chest. Julian inhaled, stroking his thumbs softly back and forth over her dark nipples. When she began to slide his briefs down, he glanced at Emma. She looked back at him intently, encouragingly. He knew he didn't need to worry about her; she'd made it very clear that this was what she wanted. Lena knelt before him. He watched the top of her head slide forward and back until the sensation caused him to close his eyes. Then he angled his face upward, releasing a moan at the ceiling.

# CHAPTER TEN

Even though Julian had been diligently turning up to the library most mornings for a month now, words continued to evade him. He groaned, rubbing his hands over his face in frustration and inciting glances of annoyance, or in some cases pity, from the others in the room. A student across from him immediately packed up his belongings and shifted to a bench further away, as if Julian's condition might be contagious. He had never been able to rid himself of the idea that writing his paper should have been effortless, that true talent, true originality, would protect him from toiling. Even after completing his doctorate and earning a visceral understanding of hard intellectual labor, he still believed that his paper would birth itself. He stared at the document now, watching his cursor blink to mark each wasted second.

He thought of his sister, Desi, and tried to imagine what she was doing right now. Most likely she was sitting at her desk, staring at a screen, the gray buildings and gray sky of

London visible through the window behind her. It was after lunch, but she still would not be halfway through her workday. At that moment, the sympathy he felt for himself extended to her too. She had the same affliction that he did, the striving and yearning, the aspirations so all-consuming that they could only be born of some deep-set childhood insecurity. Desi was smart, gifted even, but she had a rebellious streak, and despite being fearless in a way that Julian was not, her time spent cast out in the cold by their parents had eventually worn her down. After finishing school, she studied hard to become a solicitor, working in civil litigation, before moving into family law. Now she worked in a tier-one boutique firm that dealt predominately with the divorce proceedings of "high net worth" clients. These were almost exclusively heterosexual couples who fought over a chalet in the Swiss Alps or a vineyard in Bordeaux with more enthusiasm than they did their own children. She worked long hours, but she'd done well for herself, and she had a wonderful wife, Camilla, who gave her nothing but stable and unconditional love. Still, Julian believed that, like him, Desi would never be free of the sense that her accomplishments would one day accumulate to form something so large and solid that its existence was undeniable.

He wondered whether there was another life he could live—some sideways leap he could make into an alternate reality. He saw a vision of himself: a house in the countryside, a dew-covered garden, a job as a schoolteacher, Emma and their children running to meet him at the gate when he returned from work. He saw himself reading only for pleasure in the evenings, Emma's head in his lap. What could be more honorable than raising children and prioritizing your family? What would be more satisfying? Certainly, he concluded dramatically, his paper would not stand by his bed and hold his hand years from now as he took his final breaths.

He decided then and there—his mind still wandering through rolling meadows, only this time with the addition of a well-trained border collie by his side and the smell of wood-burning stove smoke in the air—that he would go back to Emma, fall at her feet, and tell her that he was finally ready to prioritize having a family with her. They would live a quiet and calm life, full of love and purpose anchored to the familial unit. He was done with his consuming, egotistical, and selfish academic dreams. He was ready to do something *real*.

Hastily, he packed up his things. He did this loudly, without any concern for the others. Only moments ago they represented his fellows, but now they were something to pity. Their piqued glances bounced off him unnoticed. He left the library, like a prisoner emerging from Plato's cave into the bright light of clarity and truth. He'd been stripped of all illusions. He imagined himself throwing his books into the fountain at Syntagma Square. It was as if he'd released the trained focus he'd held for so long, and now his energy raced around inside of him, scattered and uncontrolled.


When Julian arrived back at the apartment, he found Emma in the bedroom. She had pulled all of her clothes out of the wardrobe, piled them on the bed, and now appeared to be trying them all on. Three standing fans were positioned around her with their faces angled toward her, like a group of attentive maidservants.

"Oh, you're home," she said, holding a black dress against

her in front of the mirror. "Did you get my message?" Her face was flushed with heat and excitement.

He looked at his phone and sure enough an unread message was sitting there: *Lena has the night off and she invited us out to a club with her friends. We should go.*

He'd entered the apartment intending to immediately share the transformative epiphany he'd had in the library, but instead of a receptive audience, he was met with a force equal to his own.

"So," she said, now looking at him, "do you want to come too?"

*Come too.* So, the decision had already been made on her side.

He sat down on the bed and began taking off his shoes, feeling betrayed.

"Do you really want to go and drink with a group of twenty-somethings?" he asked.

"Well, we could do that, or we could sit at home."

"Or we could go out to a taverna—just us." Even he disliked his sulky tone.

She turned to him. "We've done that so many times since we got here, but how many invitations have we received to go out and have fun with some strangers like this?"

"We could contact Alistair's friends and drink with some people our own age."

He was surprised by his stubbornness. He struggled to recall why he had set himself so firmly against this turn of events. It had been a week since they'd seen Lena—he wasn't against the idea of seeing her again.

"Just say yes, Julian." Emma sighed, selecting another black dress and holding it against herself. "Or say no, if you must. But I'm going."

She stood before the mirror, assessing herself.

"I wanted to talk to you," he said. "I had some interesting realizations in the library today."

"Oh?" She was now pulling the dress over her head.

"It's about our future—our future family. I was thinking I could put my paper to the side and focus on that for a while."

Emma's head emerged through the top of the dress, her face flustered with annoyance. "Julian, let's not do this now."

"Do what?"

"Have this discussion." She smoothed her hair down in the mirror. "Let's just go out and have fun. We can talk about that stuff later."

There was a pause before Julian responded, annoyed. "I mean, I'm only trying to talk about our future. I'm only trying to have a very important conversation. I would have thought few things were more interesting than that." He resented the hurt and frustration roiling between his words. "I would have thought you'd be excited to talk about our future."

She looked at him imploringly, then despairingly. "No, I know, I know," she said, attempting to appease him. "I understand. We can talk about it, but please just not now." She crossed the room and stood before him, placing her hands on his shoulders. "All I want to do is have a few drinks, maybe dance, and just forget about everything for a little while. I promise we can talk about all this after, but maybe tonight we can just pretend we're twenty-two again and have an uncomplicated good time?"

He looked up at her; the dark freckle at the top of her lip, her light brown eyelashes, and the pale green pools of her eyes were like a room full of old friends. "Okay," he said, resigned. "Okay, I'll go."

# CHAPTER ELEVEN

Lena gave them the name of a place in Kypseli. They arrived to find a small bar, where tables spilled across the road to the footpath of the *plateia*. Despite the crowded look of the place, the atmosphere was intimate. Lena was sitting with two other women at a table next to a row of parked scooters. When she saw them approaching, she grinned and stood to greet them.

"This is Sophia," she said, gesturing to the woman on her left. Sophia smiled, her dark, straight eyebrows pressing down upon her round brown eyes, making her appear to be giving them a slightly flat look. A cloud of fine curls framed her face all the way to her shoulders like a halo. Emma recognized her from the bar where Lena worked.

"And this is Nefeli." A woman with straight dark hair and heavily kohl-lined eyes smiled at them as she reapplied lip gloss, rolling her shiny, pillowy lips against each other. The two women stared openly at Julian, a knowing lurking beneath their expressions, and Emma knew immediately that

Lena must have told them about their arrangement, maybe even in detail. She wondered how they saw the situation. Was Julian the handsome, older man Lena was sleeping with and Emma his strange, perverted partner who encouraged it? The thought that Lena might not be discreet had not occurred to Emma until now and she found herself feeling indignant and betrayed. But Lena was only twenty-two, she reasoned, and it was undoubtedly an interesting story. What twenty-two-year-old wouldn't tell her friends about this? She shook her annoyance away, offering to buy them all a round of martinis, and left with the purpose of locating the bar.

Emma and Julian paid for two more rounds of drinks, Lena beaming proudly each time as if they'd fulfilled some hope or expectation of hers. Nefeli and Sophia seemed quietly impressed. The conversation carried itself, mostly by following Sophia's corroboration of Lena's complaints about the owner of the bar where they worked. The two of them shared more anecdotes to illustrate his character, while Nefeli, clearly having heard it all before, only intermittently lifted her eyes from her phone.

At 1 A.M. they left for the club. Emma and Julian followed the women through twisting, narrow streets, until they arrived in a laneway where groups of people crowded the path. Bass hummed, audible from the moment they turned onto the street, and Emma felt a lifting sense of anticipation. She hadn't been to a club in a long time, but the alcohol had relaxed her, blunting any anxieties. She felt pliable and happy to be led. They followed the three women, who were speaking and giggling excitedly, to a single door that took them directly into a small room dominated by a DJ deck and a heaving pool of people. Sticking to the outskirts of the writhing mass, Emma followed behind Julian, watching as eyes were drawn to him in passing, while she was paid no attention. At first she thought she was simply being sensitive, but soon she began to feel entirely invisible.

Alice, Emma's cousin, took her clubbing when they were in school. Emma had been only sixteen, but Alice had a friend who had the same color hair as Emma, which meant that she could use her ID. As long as you had an ID that wasn't expired, the bouncers at Leroy's would pretend they didn't recognize you, or know your parents. Leroy's was a pub on street level, but if you followed the faded red carpet up a flight of stairs you arrived in a disgustingly hot room that smelled strongly of aftershave and the heady, stale musk of lust, alcohol, and body odor. She and Alice would buy a cranberry vodka each and find themselves a spot on the dance floor, twirling their hips and spinning around like kebab meat, while the grown men salivated and jerked their pelvises toward them. The draw was undoubtedly Alice with her long blond hair, long, thin limbs, and a full C cup, but by her proximity to Alice, Emma always captured the surplus attention that Alice did not have the capacity for. It was then, at that slightly premature age, that she became accustomed to—and then quickly bored by—the attention of drunken men.

As they continued to the bar now, Emma felt the eyes of the men sliding straight over her to return to Lena and her friends. The three of them were wearing tight, thin dresses, even Lena—her body strapped into a ruched and strapless black minidress, which she'd combined with her usual combat boots. Emma felt out of place in her demure, though admittedly expensive, linen shift dress. By the time they reached the bar, she had progressed to chastising herself. For so long she'd wanted to escape the leers and advances of men in clubs just like this. Practically all of her young adult life, she'd complained to her friends, creating safe words so they could rescue each other, and squealing or pulling faces behind the men's backs. Now she was surprised, and a little disgusted with herself, that she missed the attention. It was as if her currency had lowered in value and she'd never realized, not until she entered the market and was met with visceral disinterest. Meanwhile, the opposite had happened to Julian's value. He stood out confidently among the poorly dressed and desperate younger men. It was a shifting of the scales that Emma had not expected. It was ridiculous to feel this way, she told herself. She was above it. She should just enjoy watching the women pine over Julian, comforted by the knowledge that she was the one who held his interest.

Julian asked Lena and her friends what they wanted to drink and ordered them all a round of cocktails. The three of them whispered and giggled flagrantly into each other's ears, as if Emma were not there at all. The drinks arrived, purple in color and sickly sweet yet lethally strong. They took them to the outskirts of the dance floor, where they could move and drink freely. It was then that Emma realized Lena and her friends were drunk, swaying slightly as if the effort of standing still and upright was too much. They'd only had three drinks each at the previous bar, but Emma did not know how long they had been drinking prior to that.

"This drink is disgusting," Julian whispered in her ear.

The flattering blue and red light flashed over his features as he forced half of it down in one prolonged sip. She handed him hers too. Lena and her friends began to dance, nodding their heads and sweeping their hips from side to side, while scanning the room for interest. Occasionally, Emma saw Nefeli make eyes at Julian, who seemed oblivious or was at least pretending to be so. Lena shifted places in the circle so that she was next to Emma and began to pull at Emma's hands, inviting her to dance. She smiled politely and indulged Lena, who began to draw herself closer to Emma. They danced with each other for a moment, until Emma saw that Lena's eyes were seeking Julian's and it became apparent that she was using Emma to flirt with Julian. Emma had the sudden urge to go outside.

"I'm just going to get some fresh air," she told Julian.

Sitting on the curb, she rummaged through her bag to locate the lighter and cigarette pack she'd purchased the night she'd met Lena. She lit a cigarette and observed a woman nearby who was chewing on a fingernail as she whispered angrily into her phone.

"Are you all right?" Julian asked, appearing by her side. "Not exactly fresh air."

She gave him a guilty smile and ground the cigarette out on the curb beside her.

"I wasn't really feeling it in there," she said, knowing that if she gave him a small offering of truth, she would be spared from having to divulge it all. "I think I just want to go back to the apartment."

"Okay." He nodded. Lena, Sophia, and Nefeli were crossing the road toward them, having followed Julian outside. He turned to Lena and explained that they were leaving.

"Should I come with you?" she asked, looking only at Julian.

"Yeah, sure," he said, without hesitation, without even a cursory look at Emma. Lena turned to her friends, who now stood nearby talking to a group of men and vaping. She kissed them goodbye and they gave a perfunctory wave to Emma and Julian.

"We can get a taxi from a street down here," she said, reappearing by Julian's side and pointing to the right.

In the taxi, Emma sat in the front passenger seat and rolled the window down. The air that came through the window was warm; whenever the car stilled, it gathered until it was so thick she felt she could almost rest her head on it. When they arrived at the apartment, she turned to unclip her seat belt. From the corner of her eye, she saw Lena's hand resting on Julian's thigh. Irritation flared through her chest. But why? How could Lena's attraction to Julian, which had been a source of such arousal, now become a source of annoyance? Why did she suddenly feel left out? The alcohol encouraged her to feel self-righteous. Julian should have known the energy was off. He should have told Lena no, or at least consulted Emma before saying yes. But wasn't that exactly what Emma had said turned her on the previous times: the idea of Julian leaving her behind like she wasn't there at all? Lena and Julian weren't doing anything Emma hadn't allowed previously, only now she simply felt different about it—how were they to know that? As she paid the taxi driver, her thoughts circled and spiraled, self-righteous and self-pitying one moment and chastising the next.

In the elevator Julian and Lena chatted happily and obliviously, while Emma wallowed in stony silence.

She left them in the living room, while she went to get a glass of water from the kitchen, and when she returned Lena was searching for a song to play.

"Something to make us dance," she said, putting the phone back down on the coffee table. "Bizarre Love Triangle" began to play, the opening bars instantly recognizable. Julian laughed in surprise. "Really? I never would have guessed."

Lena spun and laughed. "It always makes me want to dance!"

She swayed over to Julian, pulling him by the arms. He acquiesced. Despite her mood, Emma found herself smiling at the sight of Julian leaping around and overusing his shoulders in a 1980s tribute. Failing to be seductive, his and Lena's dancing was genuinely joyful. Hearing Emma's laugh, Lena waved her over to them. "Join us," she said, twirling again. Emma sauntered toward them, eliciting wolf whistles of encouragement. They stood together, singing and jumping around, each of them lost in their own solo performance. Emma felt herself begin to sweat. The song ended and she left them in the living room to get another glass of water. When she returned, they were kissing and her mood flattened once more. She took a seat on the couch and watched as Lena began to tug at Julian's clothes. Still kissing her, he slowly pushed her backward until she fell onto the sofa chair. He removed his glasses as she giggled, and he knelt before her, hitching her dress up past her hips and lowering his head into her lap. The arm of the chair prevented Emma from seeing his face; she saw only the movement of the top of his head. Neither Julian nor Lena observed that she made no attempt to touch herself, or to participate. In the end, at the moment when Lena's moans rose in pitch and culminated into gasping cries of pleasure, Emma stood, unnoticed, and went to the bathroom to have a shower.

The next morning Julian awoke alone in the bed. He rose and staggered into the living room, relieved to see the couch was empty, meaning Lena had already left. He found Emma sitting on the balcony. Her knees were drawn to her chest and a quiet, impassive mood enclosed her like a fog. Julian thought it was likely just a hangover that was turning her inward. Sometimes this would happen—Emma would drink too much and emerge from the bedroom the next morning ready to repent with a forceful and quiet determination. She'd pull out a pair of rubber gloves and doggedly clean the entire flat in complete silence, as if in self-imposed punishment. Julian's hangovers manifested more in a desire to mope around self-pityingly in bed, indulging in physical affection, carbohydrates, and sleep.

When Julian opened the balcony door, Emma was typing placidly on her phone. He interrupted the scene, dragging her back as if from a dream. "Was Lena here when you woke?"

"No, she'd already left," she answered without shifting her eyes from her phone.

Julian suggested they go to a café nearby for breakfast, thinking the fresh air and the sun would help to shift their stale, hungover moods. In response to this suggestion, Emma gave only a reticent nod.

They found a café, sharing a rickety bench under the dappled shade of a large leafy tree and nursing a mug of bitter black coffee each. Emma remained quiet, unable to be encouraged into a discussion. Julian began to grow uneasy. Her vacancy invited him to project his own ideas across it, and his desperation only grew as she continued to be inscrutable. He began to throw himself against the wall behind which she kept her true feelings.

"Did you want something to eat?" He examined the menu seriously like an amateur actor. "There's omelet, eggs Benedict—"

"No, thanks."

He watched her as she regarded the contents of her mug,

his eyes landing on a clump of black mascara that sat just below her eye.

"I think I'm fine with just the coffee too, actually," he agreed, dropping the menu.

He reached for his mug and shifted his focus to the street, leaning back with a contrived sigh of satisfaction. "Nice morni—"

"I don't want us to see Lena again," Emma said suddenly, without emotion. "I'm finished with that now."

The statement carried no trace of affection for Lena and such firm conviction that it made him wonder whether something had happened the night before that he was not conscious of. Emma had enjoyed herself, hadn't she? He tried to recall an image of her, but he was ashamed to realize he couldn't. Lena and her friends had forced a double shot of something incredibly strong on him before he left the club to find Emma, and he'd finished both of their purple cocktails; the alcohol, which was more than he'd drunk in one evening in quite a while, had cast stretches of shadow over his memory.

"Oh, okay, sure," he replied, knowing there was only one acceptable response. "We won't do it again."

He drank from his mug in an effort to conceal his disappointment. Panic that he was at fault for this decision began to rise within him, conspiring with the caffeine. He relented to the urge to clarify. "Did we do something that you—"

"No, no," she interjected, reaching for his hand and squeezing it. "I think it's just run its course. It's done."

"Okay." He nodded, relieved.

They sat in silence and Julian was surprised to identify a small feeling of regret for the fact that he would not see Lena again. When he had imagined all the ways the situation between the three of them could have ended, he'd never imagined that Emma might simply say it was done and that it would be him who would feel sad to see the end. He'd assumed that he would bear the eventual responsibility of saying enough was enough.

A scooter whizzed by. An elderly man with a newspaper held firmly under his arm claimed a seat nearby, crossing one leg over the other. He would recover quickly, Julian thought gallantly. His feelings for Lena were small—seedlings, really. Without nurture they would die off quickly, leaving only the now uncomplicated memories of their sexual relations behind, which he could fashion and use privately. He smiled then, enjoying the fact that they had navigated the end rather well, all things considered. He was glad that it was not his foot that needed to be put down; he was glad that his relationship with Emma had emerged entirely intact, that it had suffered no damage in the process. He picked up the menu once more, finding that his appetite had returned.

# CHAPTER TWELVE

When planned correctly, a route around the National Garden could provide a jogging path nearly three miles long. Since discovering it, Julian had refined and repeated the path often enough that he could now follow its specific turns without thinking. He would enter the park, running past the line of palm trees until the tree cover thickened and provided more consistent shade. As August crept closer, the daily temperatures continued to rise, and the full blast of the midday sun became increasingly intimidating. What had been an oppressive heat had now become downright hostile. It signaled a strength he'd been unaware the sun possessed, as if he were witnessing the sun flex its enormous biceps. It was common now, around midday, to see tourists on the street dousing themselves in bottled water or complaining loudly. It seemed to only be the visitors, like himself, who attempted to assert themselves against the heat. At midday, the locals retreated to their apartments, their offices, or places of work, hiding as best they could. The tourists, usually here for only a day or two, walked around flapping their shirts or holding small battery-operated fans before their grimacing faces.

Since he'd begun avoiding his paper, he'd directed his energy toward running, waking early most mornings and heading out even before Emma emerged. That morning, she'd barely stirred when he rose from the bed and pulled on his sneakers.

The distance between him and his paper had left an abyss, and even though running was able to fill some of the space, Julian felt strongly that he needed to recalibrate, redirect. His vision of the future had returned to him, or rather had never left his side since it had formed in his mind. He frequently indulged it, floating blissfully off to daydream of crackling fireplaces, muddy boots, and joyfully squealing children. He often reemerged as if waking from sleep, confused and disoriented. He imagined it now as he ran: the blanched hills of Athens in the distance exchanged for a rolling green meadow; the gurgling park fountain nearby became the sound of a river; the dappled light now filtered through the branches of an old moss-covered oak tree. His phone began to vibrate in his pocket, and, unable to accommodate it into the vision, he stopped running and took it out of his pocket. Lena was calling. He screened the call and waited. A message arrived quickly.

*Can I see you?*

She'd messaged him the day before as well. He'd ignored that, too. He hadn't responded to her messages since Emma had put an end to the arrangement over a week ago. He didn't feel safe sharing his sadness with Emma, knowing she'd assume he had developed feelings for Lena—which was in some ways true, though the statement sounded worse than the situation was in reality. He knew Emma expected that he'd ended the connection with Lena instantly and conclusively. To be still talking to her seemed dishonest and secretive. Julian made a mental note to inform Emma of the messages so that together they could end things with Lena a little more clearly. Before he could resume running, another message arrived.

*Please respond.*

He had to admit that the desperation of the messages gave him a small thrill. It was obvious that Lena had developed feelings for him. Perhaps she was sensing that the arrangement had come to an end, and she had some plan to convince Julian to continue seeing her. Maybe she would even try to convince him to leave Emma for her. It was a flattering idea that Lena would be willing to fight for him and he allowed himself to be flattered by it as he continued his winding run around the gravel paths. His thoughts soon tracked back to Emma, and he realized that her declaration of being "done" with Lena could also be taken to imply that she was done with this current way of living. Did that mean that now was the right time to share his vision? That maybe now she would be more receptive to the conversation? The thought sent surprising feelings of affection and excitement through his chest. Why should they waste another moment here treading water instead of striding toward their new life? He stopped dead, then turned on his heel and headed back to the apartment.

"I guess what I'm trying to say is our future family is the most important thing to me," Julian said.

Emma stared across the kitchen at him; she had a knife in one hand and was in the middle of slicing a tomato she intended to put on some toast. She thought Julian looked disheveled, vaguely manic. He'd arrived home sweating and panting and had immediately begun relaying some breathless and barely coherent scramble of thoughts, the crux of which began with the realization that his academic dreams of publishing his paper were superfluous and driven by ego, which then made a considerable leap to suddenly find connection with the idea of parenthood.

"I've been having this vision," he continued, pacing the kitchen.

Emma eyed her laptop; it was sitting on the counter next to him, open to the typeset proof of her article. She wondered if she could reach it and shut it while he was distracted.

"It's us, living in the countryside, in Dorset, in a lovely old house. We have children and a dog. Emma—" He walked over to her, taking the knife from her and holding her hands in his. "I'm ready to do something else. We decided to come to Athens for a sense of change and adventure. I think we've achieved that. We've explored new things, and now that's done, we should think about the future."

"Julian—" Emma interjected uselessly.

"I'm done with all this academic nonsense." He dropped her hand and began pacing again. "All this pandering and striving for validation. It's shallow." He seemed to be working through the realization in real time, processing what he was saying as he said it. "You know, I've always wanted to be like my father, to be respected for my achievements, but the truth is, he wasn't a good father to me. When I was young, he was mostly absent. I always felt I had to earn his love. I *still* feel like that."

Emma knew this was true. She'd spent many weekends at Gramercy. She could remember the first time they'd made the trip together. They'd arrived in the evening, crunching slowly up the gravel driveway, and were greeted by the housekeeper. Their bags were collected and taken to Julian's old room. Once they were settled in the room, the housekeeper returned and served them soup and bread. They ate and went to bed, all without having even glimpsed Julian's mother or father. Emma had found this bizarre, but she kept her thoughts to herself, understanding that all families had their customs that seemed unusual to outsiders. It was over breakfast in the garden the next morning, among the moss-covered walls and rhododendrons, that Emma had first marveled at how Julian's parents' pride—the shape their love took—was only given transactionally in response to some achievement. She'd watched Julian transform into a trained animal, forced to boast about his studies in the hope of receiving some crumb of affection. Later, upon meeting Desi, Emma would witness similar tricks. Emma could sympathize; she was not immune from the urge to impress Julian's parents either. Julian's mother, Eleanor, rarely smiled in conversation, which always made Emma feel as though she were failing to fulfill some responsibility. It was as if Eleanor expected her guests to be responsible for her entertainment. During these conversations, Emma would feel time passing acutely, as if some faraway clock were counting down toward an alarm. Suddenly, when Eleanor did smile, relief would flood through Emma until the smile inevitably slid from Eleanor's face, and the ticking began once again.

"I want to be a good father to our children," Julian continued. "I want to be around more to play sport with them or read to them. I could be a schoolteacher—the hours are good. We could have the most wonderful, quiet, simple life."

Emma saw that the conversation was like a rock rolling

down a hill, rapidly gaining velocity. If she didn't halt it immediately, it might become impossible to stop. *Quiet*—the word repulsed her.

"Julian," she interjected again, this time more forcefully, "I don't want to live in Dorset."

His momentum halted, and he looked at her blankly for a moment. "I thought you liked—" he said. "That's fine. We could look at Devon, or Cornwall. There's East Sussex as well. I don't mind where exactly, I just—I think we're ready now . . ." Her laptop screen caught his eye. "What's this?" He moved closer to the screen. "Are you writing something?"

Emma grimaced inwardly. For all her tiptoeing around the act of telling Julian about the article, she had now inadvertently released the truth in the least ideal way.

"Anika couldn't meet a deadline. She asked me to take over. It's an exclusive about the illegal sewage-dumping practices of water companies in the UK. It's actually fascinating and horrifying, it—"

"How come you didn't tell me about it?" He was now scanning the editor's email address. "It's going to be published in *The Observer*?"

"I knew you were struggling with your paper, and for some reason you weren't telling me, and I just didn't think now was a good time to tell you about my article."

Julian stared at the laptop screen, his eyes darting back and forth as he read. "This is a proof. How long have you been working on this?"

"About a month."

He flinched. "I can't believe you didn't tell me."

"It's not a big deal, Julian. Of course I was going to tell you. I was just trying to be . . . considerate."

He scrunched his face up in offense. "Because I'm a failure

on the brink of a mental breakdown, and you didn't want to push me over the edge? That's a little condescending."

"*See,* I knew you weren't going to take this well—"

"You *hid* this from me!"

"I was going to tell you. I was waiting until—"

"Until it was published?" He scanned the email again. "It's being run in a fortnight!"

"I want to write more articles—maybe make a career out of it. The editor is very happy with what I've written," she blurted frantically, hoping to bury his grievance in context. "They asked if I had any other pitches. I was just trying to find the right moment to tell you. I didn't want to get ahead of myself until the article was definitely going to be printed."

Emma could sense the conflicted feelings moving around Julian's brain. She knew he'd feel reactively threatened by this; he'd feel betrayed that she'd started writing, that she was going to be published first, even though it had nothing to do with him and his paper. But he'd also know that his feelings were irrational. He'd know that he wanted to be angry and he'd have to find another, more logical reason to be.

"Julian, please." Emma stepped forward, closing the laptop. "This isn't a big deal."

He took a breath, smiling tightly. "You're right. I'm sorry I got upset. I'm happy for you. Really, this is great." He pulled her into a hug. She wrapped her arms around him, feeling relieved.

"It's actually perfect," he continued. "You can set your own schedule and work remotely. We could build a little office with a view in the cottage. The schedule flexibility will be helpful while you're pregnant and later when we're looking after a newborn—"

Emma saw immediately what he was doing. He'd let up

easily with the expectation that she would now let up in return and go along willingly with his new plans. Her heart
sank with disappointment. The moment when she would need
to remind Julian that she didn't want children, and the strength
of the conviction she felt about this topic, had arrived. She felt
unprepared, but the damage done by being passive now would
be worse than a poorly handled divulging of truth. She closed
her eyes and took a deep breath.

"Julian, I don't think . . ." She paused to begin again with
more conviction. "I don't want to have children. I don't want
to be a mother."

The loud buzz of the doorbell cut through the silence, both
of them flinching against the grating sound before the silence
resumed.

Julian stepped back and stared at her. "Do you mean that?"

"Yes."

He swallowed, grimacing. "How long have you felt this
way?"

"I've always felt this way. Julian, you know that. My feelings never changed."

"But when you were pregnant, I thought—"

"When I was pregnant, I reconsidered the idea because I
had to. After the miscarriage, I knew for sure."

"But you seemed—"

"Julian, when I miscarried, I was sad, but I felt"—she
hesitated—"I felt relieved. I don't think I could have had a
clearer realization."

The doorbell buzzed again, and Julian swore under his
breath in frustration before storming out of the kitchen and
into the hallway. Emma followed him, watching as he stood
staring at the intercom, attempting to figure out how it worked

as he did every time he was obligated to use it. He pressed a button and spoke tentatively into the wall. "Hello?"

"It's Lena," a voice replied. Julian looked back at Emma, their faces mirroring confusion and surprise. "I'm sorry to just turn up."

"No, no, it's okay. I'll let you up."

Lena's voice fell silent, and the intercom crackled softly. Julian pressed another button, hearing the click of the door unlocking on the other side. The connection ended, and Julian looked back at Emma.

"Why is she here?" she asked.

"I haven't returned her messages," he admitted. "She called me today, and I didn't pick up. I've been meaning to tell you. I think she'll probably be wondering what's going on."

Emma pursed her lips. "We should end things properly."

When Lena knocked, he opened the door to reveal her standing there in denim shorts, a tank top, and black combat boots. On closer inspection, Emma noticed that her eye makeup was smudged under her eyes, and her skin looked patchy and pale as if she'd been crying. The sight of her like this was startling. She looked vulnerable in a way that Emma had never imagined her capable of looking.

"Are you okay?" she asked.

"Why don't you come in," Julian added, stepping to the side to let her through. Lena shook her head and remained standing in the doorway, biting her lip as tears welled in her eyes. In the short silence, Emma felt the beginning of a realization form, a terrifying prophecy of what was about to be known. Lena took a deep breath.

"I'm pregnant."

# ACT II

O god, what shall I do?

Sophocles, *Philoctetes*

# CHAPTER THIRTEEN

Emma was standing on the edge of a cliff. She was in Corfu, she realized, standing on the precipice she'd watched others jump from. Over the edge and far below, the water was still and inviting, glittering as if sequined. It was obvious that she was lucid dreaming because she felt no fear. She often lucid dreamed; sometimes the realization that she was dreaming took any fear away, other times—like this—the lack of fear was the giveaway.

She leaped from the edge, her stomach lurching and rising toward her throat. The feeling of plummeting from a considerable height was something she had never experienced before. She wondered, even through the exhilaration of free fall, how her brain knew how to manufacture this feeling. Suddenly her descent slowed, as if she were pressing against some invisible but continuing resistance. She contemplated closing the scene—she could do that too when she was lucid: end the dream and manifest something else. But before she could make a decision she began to fall faster once more. The ocean

approached quickly and just before she hit the water she
screamed in surprise. In dreams, she rarely actually landed.
Her scream was muted by the water as she sank. She began to
swim, breaking through the surface and gasping as a dull pain
throbbed in her lower back. Around her the water began to
turn red. Was she badly hurt? Panic rose. The blood spreading. She screamed and woke.

Emma remained in bed for a moment, her lower back ach-
ing. Then she carefully made her way to the bathroom, climbing into the shower and washing the blood off the inside of her
thighs. It was 6:48 A.M. and she knew she wouldn't sleep again.
She made coffee and toast, located some ibuprofen, and sat on
the balcony in the still air of the early morning. It was peaceful without the hum of traffic and the sound of voices. Birds
swooped and sang in the surrounding trees. Emma closed her
eyes and took a deep breath in.

"You all right?" Julian asked, opening the glass door to the
balcony, his eyes bleary.

She nodded.

He left, returning from the kitchen with a mug of coffee
and joining her at the table. His face looked tight and pale. In
moments of high emotion, color never rose in Julian's cheeks,
like it did in Emma's; instead it fell away, leaving him looking
stricken and unwell. He wore now the bewildered look of
shock that often attaches itself to the faces of the grieving.
Years ago, when her uncle had suddenly passed away, her father had worn the same look for weeks. It made sense to
Emma that sudden life could shock you like sudden death.
The situation was not the same as when Emma had told Julian
that she was pregnant. They had been shocked, but together
they'd allowed the conversation to venture everywhere it

needed to, leaving no option unexplored. When they made their decision, Emma had the pleasure of watching it slowly transform Julian with excitement. The thought of Lena carrying Julian's baby created so many questions and unknowns that the whole image could not be viewed at once. Every time Emma thought of one detail that would need planning, it split like the frayed end of a piece of rope, branching into more and more unknowns. Lena herself represented another piece of rope, equally frayed with unknowns.

As she'd sat on their couch the afternoon before, they'd dutifully consoled her when, truthfully, Emma wished that she and Julian could console each other. There had been no mention of termination. It seemed like Julian was being careful not to be the first to say the word, though Emma assumed he would desperately want to know the full scope of their options. They had used the word "support," although it had the potential to contain vastly different meanings, and the conversation had been circuitous and unproductive, broken in places by Lena as she momentarily sobbed, and they tended to her with offerings of water or tissues. About an hour after she arrived, Lena stood and told them she needed to leave for her shift. After letting her out of the apartment, Emma and Julian had resumed their places on the couch, where they sat in a shaken silence before Emma finally spoke.

"Do you believe her?" she'd asked.

Julian slowly lifted his head to look back at her. "Do you think she's lying?"

"I just don't know if we can fully trust her," Emma replied. "The first time I met her—that night I went to the bar during the dinner party—I saw her kissing some young guy in the alleyway."

Julian's eyes narrowed. "As in you think I might not be . . ."

"I don't know, possibly. Or possibly she's not even pregnant—I mean, we were careful, weren't we?"

Julian's gaze fell away from Emma's, guilt radiating off him.

"That third time," he said, "I was so drunk I don't remember."

Emma's heart sank. The betrayal she'd felt on the evening when he'd gone ahead and slept with Lena without checking with her surged back into her body.

"Lena needs to go to the doctor and confirm the pregnancy if she hasn't already," she said. "And we should discuss termination with her as soon as possible."

Julian drew a breath. "I was thinking perhaps I should discuss that with her alone."

Emma felt that the conversation was probably one she would better handle. Sometimes when attempting to instigate difficult conversations, Julian approached the crux at speed, as if to lessen any wobbles that might result from overcaution. This was sometimes misread as insensitivity, or at worst, hostility.

"You don't think we should have that discussion together?" she asked.

"I'm a little concerned that she'll feel like we're ganging up on her." The furrow of his brow deepened. "I'm conscious that we outnumber her. I don't want her to get defensive, or to stop listening to us."

Emma was unsure whether she agreed, but she was beginning to see where her involvement had limits that Julian's did not. It seemed wrong that she should attempt to govern the situation or overturn any decisions that Julian was sure of, given the baby would share his DNA and not hers.

"Okay, if you think that's best," she agreed. "I just think it's important that we're very clear with her about our prefer-ence."

Julian swallowed and blinked slowly.

"It's early," she went on. "There are less invasive options if we act quickly. If we make her aware that she won't need to pay for the costs, she might feel more reassured. It's really the only logical path. The alternative being that she has the baby, but that's unthinkable. It would be insane—I mean, what would you do?"

Julian pressed his lips into a tight frown.

"It's *we*," he said quietly. "It's what would *you and I* do."

She saw then how easy it would be to take her feelings of helplessness and fear out on him, to let this situation create a division between them; how quickly the desire for self-preservation arose, encouraging her to reflexively make this his problem and not hers; how zealously she guarded her free-dom and how directly this turn of events now threatened it.

"I'm sorry, I didn't mean it like that." Emma reached across the table for his hand. "It's we—of course."

Julian smiled weakly. He removed his hand to reach for his coffee, his face still stricken and pale.

"When will you go and speak to her?" Emma asked.

"This afternoon," he answered. "I'll go to the bar."

When Julian ventured out to find Lena, he was distracted and harried. Attempting to shed any light on the situation seemed only to reveal how much darkness there was. He found him-self capable of only looking one step ahead; beyond that he was assailed by unwanted images: Lena with a heavily preg-nant stomach, an image of him standing by the side of a hospital bed holding a swaddled newborn. These images made his heart lurch, not in the least because he could not rationally place Emma in the scenes next to him. In light of Emma's recent admission, which had been overshadowed entirely by Lena's news, he struggled to imagine Emma standing next to him, smiling and teary-eyed as she gazed into the baby's bewildered face.

When he'd stood in the kitchen and declared his vision for the future and his desire for them to start a family, Emma hadn't responded the way he had imagined she would. In his anticipatory visions of that moment, Emma had crossed the room and fallen into his arms, her brow free of its usual creases of concern, and said something like, "I've been waiting for you to say this." Instead, the real-life version of Emma had stood in the kitchen, looking back at him somewhat mournfully, lines etched into her forehead in multiple directions. She'd shattered the vision entirely and replaced it with an image of the future that was largely the same as that very moment. Julian barely even had a full second to process Emma's admission before Lena had arrived, eclipsing everything. Reliving it now made his chest grow tight and his vision begin to darken around the edges. He attempted to take deep, slow breaths to ward off the panic, and in his distracted state, didn't see the tourist in front of him until he collided with the vast wall of the man's warm, damp back. The man grunted in surprise. "Sorry, excuse me. Sorry," Julian mumbled, as the man slowly turned around to see what the cause of the impact was. By the time he turned entirely around, Julian had already slipped away down the street without looking back.

When he arrived at the bar and opened the door, he saw Lena drying glasses with a towel. If he had to pick the act in which he would find her, this would be exactly it: a bartender wiping glasses with a dishrag. It was like finding a frog sitting on a lily pad or a shiny, red apple underneath the letter "A." She looked up at him, her eyebrows flickering upward in surprise before she reined them back down.

"Julian?"

"Hi," he replied, breathless from the fast walk and narrowly avoided panic attack.

There was a silence as she placed a glass rim-down into a crate with the others and looked back up at him expectantly.

"I was hoping maybe we could have a chat?" he asked.

She took a look around the empty bar. "Okay."

Sophia, who Julian only just realized was also in the room, was slicing through a pile of citrus further up the bar.

"Hi, Sophia," he said, receiving a smile from her in return that was pulled so tight it resembled a straight line running parallel to her eyebrows.

Lena dropped the dishrag on the counter and led Julian back through the front door into the alleyway next to the bar, where she leaned against a nearby wall and watched him silently.

"Obviously this is a big shock for all of us," he began. He was standing in the middle of the alleyway, blocking the exit in what suddenly felt like an overly aggressive stance. He crossed over to lean against the wall next to her.

"For you especially," he added hesitantly.

She pulled her vape out and began to smoke. He watched her, wondering whether she was aware that wasn't a good idea.

"For you most of all," he persisted.

Lena frowned and brought her eyebrows together as she exhaled vapor. Her gaze was now on the ground in front of them.

"I guess I wanted to check in on you to see how you are feeling about"—he hesitated—"it."

She glanced at him then. Suspicion in her narrowed eyes.

"I just wanted to see how you were doing," he backtracked.

"I'm okay." She ran the top row of her teeth over her bottom lip. "I need to tell my parents. They will be upset."

He left a space for her to continue.

"They're Orthodox," she concluded.

"I see. When will you tell them?"

"Soon." She frowned and inspected her thumbnail.

"Have you gone to see a doctor yet? They usually do a blood test to confirm."

"No, not yet," she said, inspecting another nail. "I want to see a private doctor. The public system is very slow."

"Okay." He nodded again, feeling this was reasonable.

"But the private appointment costs money," she said. The statement was followed by a brazen silence.

"I'll pay for the appointment," Julian said, relieving them both.

She turned to look at him. "Will you come with me to the appointment too?" Her eyes were wide once more. She looked young and scared, recast as someone he had a significant responsibility to protect.

"Yes, of course," he replied resolutely.

She smiled at him with an expression so clear and open that he felt encouraged.

"But when we see the doctor, I think we should make sure we ask about all our options," he said.

Lena shrank from him slightly, her gaze hardening.

"I knew you would come to me and ask me to do that," she said, a sharp edge to her voice. "Just so you know, I will make the decision for myself."

Julian floundered. "Of course, I'm sorry if I offended you. I know it's your decision. I didn't mean—"

"So that's what you want me to do?" she asked, the question holding tension like a test.

"Well, I think, ultimately . . ." He watched her brow furrow with disappointment and realized that to lose her trust entirely at this point would be the worst outcome of all. "I want you to explore the options you're comfortable with."

At that moment, Sophia appeared at the entrance of the alleyway, calling out to Lena and making some request in Greek before leaving them alone once again.

"I need to go back," Lena said.

"Okay. Sure." Now was clearly not the time to press the discussion further. Julian felt guilt rise within him. If Emma had witnessed the interaction, she would be disappointed in him.

For a moment, they stood in silence.

"I'll let you know when the appointment is," Lena said eventually, looking down at the ground between them again, her tone softening.

"Please do," he replied.

"It will cost a hundred because of the blood test." Her eyes met his expectantly. "Do you have any cash?"

"Oh, right." He pulled out his wallet. "Actually, I do."

She took the money silently, folding it into her back pocket.

"If I . . ." She spoke timidly, but with a force underneath her hesitancy, as if she were compelled to continue. "If I have our baby, do you promise to help me look after it?"

She looked up at him again. His heart now palpitating in distress. He hadn't expected her to speak so candidly, or to display such vulnerability. He hadn't prepared himself for a question like this. Still, he was thankful that the question set no clear terms, that he could take its ambiguity and hide within it.

"I promise I will try to do everything I can," he said, his words firm but comfortably vague.

Lena smiled at him and his lips curled inward to reluctantly return the smile. Somewhere along the way he'd lost control of the conversation; he'd wanted to discuss termination and somehow he'd arrived here, handing promises over to her instead.

In a slightly clumsy but fast motion, Lena then stepped forward and kissed Julian directly on the lips in a way that left him wondering if the kiss was actually intended for his cheek. As she turned away, he saw a blush rise in her cheeks, which didn't make her intentions any clearer.

Emma was waiting for him when he returned to the apartment. She stood in front of the couch, surrounded by a splayed copy of *Medea* and a cold mug of coffee—like a still life of anxious waiting.

"So?" Her eyes were moving around him, searching for answers. "What did she say?"

Julian had always believed that the best course of action to alleviate the suffering of another was to tell them what they wanted to hear. In this case, his standpoint would benefit them both: Emma's hope could remain intact, and he wouldn't have to reveal the details of how badly he'd fumbled his interaction with Lena.

"She agreed to consider it," he said, taking a seat on the sofa chair. He would still have other opportunities to discuss termination with Lena, and when he envisioned these future conversations, they were more successful. Lena was probably in shock; it would take time before she could objectively view her options and assess what would be for the best. He felt he wasn't lying so much as predicting a very likely outcome.

"Okay." Emma nodded. She seemed to have deflated slightly in response to the uncertain answer. "Did you explain that we will pay for the costs? And—actually, I was thinking maybe we could offer her some extra money. Then she could take some time off from the bar if she felt she needed to."

"We didn't discuss money," Julian admitted, relieved to be able to blend his lie with some elements of truth. "But she said she will think about it. I think we should give her a little time first."

Emma sat back down on the couch, nodding to herself as she processed the information. "Okay, this is good. The fact that she's considering it is very good." She released a sudden sigh of relief. "Oh god, I've been sitting here just staring at the walls waiting for you to get back."

He watched her with a frown on his face, feeling undeserving of her optimism. When she looked up and met his eyes, she gave him a small sanguine smile. He returned it to the best of his ability, a tightness rising in his chest. He felt trapped; his control over the situation seemed to be diminished with every passing moment. It felt as if he had no other option but to stand and watch as the walls around him inched forward slowly, closing in.

# CHAPTER FOURTEEN

Julian, Emma, and Lena were sitting in a row on the same distinctive chairs: beige plastic with a vinyl-covered cushioning that wheezed pneumatically every time it was sat on. The room had the distinctive smell of a medical center, not the sterile smell of a hospital but rather something mustier, more human. Julian tried to swallow, but his throat was dry. He'd long ago noticed that there were no plastic cups left in the sleeve of the water cooler and since then it had stood in the corner of the waiting room like a glimmering untouchable oasis. There was a stack of magazines on a low table next to him, inside the pages of which he imagined thriving colonies of germs and pathogens.

Across from them was the only other person in the waiting room, an elderly woman who sat with her head resting against the wall behind her. Her eyes were closed; she was possibly asleep. Julian saw that her ankles and feet were swollen and mottled red and purple, the skin scaly and bleeding where she had scratched it. On the wall above her head was a large framed photo of Santorini: a white church with an azure dome roof took up the foreground and behind it the vast ocean, almost the same shade of blue, reached all the way to the horizon. Julian could recall that on the waiting room wall of the doctor's surgery of his youth, there had been a large image of a café in Paris, the Eiffel Tower sitting in the distance. The clinic he and Emma had visited after discovering that she was pregnant had an image of the Amazon rainforest on one wall and Machu Picchu on another. He wondered whether these images were intended to remind the viewer of Earth's vastness and vibrancy, the pulse of life outside, which was never more appreciated than in a place like this. Perhaps it was to balance out the less inspiring pin-up board that usually coexisted on the wall. In this clinic it was covered in overlapping posters in Greek, warning of pathogens—which Julian could identify by their universal rendering as green amorphous shapes with malicious expressions.

Lena sat on Julian's left and Emma on his right. The three of them, having exhausted all conversational options available to them long ago, remained in silence. It was an absurd scene. Julian sensed the receptionist's curiosity in the tilt of her head and the frequent flash of her gaze.

When a door down the hallway finally opened, a middle-aged woman emerged, thanking the doctor. She turned, moving slowly with a limp that caused her to hitch her left hip up and grimace with each step. The doctor shut his door softly behind her. When she reached the reception desk, her presence animated the receptionist with renewed purpose. A moment later, the doctor stepped out into the hallway and strode toward the waiting room. He was an older man with thick, dark gray hair. A pair of glasses sat on the end of his nose.

"Lena?" he asked the room.

"Yes," she answered, standing.

Julian stood too, turning to Emma and giving her a lop-sided, regretful smile. When they'd discussed Lena's request for Julian to attend the appointment, they'd made the decision that Emma would not come into the exam room with them. As much as he would have liked her to be there, he was unsure how they would explain her presence.

"I'll be out the front," she said, squeezing his hand.

As Lena and Julian walked down the hallway, the doctor began speaking in Greek.

"Sorry, do you mind if we speak in English?" Julian interjected.

"No, of course." The doctor smiled, though he did not resume speaking.

Inside, the consultation room was dominated by a large desk scattered with papers and a relic of a desktop computer. They took a seat in the two chairs facing the doctor's desk.

"So," he began, sitting in his chair and swinging it around to face his computer screen, "you believe you are pregnant?"

"Yes," Lena answered.

"And you are the father?" He turned his gaze from the screen to Julian, who hesitated.

"Yes," Lena answered for him.

"Sorry, yes." Julian nodded.

"Okay." He began typing, slowly poking at each key with his index fingers. "We will first do a urine test. Then a blood test."

He stood, moving across the small room to a cupboard where he took a small specimen collection jar and held it out to Lena.

"Please collect a sample in this and bring it back. There is a bathroom down the hallway."

She took the jar and left the room. The doctor turned back to his computer and began slowly typing again.

Julian cleared his throat. "Uh, I have a question."

The doctor lifted one eyebrow and turned to him. "Yes?"

"How early can paternity testing be done?"

The doctor looked at Julian for what could have only been a second or two and yet felt like an eternity. "From week ten," he replied eventually.

"Is it invasive?"

The doctor's eyes slid back to his computer screen. "It's a cheek swab for you and a blood test for her."

"Okay, thank you."

Julian was left to sit in silence for only a moment before the door opened behind him and Lena returned with her sample. The doctor stood, putting on a pair of rubber gloves and retrieving a test kit from his cupboard. He placed a strip in the sample and held it there for a moment before placing it down on a pad of paper towel. He turned back to his computer and looked at the time before adding more notes to Lena's file. Julian took a deep breath. He was suddenly conscious of his own heartbeat and the speed at which it was pumping.

The doctor turned back to the strip. "Congratulations," he said blandly. "You are pregnant."

He then asked Lena a series of questions about when she did the first pregnancy test and the details of her menstrual cycle, all of which Julian heard as if their voices and the clicking on the keyboard were in the room next door. His heart was now pounding and each breath he took was increasingly difficult, like a weight was being slowly lowered onto his chest. He swallowed back a sudden rush of saliva, trying to focus on what was happening in the room as his mind raced out of control. He tried to take a deep breath in and his attempt was audible. The doctor and Lena paused to look at him.

"Are you okay?" the doctor asked. The sudden attention was too much for Julian to handle.

"Sorry," he said, standing. "I'm sorry."

He left the room, lurching down the hallway, past the questioning eyes of the receptionist and out the door into the fresh air.

Emma was sitting on the curb outside the clinic where the world was once again alive and thrumming with energy. She hated hospitals and doctors' clinics: the stale stillness; the vitality of life reduced to the simple goal of survival. The world was made so small in these places, confined to the physical borders of the body. It was how she felt when she was pregnant, her body's sudden and constant changing forced to the forefront of her mind. Before she was pregnant, she would drink three cups of coffee before midday and eat nothing until nearly 3 P.M. She would sit at her desk, or present to clients, or hold meetings, all the while giving her body barely a thought, and it would reliably perform as needed. Until suddenly it asserted its presence in her every thought. She was forced to leave meetings to use the bathroom; forced to avoid a colleague who wore peppery cologne; forced to procure a specific mango juice from the café downstairs for lunch every day, which was basically the only thing she could stomach. She'd become a slave to her body. She wondered if Lena would soon feel the same way. Would she more passively accept it? Emma realized that she would be thinking about Lena frequently from now on. This gave her a claustrophobic feeling, which was

ironic given Emma and Julian's world had been forced to expand in order to accommodate Lena. She wanted to return to
the world of just Emma and Julian, to the place they had
carved out for themselves over the years, decorating it with their
memories and inside jokes, strengthening its structure each
time an experience left them with a deeper understanding of
each other. She remembered when she and Julian, having only
recently spent the night together for the first time, were walking barefoot across London Fields. They were "earthing"—
a concept they'd both heard of despite inhabiting two entirely
different streams of media exposure. Everyone was suddenly
walking barefoot through parks.

"Are your feet getting cold?" Julian had asked her. It was
late spring and the sky was almost violently aflame behind
him, smoldering slowly into a shade of violet. It was a still
evening, but not a very warm one.

"My feet went numb about five minutes ago," she answered.

They laughed, grinning at each other through the flattering pink light.

"Am I supposed to *feel* the grass?" she then asked somewhat rhetorically. "I think I am. I think that might be the
whole point. I'm going to put my socks and shoes back on."

When they got back to Emma's apartment, her roommate
was in the midst of another argument with her long-term on-
and-off-again boyfriend. They crept silently past the living
room, up the stairs, and into the bathroom, where they sat on
the edge of the tub with only their frozen feet immersed in hot
water because there was never enough hot water left at this
time of the evening for them to shower.

"Again?" Julian asked, referring to the fight going on below
them.

"Oh, yes." Emma nodded seriously. "At least twice a week."

The voice of her roommate's boyfriend momentarily rose through the floor. "And it was *fifteen* quid, not ten."

"How do you put up with this place?" Julian muttered.

"I wear headphones," Emma answered. "I try not to look too closely at anything. If you squint, it's not so bad."

The fighting couple were not the only issue that required accommodating in the house. There was her other roommate, Sad Gillian, who believed herself to be known only as Gill. Sad Gillian would corner Emma whenever they were both home for the evening and suggest a "movie night." If the invitation was accepted, she would proceed to drink a bottle of wine and weep onto Emma's shoulder, talking all through the movie about her high school sweetheart, who broke up with her before they went to separate colleges and now, years and years later, still intermittently visited late on the weekends, despite being married and having a two-year-old. Emma would be offered only a stale chocolate digestive biscuit for her troubles, and the next day Gillian would wake up and act as if the conversation had never even happened. Emma's third roommate was a law clerk who moonlit as a sort of poltergeist in their house by being mostly invisible yet leaving a trail of dirty dishes, mess, and long black hairs in her wake. There was also a considerable ventilation and black mold problem.

"Move in with me," Julian said. "Come live at my place."

Emma turned to look at him.

"I mean it, just pack a bag and we'll leave," he continued. Excitement was growing in his voice. "We'll come back for the rest tomorrow."

Emma laughed in surprise at the sudden offer, both for what it meant explicitly and what it meant implicitly, which was that Julian was very serious about her—something she had hoped but had not yet let herself believe.

The next day, when she moved into his flat, they began creating a world together. It was simple, absolutely no one else could encroach on their shared life: the center of the Venn diagram. They were best friends—preferring the company of each other over everyone else; they were lovers and they were family. But that had changed now. Lena was pregnant with Julian's child. There was a newly formed space that Emma was excluded from, an experience that she would not fully share with Julian. She stared at the concrete before her as tears began to prick in her eyes. What if she was now redundant, condemned to uncover this fact at an excruciatingly slow pace as she watched Lena make herself comfortable within the world they'd created? What if Lena insisted on having the baby? Lena would be the mother of Julian's child, but what if it turned out she was suited to be more than that? What if it became easier to source everything from one place and Lena became the center of the Venn diagram? What if Julian didn't need Emma anymore?

At the sound of the clinic door opening behind her, Emma turned. Julian, with a pale face and wide eyes, was crossing the footpath toward her. He looked as if he might faint. She stood up and ran to him.

"I can't breathe," he said, staring past her. "I'm going to be sick."

"It's okay," she said, taking his hand and leading him to sit on the curb. "Just breathe. It's okay."

He sat, resting his arms on his knees and his head on his arms.

"Oh god," he said, his chest heaving. "Oh god."

Emma began to rub his back.

"He did a test," he explained, in between frantic breaths. "She's pregnant— I'm going to be a father— I don't know what to do— I can't do anything— There's nothing I can do."

"It's okay," she said, still rubbing his back. "Just try to breathe slowly."

He inhaled in a gasping, unproductive way. "There's nothing I can do— This doesn't feel like my life— This isn't my life."

"It's okay," she repeated. "It's okay."

Even though she had entirely expected the appointment to confirm that Lena was actually pregnant, she should have predicted this reaction from Julian. Since the news had been shared with them, he'd moved from shock to a sort of short-sightedness—a fixation on the next small step. Maybe this was a moment he needed to experience to feel the gravity of the situation.

After a few minutes, when his breathing slowed, she suggested they get a cab and return to the apartment, where he could lie down. She would make sure they texted Lena to explain his sudden disappearance and apologize—they would make it up to her somehow.

At the apartment, Emma led Julian to the bed, bringing him a glass of water and then leaving him in the darkened room. Later, when he emerged, his hair sticking up in odd places and lines creased into his face from the sheets, he showed Emma a missed call and two texts from Lena.

*Where are you?*

*Did you leave?*

They sat on the couch and Julian crafted an apology, asking if there was anything he could do to make it up to her.

*OK,* she replied cryptically.

Another message followed.

*I did the blood test.*

She sent a screenshot of a pathology document from the lab. They sent the document to Julian's laptop and ran it through a translator. Έγκυος. *Pregnant.* As Emma tried to read the rest of the document another message arrived.

*I want you to meet my brother.*

# CHAPTER FIFTEEN

The street where Emma and Julian found themselves was lined with utilitarian-looking *polykatoikia*. It was so narrow that if two people stood on opposite balconies and reached a hand out to each other, Emma imagined they could probably touch. Although it was bordered by Kolonaki—a well-known haunt of the young and wealthy—Exarchia, the neighborhood where Lena's brother lived, was another world. When they'd looked up the address, they'd stumbled upon article after article about the place: an anarchist, anti-racist, socialist state within a state that had a tumultuous history of refusing to be controlled and choosing to exist instead under its own set of rules.

Lena's brother's apartment was not too far from Alistair's, but after deciding the walk would be too punishing in the heat, they'd arrived via the metro and exited onto the street at Omonia station. Following the guidance of Julian's phone, they were led past the polytechnic and straight into the remnants of an earlier demonstration. A dumpster in the middle of the street was smoldering, and tear gas lingered in the air, irritating their eyes. Further down the street, a group of bored-looking police officers wearing vests and helmets and armed with truncheons blocked the way. Intuiting that they were not local to the area, the police officers shouted to them in English that the road was closed.

They were forced to navigate a convoluted detour, eventually arriving at their destination: a street that was surprisingly, almost jarringly peaceful, where merciful patches of shade were cast over the concrete by fragrant bitter orange trees and wisteria.

"She said she'd meet us out the front of the building," Julian said, looking around with his phone in his hand. "I guess we just wait for her."

Emma stood idly, continuing to take in the surroundings. Graffiti covered the yellow walls of the buildings in a combination of murals and hastily scrawled battle cries. Next to Julian's head were the words DEFEND EXARCHIA.

She tapped her foot lightly against the pavement and gazed up, past the trees, at the roofs of the *polykatoikia,* most of which were five, sometimes six stories high. There were thick knots of wires, cables, and TV antennas hanging above the street. She traced the powerlines until she noticed something dangling from one, a shoe perhaps. She moved closer so that she stood directly underneath it. The color of it—brown and pink—and its shape began to resemble something else. It was a dead rat, somehow tied to the powerline by its tail. Emma blanched and looked away.

Lena's voice echoed down from further up the street. They turned to see her approaching. She greeted them both by kissing their cheeks and led them through a set of heavy glass doors to a linoleum-floored lobby and up a flight of stairs to the first floor. The door to the apartment opened straight into the kitchen and living room space, giving Julian and Emma very little time to prepare and revealing a man sitting on a couch, one leg crossed over the other as he scrolled on his phone. Nearby, there was a white plastic table and chairs where three more men sat. One of them was eating from a plate of rice and meat, which explained the charcoal smell in the room.

"Darius, this is Julian," Lena said, walking toward the man on the couch. He sat forward a little, making Julian and Emma bend to him to shake his hand. Even seated, Emma could tell he was a short man. His head was shaved, and he wore a pair of jeans and a navy polo shirt. His narrowed eyes and the upturned corners of his lips gave him an unpleasant aura of smugness, as if he found everything amusing—the same expression that Lena's face often held, only hers was not so harsh.

"I'm Emma." She shook his hand. "I'm—"

"She's Julian's sister," Lena explained.

In her surprise, Emma's hand went limp, and Darius released it.

"Come, sit." He gestured to the couch and sofa chairs, not bothering to introduce the other men, whose presence now seemed more menacing.

They took a seat, and Emma glanced at Julian to see if he'd heard her introduced as his sister. He was holding his face very still.

"I'm staying here at the moment," Lena explained. "I told my parents I was pregnant after the doctor's appointment, and my father kicked me out."

"They are very religious," Darius added, placing a cigarette between his lips and attempting to speak around it before removing it to continue. "They don't understand the modern world. They lived closer to a time when they still had to fight for their faith. These days, you see priests driving around in fancy cars and not helping anyone. It's not the same anymore, but they don't understand."

Emma found his statements fragmented and difficult to follow. She wasn't sure how to respond. Julian remained silent next to her.

"All the fasting and the bribing," Darius went on. "They take advantage of sick, poor people. They create fear and use it against them. They tell them to give more money to them, and their sickness will be taken away. It's all lies."

In the stunted silence, Darius put the cigarette back in between his lips, holding it like it was a dart he was about to throw, and lit it. He exhaled with his head turned toward the balcony and then looked back at them with his eyebrows raised, as if he was amused by their silence.

"So," he continued, still smirking, "what is your work, Julian?"

"I'm an academic," Julian replied. Emma was thankful in that moment for the confidence in his voice. It felt as if they were able to claw back some power.

Darius then turned to Emma, raising his eyebrows instead of repeating the question.

"I work in publicity for an advertising agency," she lied, feeling it was important she had something to say.

Darius shifted slightly in his seat so that the gold cross he wore around his neck emerged momentarily from the thick, dark hair on his chest. In a normal conversation, one of them would ask Darius what he did, but Emma intuited that wasn't the right question to ask and Julian seemed to agree. The conversation was interrupted when two small children appeared out of the bedroom door by the kitchen. The smaller child, a boy who was maybe five, was crying, while the slightly older one, a girl, followed behind with an exasperated look on her face and an iPad in her hands.

The boy ran to one of the men sitting at the dining table, flinging his arms around the man's knees and appearing to cry to him in Greek about some injustice. The older child followed—her body language defiant. When she spoke, she seemed to be rebuffing whatever statement the younger child had made in a desperate, guilty tone. The man murmured to the boy, undoing the child's arms from around his legs, and then turned to address the girl, his voice level. The boy seemed happy with whatever verdict had been made, but the girl was not. She now cried out in protest, and the two children's roles reversed. It was then that Darius, in one fast movement, rose from his seat and lunged toward the children, hissing a string of stern words at them. They flinched in fright, dropping their grievance instantly and running back to the bedroom. Satisfied, Darius sat back down. The man, who appeared to be the father of the children, went back to looking at his phone, entirely unbothered by Darius's aggressive intervention.

Emma glanced sideways at Julian and met his eyes briefly before he glanced away and swallowed.

"Lena has to go to work, but I thought we could get some lunch," Darius said, standing and putting his cigarette out in the ashtray on the coffee table in front of them.

"Oh, we don't want to intrude on your day," Julian said, attempting to extract themselves.

"You aren't," Darius responded. "Let's go."

"Sure, okay." Julian's reluctance was only visible to Emma. They all stood, following Darius's lead as if they were being pulled by a strong current. Out on the street, Lena said goodbye, kissing them each on the cheek, before placing her earphones in as she walked off. Emma watched her, feeling uneasy about her sudden departure and wishing that she and Julian had had the foresight to place an inexorable time limit on this meeting. They'd been outplayed.

As they followed behind Darius, Julian was able to observe him more freely. He was not a big man, neither tall nor particularly broad, which was reassuring. Julian often unconsciously measured other men like this, finding himself relieved whenever his height and size warranted him a physical advantage.

Since they'd left the apartment, Darius hadn't asked any questions. Instead, he'd spoken in a proud, practically unbroken monologue about the neighborhood.

"The government doesn't help refugees," he was explaining. "They put them in camps and treat them like they aren't human, but Exarchia opens its arms when everyone else shuts them. They are given abandoned buildings to occupy so they have somewhere to live."

On the street corner ahead of them, a group of four men had arranged plastic chairs on the footpath and were smoking. Behind them, the graffiti-covered building had the look of desperate occupation. Darius called something out to the men in a language that didn't sound like Greek to Julian. The men laughed and responded.

"They came from Tehran," he explained as they turned the corner. "It's been very hard for them."

Julian didn't know whether he was referring to their passage from Tehran, or perhaps to the fact they were stranded in Athens, or maybe just to their lives in general.

"It's all changing now," Darius continued, his tone darkening. "A new prime minister was elected. He says he wants to 'fix' Exarchia. They want to seal the abandoned buildings and paint over the walls. The raids will increase."

They passed a wall where words had been stenciled in bright red ink: WE LIVE. WE FIGHT.

Darius had slowed down so that he now walked alongside Julian and Emma. "Do you know what the police do?" he asked, perhaps rhetorically. They said nothing and, without looking at them, he continued, "They come in wearing black masks over their faces. They hold guns to people's heads." His lip curled in contempt. "There are children living in these buildings."

"That's horrible," Emma said. Julian watched Darius glance at her.

"They drag them out and move them off to camps," he continued, "but these camps are already full. My military service was on an island near the Turkish border; I have seen these places. They have no space, no privacy. There is a lot of abuse. Here, they have lives, schools and doctors that help them."

They walked past a building that appeared to have previously been some kind of office. Julian could see the signs of occupation from where they stood: makeshift curtains covering the windows, shapes moving within. Two banners hung from the windows on the third and fourth floors that read REFUGEES WELCOME and HOME. Darius, having reached the end of his tour, fell silent as they continued walking, and Emma and Julian, both processing the candid glimpse into an incomprehensibly difficult life, said nothing either.

Eventually Emma broke the silence. "There was a demonstration earlier near the polytechnic. Do you know what that was about?"

"It was about the police being allowed back into the university."

"The police can't go into the university?"

"The law forbids it. There was a student uprising against the junta many years ago. The police sent a tank in and killed a lot of people. It is a very sad memory for Exarchia. Now, the new prime minister wants to get rid of that law. Of course, many people are unhappy with that. The murder of those innocent people is still very emotional for them."

After taking one more turn, they reached a small restaurant with formica tables and linoleum floors. Darius stopped to scratch the ears of a large German shepherd, which lay in the shade out in front of the restaurant. The dog seemed to recognize him; it wagged its tail and yelped pleadingly, dragging along the heavy chain that secured it to a nearby pole. Inside, an older man emerged through a wooden beaded curtain and greeted Darius warmly. They took a seat at a table, and Darius spoke to the man for a moment before the man disappeared back through the curtain.

"Giorgos makes the best *soutzoukakia*," Darius said, leaning back and pulling out a cigarette pack from his pocket. He tossed it onto the table in front of him. "Meatballs," he added by way of translation.

"How long have you lived around here?" Julian asked as Darius lit a cigarette.

"Many years." He paused to smoke, exhaling fully and watching through the doorway as a group of young people on the opposite side of the street took photos of a mural. "For how much longer, I don't know. It is becoming harder for the neighborhood to survive now. Investors buy apartments and turn them into Airbnbs. Then the tourists come." He looked again at the group, which was now taking photos of one another in front of the mural. "They are happy taking photos, but they don't know that they are making things worse. Exarchia is meant to serve its community—exist for a purpose—and they get in the way of that. The costs go up—it becomes harder to live here, and the rich men become richer." He reached for the ashtray, moving it in front of him before tapping his cigarette over it in a surprisingly fluid and elegant movement. "These rich men want to encourage more tourism, so they put pressure on the government. They want the police to start coming into Exarchia more. There is talk the new prime minister wants to put in a metro station in Exarchia Square." He scoffed. "They will not be able to do this easily, believe me."

His speech continued, requiring very little input from Julian or Emma, until eventually Giorgos emerged from the kitchen, carrying three bowls and delivering them to the table. The *soutzoukakia* was served in one bowl, with rice in another, and what looked like a Greek salad in the third. Giorgos left and returned with plates and cutlery for each of them, and Darius pressed his cigarette out in the ashtray.

As they ate, Darius asked how long they'd been in Athens. They explained that they were housesitting for a friend. He asked if they liked living in London, and they lamented the gray sky and the rain, partaking in habitual self-deprecation on behalf of a city they actually enjoyed living in.

After they ate, Darius lit another cigarette before leaning back and slinging one arm over his chair.

"What did you think?" he asked, raising his eyebrows to signal he was referring to the meal.

"It was good," Emma said. "Really good." Julian made a noise of agreement.

Darius exhaled and smiled, pleased.

Julian felt a natural ebb and leaped upon it. "This has been really nice, Darius." He shifted forward in his seat as if to demonstrate their impending departure. "But I think we should let you get back to your afternoon."

Darius's smile broadened. "I think first we should talk about why we are meeting," he said.

A moment of strained silence followed. Julian shifted in his seat again.

"I heard about the doctor's appointment." Darius's eyebrows drew together, his eyes settling on Julian. "Lena told me you left."

Julian sat back in his chair. "I was feeling light-headed."

"He was very unwell," Emma added.

Darius's top lip curled inward. Without the smile to balance his narrowed eyes, it was as if any warmth they'd earned by sharing lunch with him had disappeared. The effect was almost startling. Darius looked down at the empty plate in front of him. He put his cigarette stub out on his plate, pressing it slowly into a pool of leftover red sauce. "The doctor told Lena you asked about paternity testing."

"Yes, of course—"

Darius's eyes flared at him. "You humiliated her. What would he think of her now?"

"That wasn't my intention," Julian replied. "But I will be asking her to do a paternity test as soon as she can."

"You understand that doing that is shameful for her?"

"I apologize for that, but it's important."

"Maybe they could go to a different clinic for the test, then she won't have to see the same doctor twice," Emma suggested. "If that helps."

Darius closed his eyes, scratching the side of his head with an air of frustration.

"Lena is young," he said eventually. "She will rely on you a lot now, and in our family, we look after each other."

"I underst—"

"You will need to be there for her, no matter what," Darius continued over the top of Julian.

The words sounded like a threat despite being packaged with friendly sentiment. Julian found himself unable to respond. Irritation rose quickly within him with no outlet. Darius then stood up from his chair, putting his lighter and cigarettes back in the pocket of his polo shirt. The lunch was finally over, and a wave of relief came over Julian, renewing his energy.

"We'll get this," Julian said, reaching for his wallet.

"No, no," Darius dismissed him, pulling his own wallet out. "You are my guests—this is how things are done."

Again, the words were polite, but it was evident that Darius's mood had changed as if a cloud had passed in front of the sun and placed Julian and Emma in sudden cold shade. He dropped notes on the table.

"I don't want there to be any issues," Darius said as they stepped back out onto the street. "It's my duty to look after Lena—I think you understand."

"Sure, I understand," Julian responded, knowing that now was not the time to assert himself.

"And that means we will be seeing more of each other." Darius smiled broadly at them both, his eyes characteristically narrowed. "Enjoy your afternoon."

Without another word, he turned and walked away, leaving Julian seething, his heart pounding angrily in his chest.

# CHAPTER SIXTEEN

Emma had told Julian she was going to buy groceries. She stood now, hovering over the tomatoes, and watched the bar where Lena worked through the front windows of the mini-mart. Her true plan was to go and speak to Lena without Julian. There were a few pressing reasons that had driven her to this point. There was Darius for one. She would be lying if she said that meeting him the day before had been pleasant. When they left Giorgos's taverna, Julian was piqued—his ego bruised. He walked fast, blindly, through the streets as Emma exerted herself to remain within listening distance. He repeated things Darius had said and ranted about his dislike for the man. When they reached the lobby, he'd turned to Emma and breathlessly concluded, "One thing is for certain, that man wants us to feel threatened and I *refuse* to let him think he's succeeded." Neither of them felt good about his sudden presence or interest in the situation. Whether it was genuinely Lena's welfare that he wanted to look out for or not, he was a complication.

The only antidote was to find out whether Lena had given her options any more thought. Since Julian's first conversation with her about it a week ago, he hadn't even mentioned in passing the idea of following up. It was odd. If Julian truly wanted to take this course of action, Emma felt he needed to be advocating for it far more strongly than it seemed he was. There wasn't an imaginable world where Emma thought Julian might actually wish to keep the baby, but she needed, for her own reassurance, to hear from Lena directly; she needed to know that the option to terminate the pregnancy had been thoroughly reviewed and made as appealing to Lena as possible.

Only Emma now found herself procrastinating under the pressure of all that she wanted to achieve in a single conversation. She frowned at the tomatoes as she tried to plan her next move. The concern was that her sudden arrival might trigger Lena's defenses. She glanced back at the bar again just as Lena appeared in the doorway, walking over to the entrance of the alleyway and disappearing down it. Emma stared dumbly in surprise before the realization struck that an opportunity was being handed to her. She left the mini-mart, crossing the road quickly, before adjusting her speed down to something more casual. When she approached the entrance of the alleyway, Lena was leaning against the wall, scrolling on her phone with a bored look on her face.

"Oh, Lena," she said, feigning surprise. "Hi."

Lena looked up from her phone warily. "Hello," she replied. Her frown flattened into a weak smile.

"I was just on my way to the mini-mart," Emma explained, walking toward her. "Needed some olive oil."

Lena only stared back at her in response.

"Busy shift today?" she asked, then, remembering that it was still early in the afternoon, she added, "You must have just started."

"It's quiet in the afternoon." Lena pushed her phone into the back pocket of her denim shorts with an air of acquiescence. "So we are pretty bored."

"It's always better to be busy at work, isn't it? Time just drags otherwise."

Lena gave a single nod, looking placidly ahead at the street. In imagining how this interaction would go, it never occurred to Emma that she might bore Lena, but there Lena stood, practically yawning. When they had stood in this alleyway the first time they met, the interaction had felt electric. They'd seemed to intrinsically understand each other at a depth that relieved them both of having to work the clumsy machinery of the conversation. It was different now, clunky and stilted.

"Meeting your brother was nice," Emma lied. "He clearly cares about you a great deal."

Lena gave her another flat smile. "I'm glad you met him."

Emma could sense Lena's desire to end the conversation. There was a restlessness in the air between them, and she kept glancing past Emma, as if she were literally looking for an exit.

"Actually, Lena," Emma pressed onward, "there is something I wanted to talk to you about, and maybe—seeing as we're both here—now is a good time."

Lena settled her eyes back on Emma expectantly.

"It's important to Julian and me that every option is adequately explored—I'm sure you feel the same way."

Lena stiffened defensively.

"With a huge decision like this, you'd want to consider

every path that is available to you," Emma continued, keeping her eyes firmly on Lena. "There's really no way to easily discuss this subject, but I think maybe you know what I'm talking about."

Lena gave no affirming signal.

"Julian told me that you were considering ending the pregnancy—that you had a conversation about it—"

"That's not true," she interjected.

"It's not?"

"No, he told me we should speak to the doctor about all our options. I told him I wouldn't. I said that decision is for me to make myself."

Her eyes, still trained on Emma, turned steely. "Then he promised me that he would help me look after our child."

Emma carefully held her face blank of surprise. She felt a sudden desire to hurt Lena in some way, to remind her that although she held a certain degree of power over them, it still had limitations.

"Well, the truth is, it's what Julian and I both think is best."

Lena looked down once more and said nothing, and Emma knew that she needed to change tack, lay aside the hit to her pride and focus on Lena.

"It would be best for you too."

Lena's face clouded. "Why?"

"You're young—you have a long life ahead of you," Emma answered. "When I was your age, I was at university. I truly had no idea what I wanted from life. I rarely even thought about goals and plans. Time just passed, years went by, and I moved along without any destination in mind."

Lena was watching her again and she took it to be an indication of her interest. "After I left my twenties behind," she continued, "I realized how important it is to be purposeful—to find out where I wanted to end up and begin consciously moving there. Time passes whether you exert control over your life or not. I learned that I may as well control where I was going."

She remembered the conversation she'd had with Julian on the balcony, when they'd spoken about free will and mastery of fate. She had the ironic sense that she was now vouching for the existence of a causally determined world, like Julian had.

Lena was still watching her. Emma kept her focus on the path ahead. The words continued to arrive naturally and easily, and she knew this was because they were true to her.

"Having a child changes the direction of your life permanently," she went on. "It removes some of your options and replaces them with new destinations—new priorities. It shifts your perspective on everything. You will never be able to truly put yourself first again. Given how young you are, that's a significant sacrifice."

Lena was frowning, but she seemed to be considering Emma's words.

"Of course, we don't mean to put pressure on you. I just want to know you've considered your options fully. And I want you to know that if you do decide to end the pregnancy, we will fully support you. We can make sure you get the best medical care—anything you need. If we move quickly, there are less invasive options."

Emma hovered at this juncture. Lena was still silent, giving no indication of her feelings, and Emma decided that to fail to outline the full offering was to lose an important opportunity that she might not get again.

"We will also give you enough money to take plenty of time off work if you want."

Lena's eyes darted back to Emma's. "You are trying to pay me to have an abortion?"

Emma's mouth fell open as she struggled to respond. "No, that's not—"

"I will tell you what I told Julian: this is my decision to make."

"Of course."

"If I don't want Julian's opinion, then I definitely don't want *yours*."

"I'm sorry if I've offended you," Emma repented. "That really wasn't my intention."

"I need to go back now," she stated coolly.

"Right," Emma replied. "I'll let you get back. Thank you for speaking to me."

Lena said nothing. She was waiting for Emma to leave. The silence was suspended awkwardly for a moment before Emma turned away.

As she left the alleyway, Emma had the unmistakable sense of Lena watching her. She crossed the street and walked fast, chased by the jittery, uneasy realization that the conversation had not at all gone the way she'd hoped, and the larger, more uncomfortable discovery that Julian had lied to her.


At dinner, Julian thought Emma seemed subdued. She drank quickly, refilled her glass, and barely touched the plate of pasta in front of her. Meanwhile, a spectacular sunset manifested, gilding everything. Julian watched Emma glow in the flattering light while her expression remained stoic, the combination making her appear like some sort of beautiful and indifferent statue. At first he hadn't pressed conversation on her, instead leaving her to her mood, but as the evening continued, her silence had become louder, until it drowned out even the rattling hum of the cicadas.

"You're very quiet tonight," he remarked eventually, unable to sustain it any longer.

She looked up, her expression making it clear that he was in some way involved in her mood. He almost flinched, but in a second the look was gone, wiped clean off the edges of her face, and he was left wondering whether he'd imagined it.

"I'm just tired," she replied, picking up her fork. She looked at it for a moment as if it were the first fork she'd ever seen. "How did your writing session go today?"

Julian drank. He had not yet admitted to Emma that he'd officially given up working on his paper. There were more pressing complications in their life, but there was also a hesitancy drawn from the fact that Emma had not known a version of Julian who hadn't been working on this paper. When they met, he was in the thick of completing his PhD thesis and pining for freedom. He wanted time to work on another proposal, an idea which had excited a professor he deeply admired so much that the man had told him to think *very seriously* about pursuing its completion and publication.

When his PhD was completed, his passion project became his occupation. Now, years later, the paper was so much a part of his identity that if he extracted it, he worried that Emma would see him as incomplete. It was a failure, a waste of years and years of toiling that Emma had felt acutely. Over the years he'd changed plans, declined invitations, stewed silently, prioritized his alone time, at times talked about the paper obsessively and at others had sunk into despondent moods, and she had weathered it all—how could he now tell her it was all for nothing?

"It was productive," he lied. "I've made some progress on

outlining the methodical differences between ontological assumptions of the transcendental and hermeneutic approaches to phenomenology. I think I'm really starting to clarify my ideas on how they may be useful as a research methodology."

Emma nodded remotely. "That's great."

"How was your day?"

She put her glass back down and rested her elbows on the table, placing her fingertips on her forehead and tracing her eyebrows with them as if she had a headache. "I'm sorry," she said. "I'm just—I keep thinking about Lena and . . ." She broke off, picking her glass up once again and looking into it. "Remind me again what she said when you brought up termination?"

Julian swallowed. "She said that she would consider it."

He was chained to this lie now. Emma frowned at her plate. He sensed some sort of trap. She put her glass back down without drinking.

"Are you okay?" he asked. "What's going on?"

She stood, collecting her glass and plate. "I'm fine. I think I'm just tired. I'm going to have an early night."

"Okay," he said, watching her with concern as she walked past him and back into the apartment.

The light had darkened now, smoldering for a while before the sun would sink into the Aegean Sea completely. Julian sat for a moment running a hand over his chin and watching the light dim. He wanted to follow Emma, to sit down next to her and get to the crux of what was bothering her, but he couldn't. The fact that he'd lied to her kept him stuck in his chair. He had the sense that he'd escaped from some sort of confrontation, but only just. To go back inside looking for more would be to invite questions, and he'd rather not have to elaborate on his lie. He also harbored another secret: a few hours before, Lena had sent him a message.

*Can we meet tomorrow?*

*Just us two*

He unlocked his phone and viewed the messages again.

Since its arrival, the request had troubled him. He knew he had two options. The first being: to not tell Emma that he was meeting with Lena. In other words, to lie to her again. An option that made him wary. The more he lied, the more likely he was to be found out. Emma was not forgiving in this realm. If her trust was broken even in some small way, she usually curled up and sulked silently like a wounded animal; no amount of apologies, repentances, or promises could expedite the process, only the passage of time and some internal journey she took alone would eventually grant Julian remission. It was a difficult experience to be exiled like this, but the thought of enduring it now, with everything else that was going on, was too much to contemplate.

Alternatively, he could be honest and tell Emma that Lena had requested to meet with him alone. There was a chance Emma would understand this and know that he would share with her everything that was said at the meeting. But at the same time, he needed Emma and Lena to get along. If Emma knew that Lena was making requests to leave her out of the equation, it could create animosity between them, which Julian would be left to endure—possibly for years to come. The only real option then was to meet with Lena in secret and be sure that Emma never found out.

He responded to Lena, giving her a time and place where he thought they would not be seen.

# CHAPTER SEVENTEEN

Lena was late. Julian had waited at the café for nearly half an hour as the clock marched toward midday. It was a strangely decorated place, dark and cavernous with the intention of evoking luxury. The dark purple walls were crowded with large silver mirrors, meaning that whenever he lifted his head, he was greeted by his own guilty expression. He'd chosen this particular café because it afforded him privacy from the street. It was also located in Psyri, where he knew Emma was less likely to walk by.

As he waited, he used his phone aimlessly, refreshing his inbox twice before accepting that no email was going to arrive on command to engage him. Emma's article had gone live that morning. She'd been sleeping when he left the apartment and he hadn't wanted to wake her for fear she'd ask where he was going, but he'd read the article while he made coffee. Now he opened it again, rereading the lead paragraph. She had a wonderful crisp writing style, a real talent for making you read the next sentence, and then the next. He was proud of her. He only wished he could complete that thought with an uncomplicated full stop and move on. Instead, when he thought of her pursuing a career in journalism, he felt a sense of dread. He imagined her building a profile for herself, maybe even winning awards, and he wondered whether he could cope with that gracefully in the wake of his own newly abandoned dreams. It seemed unlikely, given he couldn't even read her article without a searing sense of shame and failure. Why had she hidden the article from him for so long? Did her hesitancy to tell him imply a sense of guilt on her behalf? And if she felt guilty, did that mean he did actually have a genuine reason to feel hurt by all of this?

He didn't sense Lena's arrival—she seemed to appear suddenly across from him at the table, her hair wet as though she'd just showered. He was happy to see that, even though Darius had declared they would be seeing more of each other, she had arrived alone.

"Hello," she said, leaning over to kiss him on the cheek and leaving behind the cloying artificial apple scent of her shampoo.

"Good morning," he replied.

He studied her as she hung her tote bag on the back of her chair and slid into the seat, finding himself surprised by his attraction to her, as if her beauty had waited in hiding over their last few meetings, choosing this moment to come forward and ambush him. It was strange, he thought, that their closeness now, sitting across from each other in a café, seemed more inappropriate than any of their previous physical relations.

"Thanks for meeting me," she said, glancing back at him. "Alone."

"Sure."

"I had to lie to Darius about what I was doing."

"Would he have stopped you from meeting me?"

She shrugged. "He would have wanted to come too."

The declaration that Lena was capable of lying and with-holding information from Darius interested Julian greatly. He saw an opportunity to find out more about Darius and Lena's relationship.

"Why?"

"He is trying to look out for me to make sure that you aren't going to"—she paused as if searching for the words—"take advantage of me."

"It's reasonable for him to be protective of you," Julian admitted graciously. "But I want to be clear, Lena. We won't take advantage of you. We only want what's best for all of us."

She lowered her chin toward her chest, her expression soft-ening slightly.

"Anyway," he said, "I'm also glad that we can speak—just us two."

A waiter approached their table, interrupting the conversa-tion and placing a bottle of water and two glasses down be-fore them. Julian ordered a black coffee and then gestured to Lena to invite her to order.

She spoke to the waiter in Greek, asking a few questions before making up her mind. The waiter left them.

"How are you feeling?" Julian asked, before recalling that conversations with Emma when she was pregnant often con-cerned her physical condition. "You're probably sick of being asked that," he added.

Lena observed the small silver bowl of sugar in the middle of the table and, as if by compulsion, she picked up the small diamanté-encrusted spoon from the bowl, turned it over, and put it back.

"I'm good," she answered.

"You're nearly six weeks pregnant now?" He remembered there were symptoms—nausea, cravings and aversions, fatigue—which accompanied the first trimester. He thought of Emma and her mango juice phase. The sudden recollection caused an unexpected ache of emotion.

"I'm eight weeks," Lena answered. "The doctor said they count from my last period."

"Oh, right, of course."

"Also, I don't mind when you ask how I am—I like it." She looked at him directly then, the force of her sudden eye contact causing him to redirect his own. He poured a glass of water and took a sip.

"I've been thinking of names," she continued casually.

The statement required Julian to envision a future he had not yet fully come to terms with: a pink, mewling newborn baby who required a legal name. A child who would eventually learn to speak fluently in a language he couldn't understand. He swallowed his mouthful of water awkwardly and coughed as he placed his glass back down. "Oh?"

"If it's a girl, I like Eleftheria," she stated, now smiling at the napkin holder. "It means 'freedom.'"

Julian went to repeat the name and found he couldn't. "Okay," he said instead.

"And for a boy: Darius, after my brother," she added.

The mention of Darius again was disappointing. It revealed that Darius and Lena's relationship could be both fraught and solid in a way that was far more complex than Julian had given it credit for.

"You really admire your brother, don't you?" he asked.

She only nodded in response.

"Does it bother you how protective he is?" Julian pressed, hoping to give her a chance to open up again.

"No, he's protected me my whole life. He taught me all the things I actually needed to know about the world. The things my parents didn't."

"What does he do for work?" Julian then asked. As expected, the question sent Lena's eyes sliding away from his to focus over his left shoulder. It was blunt of Julian, almost impolite, given that he and Emma had thus far avoided asking questions about Darius, but after Darius had ended their meeting with barely veiled intimidation, Julian no longer felt it necessary to tread lightly.

When Lena returned her eyes to him, Julian urged himself to hold her eye contact. Her expression was slightly stricken; a faint line appeared between her brows.

"Do we trust each other?" she asked.

They were now suspended in a significant moment and Julian saw that to answer tepidly would be to miss an important opportunity. He leaned forward in his seat, taking one of her hands in his. "Lena," he said, employing as much sincerity as he could muster, "of course we do. We have to trust each other."

"Darius was in prison," she explained. "He's on conditional release now, but he still has to report to the police every week."

"What did he do?" Julian asked, releasing her hand.

Her face, which had smoothed, became stricken once more. "Nothing," she said, before reluctantly continuing. "He was involved in a disagreement. Someone was badly hurt, but they deserved it. They were not a good person. They did terrible things. He had to take the law into his own hands. Please don't tell anyone I told you. He doesn't want you to know."

"I won't say a word," Julian promised gravely.

There was a pause where neither of them said anything.

Julian suspected there was far more to the story. He wondered whether Lena was manipulating the details, or whether Darius had told her a certain version and she'd simply believed him. He imagined that it was very likely that Darius lied to his younger sister to shield her. It occurred to him that Lena had also lied to Darius when she said that Emma was Julian's sister.

"Why did you tell Darius that Emma is my sister?" he asked.

"It was less complicated to explain," she said in a tone that implied the answer was obvious.

"Don't you think we might need to explain the real situation to him at some point? If he figures it out himself, he won't like the fact that we lied to him."

She shrugged remotely, gazing past Julian's shoulder to the street beyond. Her expression had a way of appearing open one moment and closed the next, so that Julian had the strange experience of seeing her gain or lose interest in him in real time. It was apparent that she was now losing interest and he needed to backtrack.

His coffee arrived along with a cheese pastry for Lena, which she began to eat with surprising verve.

"So," he said, smiling, "Eleft . . ."

"Eleftheria," Lena repeated.

"That's a nice name. Ele for short." As Julian spoke, he felt as though he was acting a part, that he didn't mean the words he was speaking. But when Lena lifted her eyes to meet his and beamed at him, her bottom lip glistening with oil from the pastry, he knew he'd done a convincing job.

At a quarter to one, Lena needed to leave for work. Julian paid the bill while she stood on the curb applying lip gloss. The sky was bright and clear, and a slight breeze tousled the branches of the trees that grew in the thin space between the buildings. It was a surprisingly cool day and people sat around on benches and at cafés, taking advantage of the sun's armistice. The temperature invigorated Julian, freeing him to take a moment to appreciate Athens in a way he found difficult while under the sun's direct attack.

"Athens is a beautiful city," he said, seeking to bring Lena into conversation with his thoughts.

"You romanticize it," she responded.

"That's probably true," he admitted. "You don't think it's beautiful?"

"I do, but to me it is beautiful in a way that you can't ever understand."

"I suppose you have a lot of memories to add to your feelings and complicate the way you feel."

She seemed to be considering his words, and he continued, "I mean, I only see the city's superficial beauty. You know its flaws and so the beauty you see takes on more dimension—it's earned."

"Yes," she replied, seeming slightly surprised that his assessment held some truth. He felt pleased with himself. "When I feel love and pride for my city," she continued, "those feelings have overcome a lot to exist. You have also only seen *some* of the city. If you saw where my parents live, you might not think the same."

"Is it different where they live?"

"It's not like this."

There was an extended pause, naturally drawing them to the end of their meeting.

"Right, well," he said conclusively. "Have a good shift."

Lena remained still. "There's something I want to say."

"Okay, what is it?" he asked, watching her.

"Emma came to see me yesterday."

Of all the things Lena could have been about to admit, Julian could not have predicted that. It rendered him momentarily silent. He knew that acting surprised and thereby revealing that he and Emma had a tendency to act alone would set a dangerous precedent. Instead, he nodded. "Yes, I know."

"So you sent her to offer me money to have an abortion?" She regarded him through narrowed eyes. "She told me it's what you both want."

Julian sighed, closing his eyes tightly for a moment. He lifted his hand, pinching the bridge of his nose just underneath his glasses.

"I'm sorry if she offended you," he said, attempting to quickly forge a path to forgiveness and regain her trust. "We would never want you to feel pressured to make a decision like that."

"It's okay," she said, lifting her chin slightly. "But you should both know that I am going to keep the baby. I have made my decision. You can tell her that."

It was the first time that Julian had heard Lena explicitly state her intention. Somehow he didn't flinch. His expected panic was replaced by a despondent numbness. For a moment his thoughts moved around in his mind like shadowy figures, present but unidentifiable.

"I understand," he heard himself respond tersely. "But just in case there is any confusion, we intend to do a paternity test as soon as we can. That's about two weeks from now."

He saw Lena's face harden in the brief moment before her palm connected with the side of his face, leaving a burn in its wake.

It hadn't been a particularly hard slap, but he held a hand to his cheek anyway. "What the fuck, Lena!"

"You are going to humiliate me!" she shouted. "Do you know what asking for this test does? It makes me look like a *poutana*—a whore."

Heads swiveled toward them and Julian could sense the presence of eyes on his back. He lowered his voice, hoping that Lena would follow his lead. "I understand that it upsets you." The pain in his cheek had already receded and he dropped his hand. "But you can't just attack people—you can't hit me!"

Her eyes blazed at him in challenge.

"We aren't going to change our minds on this," he continued, keeping his tone level in the hope of de-escalating the situation. "If you want, we can go to a different clinic for the test and—"

"Do you really think I sleep around a lot?" she demanded, ignoring his offer. "That I just give my body to any man?"

Julian stared back at her. The fact that she'd required very little persuading to sleep with him, not to mention that Emma had also seen her with another man, made him want to undermine her sudden moral convictions, but making either of those statements was unlikely to defuse Lena's anger. "Truthfully, Lena," Julian said instead, "I know hardly anything about you."

"When I slept with you," she hissed, "I was not *fucking* anybody else."

Julian swallowed. "Listen, it's just due diligence. I'm not trying to accuse you of anything."

Lena's expression remained unchanged. "I have to go now," she said.

"Fine, okay," Julian replied. Frankly, he was not interested in continuing the conversation while she was so aggravated.

"Goodbye," she said.

"Bye," he replied.

She stepped forward and kissed him on the same cheek she'd slapped only moments before, delivering the kiss thoughtlessly, as if she were kissing an old relative, and leaving a smear of tacky lip gloss on his cheek.

# CHAPTER EIGHTEEN

Julian returned from meeting Lena in a foul mood. He found Emma sprawled on the couch reading *Medea,* reposed with the sulky air of a bored teenager held in captivity by a family holiday.

"Hello," she said without taking her eyes from the page.

"Hello." He sat down in the chair across from her. She continued reading, unaware that she was being watched, or choosing to ignore him. Eventually, perhaps after no longer being able to stomach the stilted silence in the room, she flicked her eyes from the page to him and back again. "Good writing session?" she asked.

"Actually, I spoke to Lena today."

Without saying anything, Emma steered her eyes back to him.

"She told me that Darius has been to prison."

Emma sat up, dropping her book onto the couch next to her. "For what?"

"Some sort of aggravated assault, I think. Although according to Lena they deserved it."

"*Jesus.*"

"Also she slapped me," he added.

"She *what*?"

"I told her I wanted her to do a paternity test and she slapped me."

Emma's eyes narrowed. "She *slapped* you?"

Julian nodded. "Not very hard, in all honesty."

"Why?"

"She thinks that I'm going to humiliate her and make her look like a 'whore'—her words, not mine. I think she was pretty annoyed at us generally."

Emma looked confused.

"She told me that you offered her money to have an abortion. She thought that it was some sneaky plan of mine."

Emma swallowed, closing her eyes momentarily as if in disappointment. He took some pleasure in seeing the seriousness in the gesture.

"Well?" he pressed.

Her eyes sprang back open. "Well, what?"

"Are you going to tell me why you did that? Why you went to her alone and tried to convince her to terminate the pregnancy?"

"It's a good thing I did. At least then one of us actually pursued the option."

Julian stared back at her, realizing that his own lie had been exposed.

"She told me she never agreed to discuss it with the doctor," Emma went on, "and you told me she did."

"I was going to convince her to consider it. I just hadn't yet. That didn't mean that you should have—"

"When?" she shot back. "It's somewhat of a time-sensitive issue."

Julian felt as if the tables had turned on him. He was the aggrieved party, and yet he was now being interrogated. "Emma, you hid the meeting from me; don't you think you should have spoken to me about this? You—"

"I was under the impression that I was acting in the interests of both of us—was I not? Didn't we agree that Lena's decision to terminate the pregnancy would be the best outcome?" She stared at him and, when he didn't answer, her eyes narrowed.

"But don't you think that's a conversation I should have been present for?" he asked, answering her question with another.

"I wasn't aware that I was practically bringing it up for the first time!" She threw her hands up in exasperation. "You told me you'd already had the conversation. You lied to me, Julian. You just admitted that you also met with her without telling me, so actually, you lied twice."

Frustration boiled in Julian. Thoughts he'd tried to suppress were now rising and spilling forth. "So, what, I don't get a say in any of this? Is that it? I get no input at all?"

Emma looked at him in speechless confusion. "What?"

"It's *my* life too," he continued. "It's my child and I feel like no one gives a second of thought to what I want! How *I* feel!"

"Julian—" Emma's voice had become remote, a signal that she was about to close off, but he was not willing to give up his stance.

"It feels like things are happening," he continued over top of her, "decisions are being made—*big* decisions—all of which affect me greatly and yet I feel like I'm the last person to know, the last person to be consulted." He paused, ordering his thoughts. "God knows what Lena is thinking and planning, what decisions she's making every single day that will impact *my* life—the life of *my* child." He looked back at Emma. "Then I find out you're meeting secretly with Lena—it's like no one cares about what I want."

"What do you want? I'd like to know because it's really starting to seem like you actually want to have this child with her."

Julian said nothing for a moment. Emma stared at him, her brow creased as if she was anticipating pain. "Is that what you're saying?"

"She's having the baby. She told me today. I have to accept it," he answered.

Emma was stunned for a moment. She took a deep breath in.

"Did you try to explore all the options properly? We could offer her more money. We could—"

"No." Julian closed his eyes. "No, Emma."

"So, what, you aren't even going to try to talk her out of this?" Her voice had become panicked. "Where is this coming from? I don't understand. Is this some sort of reaction to me telling you that I don't want to become a mother?"

"It's a reaction to the situation, Emma. It's a reaction to the fact that the child exists, which is so much bigger than just a reaction to something you've said. Lena isn't going to have an abortion. She's certain. I'm going to be a father. I have to come to terms with that."

Emma fell silent, her mouth contorting with effort to suppress emotion. Tears welled in her eyes. "Well, we don't have to stay here," she said after a moment. "We could leave and return back to our life. We could give Lena some money to help and—"

"I won't just abandon the baby."

"You expect us to stay here in Athens forever?"

"To be perfectly honest with you, I haven't quite figured that out yet." Julian heard the bitter sarcasm in his own voice but felt helpless to avoid it. "There's been a lot going on."

There was a pause while the words and their meaning settled on them.

"Maybe I should just go," Emma said eventually, her eyes fixed on the ground. "Maybe I should go back to London until you figure out what you're doing."

Julian stared at her in disbelief. She'd never been one to react well when cornered. He'd known her to lash out, escalate arguments, and encroach the edges of what couldn't be repealed. Even though he'd had experience with her surprising capability for cruelty in the past, it never failed to shock him anew each time she wounded him with it.

He shook his head. "You can be so cold. Do you even hear yourself? 'I should just go.' Are you actually saying you'd see no issue leaving me here to deal with all of this alone?"

Emma said nothing. She kept her eyes on the floor.

"You're putting me in an impossible scenario. Are you forgetting that all of this was your idea in the first place?"

Her eyes flew to meet his. "You know I would never have gone ahead with it if I knew this would be the outcome."

He stared back at her, refusing to back down.

"And now that it's clear that you've decided you want to stay here and be in the child's life," she went on, "what am I doing here? How do I fit into this? There isn't a place for me—I told you I don't want any of this."

"You'd *seriously* just leave me here?"

Emma wiped a tear from her cheek with the back of her hand, and Julian looked away, a dark and cruel desire urging its way through his hurt.

"What would it matter?" he added quietly, as if to himself. "It's like you're only half here with me anyway."

He looked back at her to assess how this landed. She watched him sadly, but she didn't seem particularly taken aback by the statement. He took that to be confirmation of its truth.

"Do you know you live in a constantly dissociated state?" he asked. "It's like you don't truly care about anything. Sometimes I feel like I could be replaced by anyone. I could be any old stranger and I could get into bed with you and you wouldn't even notice. It wouldn't make a scrap of difference to you. You're so entirely checked out—"

"I'm checked out?" she shot back, reenergized by the injustice of the allegation. "What about you? You live almost entirely in a fantasy world—your perfect little delusional vision of the future where you've achieved everything you've ever wanted. You're always striving toward something—"

"So you're now saying you have an issue with ambition?" Julian laughed mirthlessly. "No, please, go on."

"What I'm saying is you're never here, in the present, and when you are it's only to perform this brief self-congratulatory appreciation of 'the moment.' You're terrified of standing still. It's your paper, your career, your *insatiable* need for validation, and then when all of that gets too hard you're suddenly chasing this bizarre idea of living the perfect little country life with the perfect little wholesome family—don't you see how deranged that is? And what happens afterward when you figure out that the perfect little country life doesn't satiate you? On to the next fantasy?"

She continued, now standing and pacing in front of the couch. "You've never even asked me what I want. You treat me like an afterthought, like I'll just happily follow you to the country, have children, and make no decisions of my own. We agreed that we didn't want children and then you decided you did. You didn't even ask me how I felt—you just decided that's what you wanted and so that's what we were going to do. It's like I'm just an accessory to your life. You expect me to make all the sacrifices."

"Well, forgive me, Emma, but you imploded your own career. What exactly was I asking you to give up?"

Emma stopped pacing and turned her narrow glare onto him. She seemed, despite herself, to give that comment consideration.

"It only seems like I make all the decisions because you've never said you wanted anything!" he defended.

"Maybe that's because everything you want is so loud!" Ironically, she shouted this statement. "It's so loud that I can't speak over it!" Her frustration implied that he was being belligerent, refusing to sympathize even a little.

"So what do you want then?" he shouted back. "What kind of life am I preventing you from having?"

Emma shook her head as if his inability to understand her grievance was so fundamental it had left her speechless. There was an element of martyrdom to the gesture; she was unjustly trying to claim the part of long-suffering partner. His aggravation rose once more. "It's pretty obvious why you have an issue with my ambition," he said coolly—her eyes blazed at him, daring him. "You don't have any of your own."

"That's not true—I do have ambition. My article came out today, which you've failed to acknowledge, by the way."

"Oh, right, the article." Julian laughed—the sound spilling out cruelly before he could stop it. "The article that someone just *handed* to you. I'm not sure that demonstrates your ambition so much as your good fortune."

Her eyebrows flinched together, and he knew he'd succeeded in hurting her. He winced as the guilt arrived.

She shook her head in disappointment. "You know your insecurities can make you a real arsehole sometimes. I can't believe you've reached the point where even this article threatens you. You're a child."

"*Insecurities?* You're the one criticizing me for having goals and trying to achieve them."

"*God,* Julian, you don't get it." All the anger had vanished from her words and was replaced by a sad, wounded despondency. "Sometimes I feel like the only version of me you're genuinely interested in is the simplified version that exists in your fantasies. The version that just says yes to everything you want. You've always wanted to change me, *fix me*—move me into your life, your vision. You don't want me to take up too much space, to exert too much control. You'll never acknowledge that my thoughts and feelings are as important as yours." She sighed again, wiping her face angrily. "You'll never see me as an equal because there's no space in your mind to even consider that idea." With one more teary, red-eyed glance at him, she stormed out of the room and down the hallway, the bedroom door slamming shut. He remained where he was, stunned and bewildered by where the conversation had left them. His anger and his self-righteousness, which had only seconds before encouraged him, had already begun to dissipate, leaving only a hollow, regretful feeling. He stared at the floor and replayed what had been said, seeking to justify his words, but each time he tried to access the motivation he'd felt, he found that even less remained.

He stood and paced the living room, grimacing as he re-lived the moment when he told Emma she lacked ambition. On reflection, she'd seemed hurt, but not shocked by the allegation: had he already made her feel that way, so that when he said it out loud she knew already the shape of the insult to come? He'd downplayed the achievement of her article; why had he said those things? He'd wanted to tell her that she was good, she had talent—it was *impressive*. On the other hand, she'd told him that he lived in a fantasy world, that he put pressure on her to conform to his visions, but when had he ever *actually* done that? Was he not just being made to repent for her projections? Did that matter? She'd threatened to leave him! The sear of injustice returned, but the feeling sat use-lessly upon him with no outlet; she'd taken that away when she put walls in between them.

He saw it then: a future without Emma. He stopped pacing and stood still in front of the couch, stunned by the vision. Without halting their trajectory, without retracing his steps and repairing the damage they'd just sustained—no matter how good it temporarily felt to voice his hurt—they would reach a point of no return. It all rose against him then: the strength of his loss and the toll it would take on him. He ap-proached the bedroom.

Emma wasn't really packing, more just angrily throwing her clothes on top of her bag to busy her hands while her mind worked. She was furious and hurt, but she was also ashamed. She now dealt with the hangover of everything she'd said, all of the complaints—genuine, but poorly timed—that deserved to be approached in a more thoughtful and productive way. She'd been crueler than necessary, and she'd stormed out of the conversation, which was something she knew Julian would never do.

It was a move that she'd learned from the man she'd dated before Julian, a man who had wounded her greatly whenever he stormed off in the midst of an argument, literally leaving the house and returning hours later in a cold silence that would thaw slowly over the following hours. Leaving in the middle of an argument broke the contract of a relationship. It showed the leaver as capable, unafraid of a more permanent exodus; a relationship could only sustain so many of those blows before it lost its shape.

Emma had learned very early on with Julian that he was incapable of leaving an argument unresolved. The first fight they'd ever had had been over something trivial that she could not entirely remember—some frustration on his behalf over her living situation, which she preferred to respond to with passivity. What she could remember was the way that she had waited for Julian to storm off and deliver that first blow. Instead, he'd stayed there and persevered through the argument, until she realized that the energy was shifting into something less intense; they were taking the time to peel back the layers and reach the true core of the issue, and with each layer they took a step back down from the height of their frustration and anger. Soon he was proposing a reasonable compromise and, after she agreed to it, he apologized, and she apologized back. The experience was a revelation. They had argued and resolved it immediately, and she didn't need to carry her hurt or her indignation any longer.

Not only had Emma now robbed them of the opportunity for resolution, but she'd also done something she'd never done to Julian before: she'd explicitly threatened to leave him. The words had rushed out of her in an effort to drive all of her points home. What she actually wanted was for Julian to leave with her; for them to manage the situation from London so they could show Lena that she was not the most important thing in their lives, that her power over them had limits. She wanted *their* freedom back. She had tried to show how important this was to her by leveling an ultimatum. She'd hoped that, knowing she'd go back with or without him, he'd realize that the decision was clear. Wiping her eyes with her fingertips, she picked up another shirt. When Julian knocked softly on the bedroom door and asked, "Can I come in?" she was not surprised, but she was thankful, thankful that she had not pushed him too far.

"Yes," she replied.

He entered the room, closing the space between them and standing before her.

"Emma," he said, looking miserably over the scene of her packing, "please, stop. Can we talk about this?"

She dropped the shirt she held onto the bed. Julian, perhaps now noticing that she was not genuinely packing, reached forward and took ahold of her hands. She acquiesced to the gesture but left her hands limp in his.

"I'm sorry for what I said," he began. "I didn't mean any of it."

She looked down at his hands grasping hers. Somehow it made her feel even more guilty that he was capable of apologizing so quickly. If she tried, she felt the words would turn to ash in her mouth and she'd suffocate on them.

"I'm just so scared. I can't do any of this without you," he continued. "You're the single most important factor in all of this—more important than anything. I know I seem like I'm always striving for something other than what I have, but I want you to know that any vision for the future I've ever had has always had you right in the center of it."

She swallowed.

"I read your article while you were asleep this morning—it's very impressive. You're an excellent writer, Emma. You have real talent. I'm sorry if I've made you feel like you aren't enough. If anything, all of my striving was only an attempt to make my life—*me*—worthy of you. I can't face the idea of you leaving right now. I just can't."

His voice broke and she wrapped her arms around his neck, drawing him to her.

"I'm sorry too," she murmured into his clavicle.

As they stood there embracing, he pleaded with her to stay, promising that they'd figure it out and move back to London as soon as they could.

"Okay," she eventually agreed.

With that, they released themselves from the emotional claustrophobia of the argument and took a few deep breaths of this fresh new air.

As Emma looked past Julian's shoulder to the mess of her clothes on the bed, she was aware that they had not truly resolved anything, but rather just agreed to suppress their troubles for the moment until they had the time and freedom to excavate them once again. Emma knew that by apologizing they had not erased the criticisms they'd leveled at each other; they would tend to their wounds privately, examining them, hindering their healing until they scarred. She knew the next time they fought they would each be prepared with defenses and rebuttals, and that was likely to only make things worse.

# CHAPTER NINETEEN

The timing of Desi's visit was not ideal. Julian knew that his and Emma's relationship would benefit little from undergoing close observation at this point. Still, he had missed his sister's presence so greatly that he could partly overcome his concern, and as her arrival approached, his excitement grew alongside his apprehension. Back in London, he and Desi met regularly for a debrief drink after work or for dinner at her and her wife Camilla's home in Islington. Their visits to Gramercy to spend time with their parents were lightened significantly by the solace of each other's company; a single look cast across the living room—meaningful only to them and completely unnoticed by everyone else—gave them strength. He longed for the comfort of Desi's unemotional advice now.

In her younger years, Desi had developed a survival-related need to be unaffected by those around her, largely due to being a closeted lesbian at an all-girls boarding school in the early 2000s—a time when the term "gay" was still wielded with the intention to wound. Later, this imperviousness loosened its grip to become a calm and constant composure, useful in her line of work as a divorce solicitor and therefore honed and encouraged. Julian often found her undramatic outlook on his dilemmas consoling. He could drag Emma into his spirals, but Desi was immune. She was suspicious of his catastrophizing and remained unswayed, like a rock parting the waters of a surging river.

He could recall the lonely first weeks of his exchange year in Switzerland, when he called Desi every night and listened, tears rolling down his cheeks, while she monologued encouragingly. Her sanguine, almost bullish personality had always countered the brittle and highly strung disposition of his youth. He often wondered what kind of adult he would have become if she hadn't been there to pull him away from himself.

Since Lena announced she was pregnant, Julian had often felt the instinctive urge to call Desi. But he'd made Emma uncomfortable in the past when he'd shared details of their lives with Desi without first consulting her. A few times a fight had resulted; on one side was Emma's protectiveness over her privacy, and on the other was the relief Julian felt from sharing all of his thoughts with Desi.

When he first told Emma that he wanted to tell Desi about Lena, she'd been staunch in her opinion that they should sit on the news a while longer. She thought it was too raw, too confusing. The last thing they needed was someone else asking questions about what they were going to do when they hadn't yet figured it out themselves. She also had reservations about how they would explain why Julian had slept with someone else in the first place—their only options were to paint Julian as unfaithful or to share Emma's private sexual desires. Julian had reservations of his own. He'd never gone to

Desi with such a large, life-altering problem. He could not see how she might downplay this one. If he watched Desi's usual unflappable demeanor be bested by his news, it might send him down a panicked spiral from which he would never emerge.

But then, a couple of days before Desi was due to arrive, Emma had returned to the apartment, flustered and resolved.

"I think I know what we can say," she'd told him, dropping her bag onto the floor. "I was sitting in a café reading when it came to me: surrogacy."

Julian stared at her.

"Surrogacy," she repeated. "We say Lena is our surrogate. She's having the baby for us."

He blinked. "But later, when Lena's still involved?"

"We could say we came to some sort of agreement where we decided we wanted to share parental responsibilities."

Julian nodded, mentally throwing different scenarios at the theory and watching as it remained intact.

"It's the perfect solution," she concluded, regarding him patiently as if she were waiting for him to catch up.

Julian was silent. He could feel that Emma was thrown by his lack of enthusiasm. She'd probably thought she was presenting him with a gift.

"Do you still want to tell Desi?" she asked after a moment. "I thought you wanted to."

"I'm not sure," he admitted. "If we tell her this, there is no going back. We will have to uphold the lie forever. I suppose that makes me pause."

He was conflicted by his desire to have Desi's support, and by the idea of lying to her. He wondered if lying would make her support feel hollow and undeserved.

Emma took a seat on the couch next to him. "We'll have to

tell people something eventually. I think I'm more comfortable with it being this rather than the truth."

Julian drew a deep breath. He considered the gravity of lying to his sister. Then, he considered the alternative of concealing Lena from Desi entirely. More and more, he wished to divulge, to at least be able to dip his toes in the warm waters of Desi's sympathy and support.

"Okay." He nodded. "We'll tell her."

Desi arrived at midday on Friday and planned to stay until Sunday afternoon. She booked a room at a hotel nearby, which had a pool and rooftop bar with customary views of the Acropolis. When she got in, she sent them the name of a café, and they ventured out to meet her, arriving to find her lounging back in her chair wearing a pair of dark sunglasses and angling her face up to the sun. A finished espresso sat on the table in front of her. Her blond hair was freshly cut so that it only just reached her earlobes.

"Julie!" she shouted upon seeing them, pulling her sunglasses off her face. Emma took a moment to adjust to Desi's boisterous energy. It was always this way, Desi's eclipsing presence causing Emma to wilt in its shadow until she summoned the strength to match it. Desi stood up from her chair and pulled Julian into a strong hug. Emma always found it fascinating to watch Desi reinforce her role as older sister. Julian, despite being taller and broader than her, seemed engulfed in her arms. Then Desi moved to Emma, drawing her into her chest as well. Emma could smell her expensive French pharmacy-brand sunscreen.

"It's so nice to see you both," she said, resuming her seat. "*My god,* isn't the sunshine glorious."

Her face was dewy, flushed and bright with excitement, though her gray eyes looked filmy with fatigue from the early flight. "Camilla is so sorry she couldn't come too. She really wanted to be here, but you know, her mother is so unwell, and she needs to be around in case . . ." She trailed off with the regretful air of having taken the conversation in an unpleasant direction. "Anyway," she resumed, returning her sunglasses to her face, "how are you both? Do you want coffee?"

They ordered and settled into conversation so familiar and comfortable that Emma could almost forget that she and Julian were harboring a monumental secret. As Desi recounted her flight, Emma glanced at Julian. He was rubbing his earlobe vigorously and wearing a morbid expression. She cast him a meaningful look, and he let go of his ear, which had now been agitated into an angry red color. They moved on to discuss Desi's time in Athens generally, and Emma suggested some tavernas to try.

"Are you planning to visit the Acropolis again?" Julian asked. Emma knew the question was intended to gauge how many plans Desi had while she was here so they could understand exactly how much time she expected to spend with them.

"I don't think so," she responded, gazing placidly at the street to her left. "The first time I visited the Acropolis, my girlfriend at the time broke up with me via text message. You"—she pointed at Emma—"wouldn't know this story. It was a long time ago, I think I was—*god,* I was probably only twenty-four at the time."

"Justine?" Julian asked.

"*Justine,*" Desi echoed longingly. "She fell in love with another woman and told me all about it in great detail. Torture.

Anyway, there I was, looking up at the Parthenon and trying not to cry. My friends and I were heading to Hydra the next day. I practically spent the entire five days in the ocean, where you couldn't tell I was crying. Hard to be unhappy in a place like that, but I managed it."

"I never liked her," Julian confessed in solidarity.

"She was terrible for me. Hard as a rock. Never gave a compliment." Desi sighed. "You know, I look back on it now, and I shudder. It was like dating my own mother."

Julian recoiled. "Don't say that."

"Come on, Julie—we're adults. We can understand the nuance." She threw her head back to face the sun again and, with her eyes closed, continued, "Anyway, I'm very fond of that dramatic Acropolis memory now. I wouldn't want to visit again and dilute it."

Emma thought of Desi's wife, Camilla. Warm-hearted, complimentary Camilla with her love for floral sculpture and white ankle-length prairie dresses. She was no match for Julian and Desi's mother, Eleanor, who Emma suspected would never truly respect a woman as—according to Eleanor's terms—*saccharine* as Camilla. Still, Desi and Camilla's relationship served as a perfect corrective experience for Desi. Camilla loved Desi for who she was, not what she did, and it was clear that she made sure Desi was constantly aware of this. It was a miracle, Emma thought, that some people were able to break the cycle of what they wanted in order to find what they needed. She thought about Julian and wondered how they brought out the good in each other, but when she could not see past the insults they'd leveled at each other only days before, she shook the thought away.

"Emma hasn't gone to see it yet," Julian then said. He had

visited the site a handful of times throughout his life, and although he'd vehemently encouraged her to go, he'd shown no interest in making the hot pilgrimage again himself.

"Oh, really?" Desi turned her gaze onto Emma. "You really have to see it up close—it's *so old*."

"I plan to go—I guess I've just been quite distracted," Emma replied, the words leaving her before she could shape them into something that wouldn't so eagerly invite a follow-up question. Luckily, Desi's attention was momentarily drawn away by a scene across the street where a tourist had spilled his iced coffee down the front of his white linen shirt.

"That's unfortunate," she murmured vaguely, leaving Emma unsure whether the remark was in response to her or the ruined shirt.

They stayed at the café until Emma and Julian finished their coffees, then they offered to take Desi to Alistair's apartment. They walked slowly, allowing Desi to stop and observe the buildings or spy through windows. The coffee Emma had ordered was her third for the day. She could feel her heartbeat rocking within her chest as she considered the lie they would soon tell.

When they arrived at the apartment, Emma went straight to the kitchen and filled a jug with water while Julian showed Desi around. She met them back in the living room, as they were observing one of Alistair's bookshelves and chatting about something unrelated. Emma placed the jug and some glasses on the coffee table as Julian took a seat on the armchair. She and Desi sat on the couch, the three of them silent for a moment as they each drank a glass of water.

"Well," Julian said suddenly, placing his glass back on the table and cutting through the silence almost violently, "I guess now is as good a time as any to tell you our news."

He looked at Emma, and she looked at Desi, who looked at them both with her eyebrows raised and said, "Oh?"

Before Desi arrived, they'd practiced the announcement a few times, but Julian was now delivering it in a flattened, rehearsed way. On reflection, Emma felt that perhaps too much practice had made the speech unnatural. She cleared her throat to take over.

"Julian and I decided that we would like to try for a baby again." Emma's body twitched in response to the lie.

Desi placed her hand on Emma's, her eyes wide and watery already, as if she were walking ahead of the conversation unaware she was going in the wrong direction.

"But given there are some complications," Julian continued vaguely, taking over from Emma, "we began looking into other options, and we managed to find a surrogate here in Athens."

Desi's face was swiveling between them now.

"It's early, but she's about nine weeks pregnant," Emma said.

Desi withdrew her hand, confusion flickering over her face briefly before recovering into surprised joy.

"Oh, congratulations!" she cried, standing to hug them both. It was the only acceptable reaction, and because they'd expected it, they were able to enjoy the moment, even though they knew it preceded the more difficult discussions where Desi—being who she was—would probe for more logistical information.

"Wow," she sighed breathily into Emma's ear as she embraced her. "This is just wonderful."

They sat back down on the couch.

"So, the baby's DNA . . . Is it both—"

"Just Julian's," Emma answered.

Desi nodded. Emma could sense Desi's lawyer persona was clearing its throat and shuffling its papers behind the scenes.

"And do you have regular contact with her? The surrogate? This . . ."

"Lena."

"Lena?"

"She's lovely. Very sweet," Julian said. "We see her every few days, actually."

"Who is she? How old is she?"

"She's twenty-two."

"*Gosh*." Desi frowned. "That's young."

"She's very mature for her age," Julian insisted. "If you met her, you'd see—"

"I'd love to meet her!" Desi replied, taking the statement the wrong way. "Can we invite her to dinner tonight?"

Julian's eyebrows crept up his forehead, his lips pressing against each other into a thin line. "Well—I think . . ."

Emma could see he was using all of his strength not to turn and look at her for help. She tried to calculate the benefits and risks of Desi meeting Lena.

"She works at a bar in Plaka, so she's usually busy in the evenings . . ." he continued, buying her a little more time to consider.

"Does she finish late? Maybe she could meet us afterward?" Desi pressed.

Emma decided that, even if Desi didn't have the true context, it would be useful to hear her opinions, particularly given her experience with family law. She knew that if they told Lena to go along with the surrogacy story, she would comply, especially given they were going along with her lie to Darius about being brother and sister.

"Why don't we message her and see." Emma smiled at Julian, whose relief to have arrived at a decision was palpable.

"Okay." He pulled out his phone.

"Oh, wonderful!" Desi grabbed ahold of Emma's arm and squeezed it. "How exciting!"

# CHAPTER TWENTY

Julian and Emma took Desi to a late dinner at an old taverna they liked: a joyfully cramped place where the waiters fastened butcher's paper over each table after you were seated. They sat on the street's edge, where the tables and chairs were arranged all the way to the next restaurant. Cats roamed all along the strip, winding their bodies around the legs of the chairs and patrons in a well-practiced performance for scraps.

The three of them spent a few hours drinking wine and working their way slowly through plate after plate of *mezedes* before they moved on to the main courses of stuffed vegetables, salted cod, and grilled lamb. Lena was meeting them after her shift, and her impending arrival gave the meal a charge of anticipation. Julian had explained the situation in his messages to her, and she agreed to go along with the surrogacy story. Her willingness was reassuring. He began to agree with Emma that this could really be the explanation that saved them from the scrutiny of their family and friends back in London.

Eventually, after the dishes stopped arriving, their eating slowed, and the focus shifted to the wine. Desi was telling them about the greenhouse structure she and Camilla had built in their small backyard, which Camilla used as her studio for her floral sculptures.

"It looks like something off Pinterest. It's positively ethereal," she explained, eyeing her empty wineglass. "*Apartamento* wanted to come and take photos of us in it for a feature. I said to Camilla, 'But why do I need to be in it?' And she said, 'It's sort of a successful couples thing.'" Desi swatted the words away with her hand as she spoke and reached for the jug of wine. "The stylist asked if I'd wear a pantsuit—more wine?"

Emma shook her head, and Julian passed his glass forward so she could refill it.

"I said, 'And why would I be wearing a pantsuit in a greenhouse? Because I'm a lawyer? Or because I'm a lesbian?'" Desi poured the last of the wine into her glass. "Anyway, I declined in the end. I have to keep a low profile. I already have to manage the egos of my clients—last thing I need is a dog of my own in the fight."

The waiter had just placed a second jug of wine down on their table when Julian glanced at the street to see Lena crossing the road and walking in their direction. Her eyes were focused on something just ahead of her, and following her line of sight, he saw it was Darius. Julian looked back at the half-finished plates in front of him, his jaw clenched. He hadn't had a chance to inform Desi of Darius yet. He felt ambushed.

"Lena's brought Darius with her." He interrupted Emma and Desi's conversation.

"Who?" Desi asked at the same time as Emma exclaimed, "What?"

"Darius is Lena's brother," Julian quickly hissed. Desi's eyes narrowed in confusion.

Darius had seen them now and was approaching. Catching his eye, Julian smiled at him before turning back to Desi. "*Listen,* we don't trust this guy," he explained, holding a smile awkwardly on his face. "Don't give him any information about us—"

"*Yassou,*" Darius said, arriving at the table.

"Darius," Julian greeted him, standing politely to shake his hand. "This is my sister, Desi, and you remember Emma."

Darius shook their hands with a bemused expression on his face. "All the siblings together," he said, holding his hands out palms up to gesture to the three of them.

Desi held her smile still, maintaining her practiced poker face and divulging no sign of confusion.

"And, Desi, this is Lena," Julian continued. Desi shook her hand. Lena's cheeks were flushed, her expression piqued. Julian wondered if she was embarrassed by Darius's presence. Maybe she had tried to argue against him joining them. After letting go of Desi's hand, she crossed her arms over her chest.

"Take a seat," Emma offered, and the two of them sat down.

"We can't stay for long," Darius explained, slouching confidently in his chair. "But I wanted to come and meet you." He grinned at Desi, and she smiled tightly back. "Of course, I also have to make sure Lena is not too outnumbered." He laughed as Lena stared at the table unhappily, the color on her cheeks deepening.

Julian was disappointed that she had told Darius about Desi. He couldn't understand why she would do that, only to then seem frustrated that he'd decided to intrude on the dinner.

"So, you are here on holiday from London," Darius said, more as a statement than a question.

"Just for the weekend," Desi replied.

Darius looked down at the remnants of their dinner.

"Did you like the *bakaliaros*?" he asked, pointing to the salted cod. "It's one of my favorites."

"It's really good," Desi said, pushing the plate toward him. "Help yourself. Have some wine."

Darius looked back at her without moving and smirked. "No, thank you."

The mood of the dinner had grown tense, and Julian was suspicious that this was Darius's intention. He needed to shift the conversational control away from him.

"How was your shift, Lena?" he asked, attempting to divert attention to her.

"It was okay," she answered. "I'm in trouble at work. Sophia told my boss that I'm pregnant and now he told me he is going to start cutting my shifts. He said he won't have a pregnant woman working in his bar—"

"That must be discrimination," Julian replied. "Surely he isn't allowed to do that."

"You should look up your rights," Desi added. "Don't let him push you around."

"Okay," Lena said, her eyes slipping away as if she wished the conversation would move on.

"What do you think about all of this?" Darius interrupted, directing the question back to Desi. "My little sister being pregnant."

"I'm very happy for them," Desi replied, her voice clear and confident. She was not allowing herself to be intimidated.

"So am I." Darius smiled. "It's important that we all stay happy."

The comment had the distinct air of threat, and Julian bristled.

"It's a wonderful thing she's done. Very selfless," Desi added.

Julian swallowed, his heart lurching. He searched Darius's face, but his expression registered no confusion. "Good, good," he said eventually, looking back at Julian. "Seeing as we're here, I have something I need to discuss with you."

"Sure, okay," Julian replied.

"Lena will need an apartment soon. I'm sure you understand that where I live currently is not suited for this." He turned to Desi to explain, "I smoke a lot." He shrugged as if to declare the matter out of his hands.

Desi shifted in her seat but kept her expression blank. Still, Julian could sense a change in the air around them.

"I think it's best you give us the money for the deposit," Darius continued. "She will need two months' rent for the bond—maybe eight thousand. Once you give us the money, Lena can look and decide—she knows the neighborhoods."

"I want to live in Kolonaki," Lena interjected. "It's a nice, safe area."

"The sooner she has a place, the better it is for the baby," Darius pressed. "And of course, it will be easier for you too—to have a place to live with her."

A flash of irritation tore through Julian. He could feel all eyes around the table boring into him: Desi's eyes demanding an explanation, Emma's pressing her distress upon him, Darius's expecting an answer, and Lena's looking upon him with a strange sort of curiosity. He clenched his jaw and forced himself to nod just once.

"Great," Darius concluded, sliding his chair back and standing. Everyone was silent; he had effectively drained the last of the conversation's energy. He looked around at each of them with a bemused expression. "I think we will leave you to enjoy your dinner."

Lena touched Julian on the arm as she stood, and he almost flinched in response.

"It was nice to meet you, Lena," Desi said, making meaningful eye contact with her. "Take care of yourself, okay?"

"I will," she replied.

Darius slid his eyes over to Desi and narrowed them. "You don't need to worry—I'm looking after her."

"That's reassuring to hear." Desi veiled the comment in insincere politeness, and Darius's face momentarily twitched with confusion.

Julian was unable to speak. He couldn't even bring himself to look back at Lena. Emma said goodbye, and Lena gave them a small wave before following Darius back onto the street.

"Isn't he an odd fellow," Desi sighed, leaning back in her chair.

Julian remained silent. Emma watched him running his teeth repeatedly over his bottom lip as he stared out at the street in the direction Darius and Lena had left. Darius had once again succeeded in aggravating him. Emma was learning that Julian was particularly susceptible to these attacks, perhaps because they represented a battle for control and, while the extent of Darius's danger remained a mystery, Julian was not willing to throw himself recklessly into the fight.

"That was only the second time we've met him," Emma said. "He wasn't any more pleasant the first time."

"Why is he under the impression that you should pay for her apartment?"

Emma looked at Julian. He looked back at her morosely. They were going to find it difficult to explain this away.

"I don't mean to overstep here," Desi continued, frowning, "but I assume you have a surrogacy contract. A formal agreement outlining the terms."

Julian said nothing.

"Julie, tell me you have a contract," she repeated, staring at him.

"Well," Julian sighed, running a hand over his cheek and down to his chin, "no."

Desi's face hardened. "Why didn't you tell me you were planning to do this?" she hissed. "I could have put you in touch with the right people. They have agencies that officiate these sorts of agreements." Her eyes drilled into him. "Do you have any idea how incredibly messy this could get? A surrogacy contract wouldn't be legally enforceable if we were in the UK, but here in Greece, it would be. To not have one is—it's *insane*."

Julian blanched under the attack.

"What if she doesn't give you the child?" Desi demanded. "What if she wants to retain her position as the mother? Julian, you're the child's father, you'll have legal—*moral*—obligations." She shook her head in disbelief. "And this Darius fellow could become a real problem for you both. He's clearly going to attempt to extort you for as much as he can. I can't *believe* you didn't call me before you went ahead with this. I mean, for *Chrissake*, I work in family law!"

Heads at the surrounding tables turned in their direction.

"Desi, please. We know," Julian said, trying to get her to lower her voice. He drew a deep, shaky breath. Emma could see him crumbling under the pressure of Desi's hurt and disapproval. She knew immediately that he was going to tell the truth.

Desi continued to stare at Julian. "Then what—"

"She's not a surrogate."

Now completely adrift in confusion, Desi closed her eyes and shook her head. "What?"

"I slept with her—at Emma's request." He glanced at Emma, and she felt her cheeks begin to burn. "Then she fell pregnant. It was all a complete accident."

Desi blinked her eyes rapidly in shock.

"That's why there isn't an agreement," Julian explained. "Honestly, it was a horrible shock, and I feel as though we haven't recovered from it yet. I have no idea what we're going to do—so if you could lower your voice and stop scolding me right now, I would really appreciate it."

Silence fell while Desi and Julian stared at each other.

"I'm sorry," she said after a moment, reaching out and taking hold of his and Emma's hands. "What a horrible shock this must be," she said. "Have you given them any money so far?"

"None," Julian replied. "Well, a hundred euros or so for the doctor's appointment and blood test."

"Right, so you have proof that she really is pregnant."

"Yes," Emma answered. "Unfortunately."

"But you don't know for sure that you're the father?"

"No," Julian admitted. "We're going to do a paternity test, but we have to wait a little longer." He glanced at Emma and sighed, rubbing a hand over his face. "And we may have an issue getting Lena to agree to do that."

"She doesn't want to do the test?" Desi asked, eyebrows raised. "That's more than a little suspicious."

"She said it would embarrass her in front of the doctor."

Desi frowned at her glass of wine. "Dubious. And Darius, I suppose his interest in this whole affair is money?"

Emma nodded. "We think so."

"He's also very protective of her," Julian added. "As you can see."

"Protective of his cut perhaps," Desi said with distaste.

"I think there is genuine care there too. They seem to be very close."

"The sibling thing . . ." She resumed frowning.

"He thinks I'm Julian's sister," Emma explained.

"Why?"

"Lena told him that for some reason," Julian answered. "Although I don't think he believes it."

"I think he's just playing with us," Emma said. "He's trying to see how far he can push us."

"His enthusiastic presence certainly makes things more complicated." Desi was still frowning. "What else do you know about him?"

Julian shifted his focus down to the table and began running his fingers along the stem of his wineglass.

"We don't know a lot," he said. "Except Lena told me that he was in prison."

The lines between Desi's brows deepened.

"Sounds like he assaulted someone, though she tried to tell me they deserved it for doing something terrible. She said he's on conditional release."

"When we met him," Emma added, "we went to the apartment where he lives, and there were these three big men just sitting at a table. They didn't say a word to us, and he didn't introduce them. I think he was trying to intimidate us."

"What do we do?" Julian asked.

"The paternity test as soon as possible," Desi began. "Then, if you are genuinely the father, I suggest you do everything you can to get her to come to London to give birth. The baby will then be a British citizen, which means that if Lena tried to take the baby back to Greece without your consent, you could ask the court for a recovery order."

Julian was now giving Desi his full attention while she organized her thoughts. "If Darius is on conditional release, then I'd imagine he'd have to frequently report to a probation officer, probably a social worker who visits him regularly."

Julian began nodding, his mind working.

"I'd imagine one of the terms of his release would be that he can't leave Greece, which is all the more reason to leave with her if you can."

"If we left and Lena was willing to keep our location secret, he wouldn't be able to find us," Julian said.

Desi nodded. "That would be a great outcome."

Desi finished her glass and placed it back down on the table. "And what does Lena want in all of this?"

Emma looked at Julian. She couldn't think of an answer herself, and it surprised her to realize that they had failed to find out something so important and useful.

"I'm not entirely sure," Julian answered.

"We haven't really asked her," Emma admitted.

"That should be the next thing you do," Desi said. "Find out exactly what *she* wants. I'm sure she has an agenda, even if it's only her brother's that she's going along with. She strikes me as being impressionable. Maybe she'd like to be given some other options."

Desi paused in thought, and Emma saw that Julian was running his teeth over his bottom lip again.

"You need to get her on your side rather than his," Desi said. "From that brief encounter, I think the further away you can move her from his influence, the better. Even if the baby is yours, I advise you not to give them a cent. Not until after the baby is born, and we've come to some sort of official child support arrangement."

Julian nodded, and a heavy silence fell over the table.

"Oh god," Desi eventually said, placing a hand over her face. "*Jesus,* you two. I was *not* expecting this." She began to laugh slightly maniacally into her hand.

Emma glanced at Julian and saw that he had taken on a remote, exhausted appearance as if the confession had drained him of the energy required to be offended.

"What are you going to tell Eleanor?" Desi then asked, dropping her hand from her face. She sat forward. Her eyes wide. "Can I *please* be there when you tell her?"

Julian gave her a flat look. "I think if we say it's some kind of surrogacy agreement, she'll have fewer questions than you did."

Desi nodded, regaining composure. "At least let me help you smooth out the details a little more."

At that moment, a waiter crossed behind her chair, and she turned, holding a hand in the air.

"Excuse me," she said. "Could we please get the bill?"

The man nodded without breaking stride.

"*Efharisto,*" she called after him, turning excitedly back to the table. "Did I say that right?"


The next morning, they met Desi for breakfast. The hotel restaurant was a sad-looking place: gleaming silver bains-marie held gray, watery scrambled eggs and anemic tomatoes. There was a giant toaster with an impressive conveyor belt–like system that, despite its industrious appearance, was only capable of toasting one vertical strip on a slice of bread. The other patrons were almost exclusively heavily cologned men in business shirts, ordering round after round of iced Nescafés and reading their newspapers, their shiny gold watches catching the light as they turned the broad pages.

News from Camilla had arrived overnight. Her mother was in a very bad way. Desi was flying back immediately and heading straight to the hospital from Heathrow. She was teary and pale, wearing her sunglasses inside and nursing a black coffee, the tragic circumstances entirely eclipsing Julian and Emma's problems. Not much was said over breakfast. Desi filled them in on the family dramas on Camilla's side, all of which would be exacerbated by their shared grief and would likely manifest in inexplicable behaviors and strangely drawn boundaries.

"Camilla's been managing her mother's finances for years," she explained. "She knows what's there, and let me tell you, it's not worth fighting over." She stared out of the large windows toward the street's edge as if considering the trials ahead of her and finding herself depleted already. Emma wondered whether Desi's predictions were objective or whether they came from her own opinion of what a sum worthy of conflict would be.

They said goodbye as a taxi pulled over to collect Desi. When they hugged, she clung to them tightly.

"Please keep me updated," she said, extracting herself and addressing them both. "And call me if you need anything—I'll always pick up." She stared at them sadly for a moment, fresh tears arriving in her eyes. "You'll be okay," she said firmly, perhaps to herself. "You'll get through this."

As the taxi pulled away, Desi's pale face smiled forlornly at them through the window. Then she was gone, leaving Emma and Julian alone once again.

# ACT III

O gods, what horror! Oh, what misery!

Euripides, *The Bacchae*

# CHAPTER TWENTY-ONE

After murdering her children and her husband's lover, Medea was flown away from Jason's wrath to safety on a chariot sent by her grandfather, Helios—god of the sun. Emma could understand how some people—viewing the story under the scrutinizing light of modern narrative convention—might feel cheated by Euripides using deus ex machina to bypass the tangle of the plot and force a resolution. But Emma did not feel cheated. She thought that Medea's unthinkable violence was supposed to represent the absurd and desperate lengths a woman in Medea's position would have to go to in order to enact revenge, to regain any semblance of control. Without a doubt, Jason would have murdered Medea had he been able to confront her. In a strange and inexplicable way, Emma felt it was almost empathetic of Euripides to let her escape. Still, Medea had not avoided all punishment; Emma imagined that the ensuing guilt and shame would condemn Medea to a slow unraveling, a spiral into madness. She imagined Medea sitting alone with her thoughts long after the thrill of escape had worn off, and shuddered as she put the book back on Alistair's shelf.

Hours of midday heat stretched idly ahead of her. She was not due to meet Lena until the afternoon, a plan that she and Julian had formed after Desi suggested they try to gain clarity on Lena's desires. Julian had been gracious this time in admitting that engineering those types of conversations was not his strong suit. Although Lena seemed to like, even prefer, his company, Emma thought two women might more easily understand each other. They decided that Emma alone would better stand a chance at more delicately extracting information. If the conversation went well, Emma would invite Lena over for dinner, where they could all discuss the plan together.

Emma left the apartment just after 3 P.M., making her way through the relatively quiet streets. Alistair had been right that the city would empty as the summer went on. It was August now, and when Emma sat on the balcony, she saw that many of the other apartments seemed to have their security shutters pulled down permanently. She had made little progress adjusting to the heat and the added demands it placed on the body and mind. She still sweat as profusely as she did when they'd first arrived, and brief moments in the midday sun could still leave her skin pink for days afterward. In London, the sun was embraced like a visiting friend, one whose energizing presence helped her view her own city with a renewed appreciation. She would take her lunch breaks in a park, partially inspired by her first date with Julian, and hold her face up to the sun in offering. Here in Athens, she kept her eyes down.

After crossing through more quiet and shuttered streets, Emma reached the meeting place they'd agreed upon and saw Lena sitting on a bench in the shade scrolling intently on her phone. Her hair was arranged in two plaits, and even though Emma knew she didn't have a shift that day, she wore her usual uniform of a T-shirt tucked into denim shorts.

"Hello," Emma said. Lena smiled, dropping her phone into her tote bag.

"Thank you for meeting with me," Emma said. "I know our previous meetings have not always gone well."

"That's okay," Lena replied, flicking one of her plaits over her shoulder. Emma waited, hoping maybe Lena would politely rebuke the comment. Instead, Lena looked at her expectantly.

"I was thinking we could go for a little walk?" Emma suggested.

They wandered through the neighborhood of Monastiraki, stopping to buy homemade lemonade from a stand Emma had discovered and grown fond of. As she ordered and paid for the drinks, she watched Lena, who was leaning against a wall, looking at her phone once more, and exuding a sort of contentment. It seemed to Emma that practically all pregnant women carried themselves in this way, as if the fulfillment of some kind of biological destiny gave them a deep, anchoring sense of purpose. However, she doubted that she had ever appeared so serene and composed. One day, very early on in her pregnancy, her face had paled, leaving her looking sickly, and her chest had flushed red and turned blotchy. It remained that way for weeks.

"How are you doing?" Emma asked when she returned, and handed Lena her lemonade.

Lena drank, swallowed, and let go of the straw. "I'm fine, just tired."

"Do you want to walk a bit more? I was thinking maybe around the National Garden—only if you feel up for it."

Lena swirled her lemonade in her hand, the ice cubes rattling against one another. "Yes, okay," she answered.

They passed into Plaka, walking in the direction of Syntagma Square. The pale yellow and pink buildings around them stood out brightly against the blue, cloudless sky. They crossed the streets back and forth to chase the shade while yellow taxis coasted slowly past them, one after another, in the hopes of being the closest chair when the music stopped. They turned down a street named Lysikratous, where directly ahead of them through the space in between the buildings, Emma could see the ruins of the Arch of Hadrian.

"Are you getting plenty of rest?" she asked, focusing back on Lena.

"Not really," Lena admitted. "Darius has a lot of visitors."

"It's good that you had the day off today," Emma offered as Lena continued to stare ahead.

"It's not a day off. My boss has cut my shifts," she replied dejectedly. "I don't have any at all this week."

"I looked it up, Lena. He can't do that," Emma said. "Have you brought up your employee rights with him?"

Lena shook her head. Emma sensed it would be kinder to let the conversation move on, but there was something belligerently vague about the way Lena was acting. She was uncertain whether Lena had a plan and was not willing to share the details with Emma or whether she was simply moving ahead chaotically with no consideration for the future. If it was the latter, Emma felt it was not fair for her to behave this way, knowing her actions could affect the welfare of Julian's un-born child—and, by extension, Julian's life and her own.

"What will you do if he doesn't give you any more shifts?" she asked to force the matter.

Lena frowned with irritation. Her eyes cast down as she stirred her drink with the straw. "I know Julian will help me," she said finally.

The offhanded confidence with which Lena made this statement took Emma aback. She'd thought she could force Lena to acknowledge the responsibility she seemed to be avoiding, but Lena had one-upped her by reminding her of the claim she had over Julian's attention, loyalty, and money. Emma wondered whether Lena would speak this way if Julian was present, or if she spoke to Emma like this because she assumed that Emma's motives for attaching her life to Julian's were not so different from her own. The fact that she hadn't said that *both* Julian and Emma would help seemed to affirm this suspicion.

They reached Vasilissis Amalias Avenue and were momen-tarily distracted by the task of crossing the lanes of heavy traf-fic. Lena was looking to her left, and for a moment Emma studied her open and trusting profile.

In a sudden, violent vision, she saw herself pushing Lena onto the road directly in front of one of the fast-moving buses. The vision was so quick and jarring that Emma barely had time to react to the image before the scene resolved itself in her mind and she saw herself simply flying away with Julian, like Medea on her chariot, returning to their previous life en-tirely free of consequences.

When Lena then turned her head, looking across the street at the National Garden, and said, "We can go now." Emma was sobered by her blank, unaware face and her interest in their safe passage across the road. She pushed the violent vision away.

On the other side of the road, they disposed of their empty cups, and Emma resumed their conversation, only now changing tack. "Have you thought about what you want your life to look like in this new future?"

Lena was quiet, and Emma consciously stopped herself from speaking to fill the silence. They entered the National Garden, choosing one of the curving gravel paths at random. The shade of the trees and the sound of water dampened the heat.

"I'd like to study," Lena said finally, in a small, almost shy voice. "I want to study pharmacy—maybe run my own pharmacy one day." They passed by rows of flowerbeds arranged around a concrete plinth that displayed a sundial. A group of small children stood on their toes, running their fingers over the object. "I want my life to look different from the lives of the other women in my family," she added.

"What do their lives look like?" Emma asked.

"They don't have any control." The disapproval was heavy in her voice. "They have no freedom. All day, they are stuck in their homes cooking and cleaning."

"They had children young?" Emma ventured, suggesting a connective thread.

"Yes," she admitted. Then, perhaps wising up to Emma's implication, she added vehemently, "I know I want to become a mother, just not the same way as that."

Witnessing Lena's conviction made Emma feel even more resolutely that she had no desire for children herself.

"I want to be more than just a mother," Lena added. "I want to also have freedom."

Desiring freedom was more relatable to Emma. She herself being a cliché: the modern woman who resented the idea of giving up the freedoms she was only now—in her thirties— truly enjoying, to have a child. Times were different now, people would say. Society has evolved and the burden of child-rearing could be shared. Apparently, she could have it all— freedom, independence, a flourishing career, and the joy of motherhood. How did that explain the way her female friends' careers so often withered or stagnated after children while their male partners' progressed? Even if the women didn't complain, even if they were content, Emma could not recon-cile what she was told with what she saw. She felt a sudden desire to be iconoclastic, to hold Lena's statement up and demonstrate its fundamental contradiction, but she knew there was little to gain from aggravating Lena. Certainly, it would not aid her objective.

"Okay, well, the next question to ask yourself is: what do you need in order to create the life you desire?" Emma knew there was truly only one answer.

"Money," Lena admitted, just as Emma suspected she would.

"You know, having a child will cost quite a bit." Emma registered the faintest guilt at her manipulation of the conver-sation. "Julian and I will help, of course, but it will also cost you time and energy. You'll find it hard to study and work for a while."

Lena stewed in silence, either considering Emma's words or withholding her argument.

"I hope you don't think I'm trying to convince you to take any one path," Emma clarified. "I'm more trying to show you your options, or at least ask you to consider them. That's something no one ever did for me when I was your age."

"What are your parents like?" Lena then asked. Emma

paused for a moment before deciding to allow this momentary switch of focus. When she thought about her parents, she found it difficult to separate them from each other, from the community they existed in, from the memories of her childhood. She wondered if it was some failing on her part that she could not outline any traits that were uniquely theirs, that couldn't be found behind the front door of every house up and down the street she'd grown up on. Their passivity was partly to blame. For them, time was like a fine that had to be paid over and over. The passage of it was a bruising, costly experience. They'd never had the luxury of truly, self-indulgently considering the future. They still lived in the first house they ever bought—a narrow, dark townhouse with low ceilings and gray carpet. They'd paid the mortgage down in the necessary increments over thirty years until they recently surprised themselves by having paid it all off. But even that respectable achievement represented their passivity. They responded to the events in their lives, but rarely did they seem to incite them.

"I'm not sure my parents could ever fully exert control over their lives either," Emma admitted. "Growing up, it seemed like life happened to them, and they sort of endured it, so I understand your desire to be different."

She was pleased that they were finding common ground.

"Tell me more about your parents," she said, shifting the conversation back to Lena. "They kicked you out of their home when you told them you were pregnant?"

Lena glanced at Emma. "I chose to leave," she admitted. "My father is violent. He beats my mother."

The bluntness of the statement surprised Emma. For a moment, she was at a loss for words. "Lena, that's horrible," she eventually said.

Lena stared at the path ahead of them. "He would beat me

too," she added, "but only very rarely. He was violent to Darius all the time."

Emma thought about Darius's prison time for assault. "Does Darius ever . . ." she ventured hesitantly.

"No," Lena replied firmly. "When I was younger, he protected me from my father. He's never hurt me."

"I can see why you would want to get away from your father."

"I don't want to bring a child into that family. I want to create my own."

"I understand that, I really do," Emma said. "I think Julian and I can help."

A vision of what Lena desired was forming in Emma's mind, constructing itself out of the pieces she was gathering from their conversation and others that she was intuiting. This is what she would do with her former clients: probe and question until she had a complete image of what they wanted. Then, she would present their own vision back to them, disguised as the perfect solution. She always took pleasure in watching their backs straighten and their eyes light up. "Yes, exactly!" they'd say. "That's *exactly* what we want."

"Can we sit in the shade over here for a moment?" Lena asked, pointing to a bench. "I'm feeling hot."

"Of course."

They took a seat, and Emma gave Lena a drink of water from the bottle she'd packed in her bag.

"Do you ever think about starting a life somewhere else, away from your family?" she asked once Lena had finished drinking.

Lena's eyebrows drew toward each other. "Sometimes . . ." She admitted, hesitating before continuing, "Sometimes I want to get away from them all."

"Even Darius?"

Lena looked ahead and grimaced guiltily. "He is very protective of me. Sometimes I feel suffocated by him." She paused, deliberating over how much information she should divulge. It felt to Emma as if she had turned the tapestry of Lena's mind over and was now observing knots and untied threads. She waited for Lena to continue. "He controls my life. He takes all of the money I earn and gives me only some of it back."

"That doesn't sound fair," Emma commiserated.

Lena glanced at her. She seemed to be uncertain about her next words.

"What is it?" Emma nudged.

"He wants you to give money to me to rent an apartment because he is going to keep the money for himself."

This admission was not entirely surprising to Emma. She and Julian had never for a second intended to hand over any sum of money to Lena. Still, in hearing Darius's true intentions so plainly, she felt a surge of irritation.

"Thank you for telling me that," she replied a little more tersely than she would have liked. "If he talks to you about money again, you can tell him that we will not be giving you any until after the baby is born. You can tell him that none of these plans of his are going to work."

Lena frowned. She was emitting a slight air of regret for selling her brother out, but this revelation about Darius was well timed for Emma. The way forward formed as naturally as the crest of a wave. Now Emma only needed to gently urge the conversation in the direction she wanted it to go.

"Lena," she began, "I want to make a suggestion, and I hope you'll consider it."

Lena turned to look at her.

"You could come to London with us. We would give you enough money so you could study and live in a flat by yourself."

Lena's face was expressionless. Her eyes traveled back down to the ground.

"We could share care of the baby. That way, you would have time to study," Emma continued. "You could get away from them all and be in charge of your own life. You could be a mother and still have your freedom."

Lena continued to observe the ground, her eyes moving to signal she was working through the proposal in her mind.

"I know it's a big decision, but if you'll consider it, then it could be an option we all explore together."

Emma watched her carefully, hoping to spy her response in the arrangement of her features.

Finally Lena turned to look back at Emma. A curtain parting to reveal a look of determination. "Yes." Her voice was small but sure. "I will consider it."

"Great—that's great. I'm so glad," Emma replied, sighing with relief. "I really think this could work out well for all of us."

Lena managed a small smile.

"Seeing as you aren't working tonight, why don't you come over for dinner?" Emma asked. "Let us cook something for you—something healthy. And maybe we could discuss this idea further?"

"Yes, okay," Lena agreed. "Thank you."

Emma noticed then the dark, purple indents under her eyes. She looked exhausted.

"Are you feeling okay?" she asked.

"I'm just very tired," Lena admitted.

"You should have a nap before dinner. You need to prioritize your rest." She stood, collecting Lena's tote bag for her. "Let me find a taxi to take you home."

They retraced their steps back to the street, where Emma flagged down a taxi, paying cash in advance for the fare and waving goodbye to Lena as the car pulled away. She stood back from the road and stared out across the flow of Vasilissis Amalias Avenue. The final moments of her conversation with Lena had rejuvenated her. She felt optimistic, which seemed to strengthen her resilience against the heat. Julian would be glad to hear this news, and she was pleased to be able to deliver it. She sent him a message immediately. *She said yes to dinner!*

*Great—I'll go to the mini-mart now*, he replied.

She slid her phone back into her bag and decided to walk back through Plaka to the apartment, taking Kidathineon Street and passing a line of tavernas where waiters wiped tables around the last of the late lunch guests and enjoyed the quiet hours before the street filled at dinnertime. She saw a popular gelato shop that she'd passed many times and decided to stop. She chose a scoop of pistachio praline, but after being handed the cone, she realized her vision of slowly enjoying the gelato for the remainder of her walk had not taken into account the rate of melting; it was dripping even as she took hold of it. She walked quickly further down the street to where the path expanded into a small square. In the center was a group of benches facing one another in the shade of a row of sycamore trees, which also acted as a barrier separating the public sitting space from the tables and chairs of the restaurants that lined all sides. She took a seat and ate her gelato.

Intending to immerse herself fully in the moment, she turned in her seat and looked around the square. A tourist, wielding a large camera with a long black lens, was failing to coax a litter of kittens out from under a bush. The kittens were too timid, too content to remain in the shade out of sight. Emma expanded her vision past the trunks of the sycamores, the restaurants, and the tourists in tank tops and sandals—their shoes slapping against the ancient stone. She watched as an elderly man with a string of rosary beads threaded around his hand walked through the crowds, rapping the concrete with his walking stick. It was then that her eyes landed on a man pacing back and forth in the shade of a building and speaking to someone on the phone. It was Darius.

Emma inhaled sharply and sat back, pressing herself against the bench to make sure she couldn't be seen. Had he followed her? Carefully, she watched him from her concealed vantage point behind a sycamore trunk. She waited, but he didn't turn or even glance in her direction. It seemed that he wasn't aware she was even there. She shifted, pressing against the metal arm of the bench so that she could better see him from behind the trees. He ended the call, slid his phone back into his pocket, and lit a cigarette, standing still but tapping his foot with visible agitation. He pulled his phone out of his pocket again, shaking his head. He looked up, away from Emma, and stared down the street ahead of him, taking only one or two inhales from the cigarette before he tossed it on the ground and set off.

Emma stood, taking one look at the melting gelato in her hand and determining that it could not come along. She dropped the cone in a bin and set off after him.

He was easy to follow. His distinctive gait—shoulders thrown back, chin thrust upward as if to make himself look larger and take up more space—helped her keep track of him. For the first few minutes, Emma trailed him confidently, protected by the crowds and shop stalls that filled the footpath. When he turned and entered a *stoa*—one of the arcades that traveled underneath the larger buildings—she was forced to hang back, knowing that she would be easy to spot if he turned and looked behind him in the narrow thoroughfare. She waited until he was halfway through the arcade before she entered, walking quickly to close the distance again. The *stoa* was shaded and cool; the sound of her fast footsteps echoed loudly on the tiled floor. Darius, perhaps hearing the sound, glanced back, and Emma was forced to duck behind a rail of beige undergarments, rattling their plastic hangers noisily. An elderly man stepped out from the small shop and eyed her suspiciously, arms crossed over his paunch. Peering over the rail to see that Darius had now reached the main street at the end of the arcade, Emma stood up from her crouching position, apologizing to the man as she quickly walked away. When she emerged onto the street, she looked around, her eyes scanning the crowds and restaurants, until she saw the navy blue of Darius's shirt.

Emma walked as fast as she could, closing the distance between them, before checking the map app on her phone—Darius was not walking in the direction of his apartment but rather leading her into the neighborhood of Kolonaki. Here, the buildings began to expand, and the streets inclined upward, becoming steeper as they approached the slopes of Mount Lycabettus. The luxury boutiques and large lobby entrances gave her options should she need to duck quickly out of sight. He continued to lead her uphill; she was sweating, the pits of her shirt growing damp. He took a left turn, and to her relief they were no longer walking uphill. She hung back, ready to hide behind one of the cars parked along the street's edge. Then he turned once more onto a narrow residential street, and she was forced to adjust her pace once again.

Further down the angled street, Emma saw a woman with brassy, artificially blond hair sitting on the steps outside a lobby, smoking a cigarette and speaking on the phone. Darius appeared to be heading toward her, reaching the woman just as she ended her call. She looked up, and seeing him, she leaped up from where she sat, holding her hands up as if to keep him at bay. Emma halted, sliding backward under the cover of another lobby so she wouldn't be seen. She peeked around the corner and continued to watch. The woman made a run for the intercom of the door behind her, desperately trying to tap in a code, her phone falling and cracking against the ground next to her. Darius grabbed the woman by the arm, jerking her back to the pavement. She wailed desperately, trying to grab her phone as he pulled her away. With the phone out of reach, she now turned her attention to Darius, attempting to hit him and evade his grip. He pinned both her arms behind her, and she tried to kick him away uselessly.

A black car arrived at the top of the street and began to creep slowly down toward them. Emma feigned interest in the glass doors of the lobby to conceal her face. When she turned and peeked out once more, the car had passed her and was now stopped alongside Darius. He was speaking to the driver through the passenger-side window. The woman was screaming and crying in Greek, the sound piercing the quiet of the street.

Emma looked around frantically. Knowing she could not reveal herself to Darius, she hoped another pedestrian would see the commotion and approach the scene.

A balcony door above opened, revealing an elderly woman.

She took one look over the railing, before quickly returning inside and lowering her security shutter.

Emma looked down at her phone, opening her browser and searching with shaking hands for the police's emergency number.

The back door of the car sprang open, and Darius dragged the woman over to it. Her wails and pleas increased. She continued to fight back, attempting to push Darius and the car away with her feet. With one leg, she managed to kick the car door shut. Darius hissed something at the woman, and she cried back in protest. Emma held her breath. The woman cried out again, her words cut off by the sudden force of Darius slamming her face against the closed car door. She was instantly silent. When he repeated the movement one more time, Emma flinched. Even from the distance where she stood, she could see that blood now covered the woman's face.

The driver, a man Emma did not recognize, got out of the car and helped Darius shift the limp, unconscious body of the woman into the back seat. Then Darius slammed the door, storming around the car and climbing into the passenger seat. The car sped off down the street, and Emma stood back, remaining frozen in the doorway. In the sudden silence, she could hear her shallow breath arriving and leaving her chest in short, forceful gasps.

# CHAPTER TWENTY-TWO

Emma returned to the apartment to find Julian in the kitchen. He spun to face her, wooden spoon in hand. "Mushroom risotto is okay, right? I was going to make a salad instead, but I didn't know if—"

"I'm sure risotto is fine," she replied, dropping her bag in the doorway.

He took a long look at her. "Are you okay?"

She told him about Darius, the woman, and the violent interaction she'd witnessed, the fact that he appeared to have orchestrated a kidnapping. Early on, around the point where she was required to admit that she'd decided to follow Darius, Julian had put the spoon down and given her his full attention. He listened intently, his response progressing from intrigue to shock to concern as he interjected and probed for more detail. When she'd eventually told him everything she could remember, they fell silent in thought.

"He definitely didn't see you?" Julian asked finally. "And the people in the car didn't either. You're sure?"

"I'm sure." Emma nodded. Her arms were crossed in front of her with one finger tapping anxiously against the other arm.

"Then I don't think we should contact the police," he said. "I don't think we should get any further involved in this."

Surprised, Emma parted her lips as if to speak.

"You could end up being called upon as a witness or something," he continued, shaking his head. "No, I think we stay out of it."

"Okay," Emma agreed.

He glanced back at the risotto. "I think we should stay away from Darius as much as possible from now on."

"Lena told me that he takes all the money she earns and only gives her some back, like an allowance. She admitted that sometimes she wants to get away from him."

"Really?"

"She also told me that he's under the impression that we're going to hand over money for Lena to rent an apartment—he plans to keep the money for himself."

Julian rubbed a hand over his forehead. "Right." He frowned pensively into the pan, taking up the spoon and stirring once more. "So she's interested in moving to London with us? What did she say exactly?"

Emma nodded. "She wants to discuss it further."

"Discuss as in negotiate?" Julian replied. "What does she want?"

"She wants freedom. That's all. She wants to be able to go to university and study."

Julian frowned again as he absorbed the information. "How does her decision to have this baby fit into her desire for freedom, exactly? Or her desire to go to university?"

"She admitted that her parents didn't kick her out. She ran away to live with Darius because her father is a violent man.

She doesn't want her child to grow up in that family. I think when I suggested she move to London with us, she realized we could provide her with a way to be free of them all, to create a new and better life. The baby is what grants her access to that new life."

In response to this description of Lena's misguided logic, Julian sighed.

"It just so happens that her interest in leaving works in our favor too," Emma continued. "If we make an offer—one that gives her freedom from her family and Darius, as well as the time and financial support to study while sharing custody of the child with us—I think she will take it."

"What if she's lying?" Julian asked. "What if she says yes, comes to London, accepts money from us, and then flees?"

Emma considered this for a moment. "I think we have to accept that Lena could sever contact and disappear at any moment," she said eventually. "No agreement could stop that from happening."

Julian's brow compacted once more, and she felt a flash of guilt at not stating the fact more delicately.

"But it's like Desi suggested," she went on, her tone lifting with determination. "If Lena comes to London, we'll have more control."

"What if she tells Darius about the offer?" Julian asked.

"Why would she do that if it will only aggravate him?"

"I don't know." He shrugged. "Do you trust her entirely?"

"No." Emma shook her head. "But I don't think she's very complicated. She has nothing to gain from telling him about this plan. In any case, we can tell her not to tell him just to be sure she understands."

. . .

The intercom buzzed just as Julian was setting the table and Emma was getting changed in the bedroom.

"Right," Julian said to himself with grim determination as he crossed the room. "Right," he repeated, only this time with less confidence.

He reached the intercom just as it buzzed for the second time. "Come on up," he said, unlocking the lobby door.

"Okay," came the grainy, distant response.

Emma let Lena in. Julian could hear them talking in the hallway. Lena was complaining that her boss was still ignoring her. She'd tried to call him this afternoon to beg for some shifts, but he was screening her calls.

They arrived in the living room, Lena kissing Julian on the cheek in greeting. He was surprised to see she was wearing a tight black dress, the same one she had worn when they went to the club together. It was an odd decision. He wondered if she was perhaps under the impression that tonight would end the same way her previous visits had. Technically they had never told her that part of the arrangement was over.

Emma and Lena took a seat at the table, and he began serving the risotto onto their plates.

"Have you been managing to eat well?" Emma asked Lena.

"Not like this," she said, her eyes watching the plate as Julian garnished it with chopped parsley. "Sometimes I don't feel very hungry, but I try."

"Were you told to have an ultrasound?" Emma asked as she poured Julian and herself a glass of wine. "It's usually meant to happen around seven to eight weeks."

"Yes, the doctor told me." Lena dropped her eyes to the plate Julian had placed before her. "But now that my shifts have been cut, I can't afford it. Darius told me to ask you to pay, but I didn't want to ask you again for money."

"Don't worry about that," Julian said. "We'll pay for the ultrasound. It's important that you don't miss appointments."

"Okay," Lena replied.

A silence fell over the table as they began to eat. Julian glanced at Lena, watching her fill her spoon and tentatively place it in her mouth. He did the same, determining quickly that he hadn't used enough salt. The result was a little bland.

"It might need some more salt," he said.

"It's really good," Lena said, placing her spoon down in a gesture that contradicted her words. "Thank you for cooking for me."

"Do you feel a bit unwell?" Emma asked. "I remember the food aversions could be pretty intense. Please don't feel like you have to eat if you don't want to."

Lena's face opened in surprise. "You were pregnant?"

Even from a cursory glance, Julian could read the regret on Emma's face. She'd slipped up; she would never have willingly entered this conversation.

"Yes—well, I had a miscarriage." Her brow creased. "At eleven weeks, actually."

Lena's face now filled with an expression of pity. "I'm sorry," she said.

"Oh, no, no, please—it was a while ago." Emma reached for her wineglass. "In the end it helped me confirm my feeling that I don't want children of my own, so when I look back on it, in some ways, I feel thankful."

Lena's expression now slipped into confusion. "You don't want children of your own?"

Emma watched her glass as she placed it back down on the table. "No."

"Do you want children?" Lena turned to Julian.

"Yes," he replied simply, looking to Emma and hoping she

would expand on her answer so that she didn't leave the conversation drifting so uncertainly.

"I don't want children of my own, but I do see an incredible opportunity in our current . . . situation," she explained, to his relief. "We can share the care of this child, Lena, and that way, we can experience both parenthood and freedom. Why don't we talk about you coming to London?"

"Okay." Lena's face was still furrowed. "How will it work?"

"Well, the rough plan," Julian stepped in, "is that we return to London, ideally in the next few days, and you come with us. Once we're there, we will help set you up in a flat nearby, and after the baby is born, we will share parental care of it."

Lena was studying Julian as he spoke.

"We would help you with the financial means to do this, of course, and support you in setting up your life there. Emma said you want to study to become a pharmacist?"

"Yes," Lena said, glancing at Emma. Emma nodded back supportively.

"If we share care of the baby, you will have more time to study. Desi will help us with your applications for a visa of some kind—she knows a few good immigration lawyers."

"This also means we would take on all costs related to the child," Emma added. "Schooling, medical bills, childcare—whatever we need."

They had decided that the best approach would be to start with what Lena was set to gain, rather than what she was leaving behind. Emma had predicted to Julian that this would better engage Lena, and as he watched Lena's eyes lift to meet hers and remain there, he felt Emma had been correct.

They waited, holding Lena's eye contact in silence. Eventually, Lena lowered her eyes to look at her abandoned risotto and drew a deep breath in. "How often will I see my child?"

"As often as you'd like," Julian answered. "If you wanted to do one weekend and then we could—"

"The idea is that we accommodate each other's needs," Emma interjected, perhaps to prevent him from getting too deep into the details so soon. Clearer boundaries could and would be erected later.

"Why are you so sure my child will be better off if they are not here?" Lena asked, suddenly indignant. "They will not be raised Greek—you seem to think this is only a good thing."

Julian was taken aback. Lena had exposed an assumption that neither he nor Emma had considered.

"If they will be taken from their home country, then I want you to know I will raise my child to know that they are Greek," she concluded.

Julian nodded, chastened. "Of course."

"Will you pay for a good school?" she then asked.

"Yes, certainly."

"How much . . ." She paused, a line appearing between her brows. "How much will you pay me?"

Julian tried to conceal his relief. It was an encouraging question, and they had prepared a sum they felt was extravagant enough to make any remaining doubts dissolve instantly.

"We will give you fifty thousand pounds to use for rent, tuition, and living expenses," he answered. They had decided it was not necessary to explain just yet that they intended to pay her the money in monthly installments, like a wage, so that she would be less inclined to flee. "As we mentioned, we will also take on all the costs related to the child."

"And that will include the pregnancy," Emma added. "If you come to London with us, we will pay for your obstetrician appointments and a birthing suite in a private hospital. We will make sure you have the best care."

Lena's eyebrows rose. Julian could tell she was realizing the full extent of their offer. He felt a surge of affection toward her. He could tell by Emma's expression that she was feeling something similar. They were witnessing a young woman bargaining for her freedom, for the opportunity to break a cycle, release herself from the constraints of her history, and alter her fate to create something entirely new. What was needed now was some final thrust of sincerity, some closing statement that would unite them.

"You said you wanted to get away from your family and create a better life, right?" Julian asked.

"Yes," Lena admitted.

"We think that's brave of you, Lena—really, it's admirable."

Emma reached out and took hold of Lena's hands. Lena gave them over warily.

"You want to forge a better path for you and your—*our*—child," Emma said. "Let us help you."

A silence began to stretch in the room, and Julian, despite his desperate desire to exact some kind of promise from Lena, knew it was crucial that it be left alone.

With her eyes cast down at the table, Lena assented silently at first, with an almost imperceptible nod. Then, she gave another, more vigorous nod. "Yes," she said, resolved. "I will come to London with you."

"That's great news!" Emma beamed, releasing Lena's hand. "Really great."

Lena smiled back weakly.

"I do think," Julian added cautiously, "it might be best to

keep this plan between us for now. I don't know that telling Darius about it would be a good idea."

Lena frowned.

"Don't you agree?" Emma pressed.

"Yes," she answered morosely.

With the initial details ironed out, Emma and Julian relaxed. They began to tell Lena more about the neighborhood where they lived in London and the walks she could take along the canal or through London Fields. She watched them as they spoke, a wary yet excited spark emerging in her eyes.

After they finished eating, Emma cleared the table and took the plates into the kitchen, and Julian stood, hoping to signal that the dinner was over.

"I'm sure you want to go home and sleep," he said, just to be sure the message was received.

Lena stretched in her seat. "I am tired," she said, dropping her arms back down. "But I don't want to go home."

"Still not getting much sleep at Darius's apartment?"

"It's too noisy." She stood, walking around the table to stand before Julian. He looked down at her in surprise.

"I want to stay here with you," she said, slinging her arms around his neck and bringing her lips to his. The sound of Emma turning the tap on to fill the sink in the kitchen reached them.

"Lena." Julian pulled away. "We can't—"

"Why not?"

"Emma and I decided that you and I would no longer—"

"She doesn't have to know," Lena interrupted, stepping forward and placing a hand on the crotch of his pants, where he hoped she would not find evidence of an interest at odds with his words.

"I'll stay on the couch." She pressed her body against his. "You can come to me when she is asleep."

She tried to kiss him again and he dodged her.

"Why won't you kiss me?" she whined, grabbing his hands and placing them on her chest. Julian heard the water stop running in the kitchen.

"Lena," he said firmly, stepping away, "listen to me—we will not be doing that again."

She flinched away from him in hurt, her face hardening. "Fine. I'll go."

She grabbed her bag, and Julian felt the immediate pressure of rectifying the situation in some way so that she didn't leave angry.

"Lena," he implored, "please stop for a moment."

She stood with her tote bag on her shoulder and arms folded in front of her.

"Look, we had fun, and I like you a lot." He was pleased to see her face soften slightly. "And as much as I might want to continue this, you have to understand that Emma no longer wants me—*you and I*—to do that. I have to respect her wishes."

"But you want to," Lena pressed. "You want to have me too."

Despite the guilt he felt at using Emma as the obstacle, it seemed more important to preserve Lena's feelings and retain her cooperation.

"I do, Lena," he admitted. "I just can't."

Lena pursed her lips indignantly and then released them. "I understand," she said resignedly.

"Here," he said, placing a hand on her back and steering her to the hallway perhaps a little too firmly. "I'll walk you out."

Lena waved goodbye to Emma from the hallway, smiling sweetly and thanking her for dinner. On the street, when she said goodbye to Julian, she hugged him tightly, pressing herself firmly against him in a gesture that conveyed a lingering hope.

He watched her climb into a cab with a sense of guilt and unease.

# CHAPTER TWENTY-THREE

The sound of Julian shutting the door as he left the apartment to go for a run woke Emma. It was early, but already the white sunlight leaking through the curtains lit up the room. She stared at the ceiling for a moment, listening to the clicking and whirring of the fans positioned around their bed, before reaching for her phone.

After wasting the first moments of her day scrolling mindlessly and avoiding the messages from friends—*How's Athens going?*—she was overcome with the desire to repent through productivity.

An idea surfaced: she would finally go to see the Acropolis. Given their plans to leave in the next few days, this could be her last opportunity to visit the site. She knew that, if she was going to go, she should arrive early to avoid the sun at the height of its power. Another glance at her phone informed her it was now 7:38 A.M. Already, heat was radiating into the room through the window. She leaped from the bed.

As she hastily ate a piece of toast over the kitchen sink, she thought of Lena and the conversation they'd had last night over dinner. It was a relief to know Lena was going to come to London with them, for many reasons, but mostly because it felt to Emma as if she had gained back some control over her own life.

She had not spent much time contemplating the existence of Lena and Julian's child once it was outside the womb, and she knew that her decision to avoid those thoughts was a form of denial. Their baby would not simply be a baby but a human being with complex, often changing and elaborate needs, a personality with a destiny of its own.

What would she be to this child? A form of stepmother? She knew that Julian's feelings for the infant, when he held it for the first time, would reach an incomprehensible depth. Would she feel the same way? How would the child feel about her? The issue was that she remained unsure of her place in this new future, and instead of approaching the issue, she simply refused to spend time with it. Any attempt she made to imagine herself in the role of mother flickered and faded, overwhelmed by the white noise of panicked dismay.

Emma stepped out onto the street, the heavy glass door of the lobby clanging shut behind her. The morning was still, and she was buoyed by the gently stirring warm air and the vast blue sky. She'd finished her coffee just before she left, and as usual, the caffeine working through her system gave the day an exciting potential—one that it rarely lived up to by the time the afternoon had arrived.

She stood for a moment, consulting the map on her phone once more to confirm the direction she needed to take to get to the site entrance. When she looked back up at the street ahead, her focus was snagged on the figure of a man leaning against a nearby wall. He was smoking a cigarette and scrolling on his phone. It was Darius. At the sight of him, her mood was dimmed by apprehension. Lena must have told him where she and Julian were living.

She sent a quick message to Julian. *Darius is waiting outside the apartment. Lena must have told him where we live.*

Upon seeing her, Darius pinched his cigarette and tossed it away. "*Kaliméra,*" he said. "That means 'Good morning'— I was thinking you should start learning Greek."

"Were you waiting outside my apartment?" Emma kept her voice level, knowing it was important to conceal her emotions from him. The incident with the woman and the car had revealed that he was not a menacing but ultimately harmless figure. She saw him now as someone explicitly capable of violence, someone who posed a very real danger. Realizing that she was still gripping her phone tightly, she loosened her fingers.

He shrugged. "I was just in the neighborhood."

"What a funny coincidence," she said, turning away. "Have a nice day."

"What are you doing?" Darius called after her.

She stopped reluctantly. "I'm going for a walk."

"Well, then," he said, his voice suddenly closer as he fell into step behind her. "I'll join you."

Her skin prickled with unease.

"Don't you have something else you should be doing?" she asked, still attempting to maintain a facade of indifference.

"No," he replied, now alongside her. "Where are we going?"

She wondered if there was any point in lying to him. If he had some motivation to speak to her, he was unlikely to be deterred by her plan.

She glanced at him. "I'm going to visit the Acropolis."

"You haven't seen it yet?" His eyebrows rose.

Emma shook her head.

"Okay, I'll take you," he said, with the air of relenting to a request even though she'd never made one. "You're going the wrong way—it's this way."

As they walked, Darius fell easily into the role of tour guide, pointing out buildings of interest and reciting from memory the dates they were built. The effect of this was strangely calming. For a moment, Emma could forget that he'd been waiting outside their apartment for reasons she still did not understand and instead believe that they were simply two friends walking together.

Julian responded to her message. *What? Did he speak to you? Are you OK? I'm on my way back.*

He tried to call her. She screened the call and sent a message back.

*I'm fine. He's just walking me to the Acropolis.*

*Don't worry. He's not being threatening. There are plenty of people around. He's being weirdly nice. I want to know what he wants. I'll keep you posted.*

"This is the Gate of Athena Archegetis," Darius said, pointing out an impressive structure to their left. Emma put her phone away. "These four columns under the portico are called Doric columns. This material"—he pointed to the stone—"is Pentelic marble."

"You know a lot about this stuff," she remarked.

"A long time ago, I was studying to be a tour guide."

"And then you decided to do something else?"

"I was not suited to it—all the begging for tips—the *progonoplixia.*"

"The what?"

"Ah—" Darius paused to translate. "Obsession with the

old. Like ancestor worship—being so in love with the past that you are ignoring the problems happening now."

"Oh, I see."

They walked past a strip of busy restaurants. In one smooth and quick movement, Darius collected a wallet from a table on the street's edge, while its owner was turned away. Without even the smallest hesitation, Darius pocketed the wallet, shaking his head, as if he were burdened by the responsibility of teaching this careless tourist a lesson. Emma's cheeks burned as she fought the urge to glance back.

"Is that what they taught you in tourism school?" she asked once they had turned down another street and slipped anonymously back into a crowd.

Darius laughed then, genuinely. His laughter burst out of him, unexpectedly high-pitched and contagious. She was surprised to find herself also smiling.

"In some ways, yes," he said, still grinning.

When they reached the ticket office at the base of the Acropolis, Emma saw there were already crowds of people standing out front. Many were identifiable as part of a group by their matching headphone devices and colored lanyards. To the left of the office, she saw a self-serve ticket machine and approached it. Darius followed her but hung back. He wasn't buying a ticket, which could only mean he wasn't going to follow her into the Acropolis after all. She felt a sense of victory and relief. Taking her ticket, she lined up in front of the turnstiles, where visitors were being herded through and urged on by the shouts of the staff members. It seemed the tickets were not easy to scan, and so the flow was halted frequently. A staff member at each turnstile was then required to manually override the machine so that the next person could enter. As she waited, Emma looked back to see that Darius was speaking to a staff member over to the side of the crowds. Emma watched as the man opened a gate and allowed Darius to walk straight through. Her stomach sank with disappointment. When she made it through the entrance, he was waiting for her on the stone path that led up to the ruins.

"How did you get in without a ticket?" she asked. "I saw you talking to that man."

"I still have my tourism student card." His eyes were focused ahead where a large group of tourists were milling on the path, all of them wearing headphones that had some sort of antennas, which gave them the look of a group of lost extraterrestrial visitors. "Come on, let's get ahead of them."

They traversed up the path until they reached the grand entrance. Despite the presence of her unnerving companion, Emma was immediately awed by the size and the sheer ancientness of the stone. She found comfort in the stone's solid and enduring perseverance.

"The Propylaea," Darius explained, gesturing to the building. "It means 'monumental gateway.'"

They shuffled through the thin hall as Darius continued addressing her over his shoulder. "Those are Doric columns, and these are Ionic. It's the first building known to have both."

After he turned away from her, Emma eyed him with suspicion. He was wearing a pair of black shorts and a white tank top. His sneakers were bright red, and Emma could see the glint of a gold chain around his neck.

They stepped out into the open again, and Emma looked around, taking in the height to which they'd scaled. She walked away from Darius, over the rocky and uneven surface, to the edge of the ruins and looked out over Athens. It was satisfying to see the city from this angle after spending so much time looking up at the omnipresent walls of the Acropolis. She looked for the apartment before remembering it would only be visible from the other side. She continued up a path alongside the largest ruin.

"This is the Parthenon," Darius said, appearing next to her once again. "It was built in four hundred and forty BC for the goddess Athena."

"It's impressive."

Darius laughed as if Emma had said something funny.

"Did you know that during the nineteenth century, an English lord came and stole many of the original marble sculptures?" he asked. "They are still in the British Museum even now. The Greek government has asked for them back, but the British refuse to return them." He added darkly, "The British are always taking things that aren't theirs."

Emma frowned. The comment was pointed. Had Lena told him of the plan to leave for London? She could not fathom a reason why Lena would do that to hinder their plans.

"What are you trying to do here, Darius?" she snapped.

He placed a hand on his chest in mock hurt and said, "I'm giving you a free tour."

Emma stared back at him, refusing to react to his sarcastic humor.

"What are *you* trying to do here?" he then shot back, no longer smiling.

"I'm trying to absorb the ancient wonder that is the Acropolis," she replied, before adding, "alone, in peace."

He narrowed his eyes and smiled at her. "I mean in Athens. Why are you still here with your brother? You must be lonely."

The way he said the word "brother" made it clear that he knew the truth of the matter. Emma immediately felt annoyed that Lena had lied, and now, as a result, Darius's tone seemed to indicate he'd triumphantly caught Emma and Julian lying.

"How could I be lonely with you following me around?" she replied.

He made the same expression of hurt once again.

"You know you make that face a lot."

He made it again and then smirked. "You hurt my feelings a lot."

Emma stared straight back at him, keeping her features perfectly still. "That's funny," she said before walking away.

Darius hung back for a while, and Emma tried to immerse herself in the ruins and their history. She approached the east facade of the Erechtheion and then made her way around to where the sculptures of six maidens balanced a roof upon their heads. For a moment, she stood there viewing the site. Then, sensing Darius lurking around, she moved across the uneven and rocky ground to the other side of the ruins, hoping that she might continue to evade his attention.

"The Theater of Dionysus is over there," he eventually called out, catching up to her after she had circumnavigated the whole site. Despite herself, she found this information interesting and turned her head to follow the direction of his hand. "It's on the southern slope. On the way down, we can see it."

She followed him down the rocky path toward the theater, which she had allowed herself to imagine as something grander than the stone amphitheater she soon saw before her.

"Where tragedy was born," Darius declared proudly. "Here in the fifth century BC, you could watch the greatest plays ever written be performed."

Emma arrived by his side and looked over the site.

"Except you would probably not be allowed to watch," he added.

"Because I'm a woman?"

"They think women were not allowed."

"Of course," she replied sarcastically.

" 'Now as I hang, the plaything of the winds, my enemies can laugh at what I suffer,' " he recited solemnly.

"Bit morbid."

"*Prometheus Bound*—do you know it?"

"I think I've heard of it."

"Prometheus is punished for protecting and helping the humans against the wrath of Zeus. He gives them hope and teaches them about fire and other things. He is forced to live forever tied to a rock. Every day, an eagle eats his liver."

"Oh right, that one."

"It's my favorite. I was Prometheus once in a performance."

"At school?"

He looked at her coolly.

Prison, she thought.

"Reciting lines from an ancient Greek play, would that be considered ancestor worship?" she asked.

A flicker of annoyance flashed across Darius's face. Without another word, he wandered away from her, the effect all the more chastening given it was Emma who had been trying to be rid of him.

Perplexed, she stood alone for a moment. She looked over the amphitheater, determined to show that she remained occupied by her own sense of purpose. Then she continued further along, feigning studious wonder to conceal her new ploy of boring Darius into distraction so that she might be able to slip away without him noticing. She committed herself to the task of viewing the theater from every available angle while edging her way to the exit. When she arrived to ponder her third viewpoint, she saw Darius was deep in conversation with one of the tour guides, a man who was watching over his group with the air of a parent at a playground. She slunk slowly toward the exit, and when she saw Darius facing away from her, she quickly left.

Back on the streets that ran along the slope of the Acropolis, she checked the time. It was 11:40 A.M. She'd walked quickly and was pleased to find that her escape plan had been successful. The sun was beginning to peak, and a throb of pain right at the surface of her forehead reminded her that she hadn't drunk any water since she left the house that morning. She stopped on the curb and looked around for a mini-mart or a pharmacy.

"I thought you might want to get something to eat?" Darius said, appearing behind her.

She spun to face him. "Why are you following me," she demanded.

"Wow." He laughed. "Are you angry? It's only lunch."

Emma sighed and placed a hand on her forehead. "I have a headache. I need some water."

He looked at her with concern before directing her to a bench in the shade. She sat down and took a deep breath as the dull pain echoed outward, wrapping her head in a vise of tension. Darius disappeared into a nearby pharmacy and returned with water and painkillers, opening the bottle and handing them both to her.

"Thank you," she said. In response, he shrugged mildly, sitting down on the bench next to her and lighting a cigarette. She took the pills and closed her eyes for a moment, taking deep breaths. When she opened them again, she caught sight of a man making his way through the crowds. He was holding a collection of balloons that billowed out above his head, most of which were the shape of animals or Marvel characters. As the man approached, Darius whistled to catch his attention. The man eagerly came over to Darius, who was now pulling out the wallet he'd stolen earlier. Emma watched as he extracted cash and gave it to the man. The man looked at it in surprise. Then he looked up at his balloon collection as if to count whether he had enough, but Darius waved him away dismissively. The man said something to Darius, holding his hand for a moment, before wandering back into the stream of people.

Emma watched as Darius flicked through the rest of the wallet's contents, unfolding receipts and looking at the man's health insurance and credit cards. She felt a frustration toward him, that he should be so hard to define, that at one moment he seemed dangerous, cold, and calculating, and then suddenly kind.

"I don't want to go to lunch with you, Darius," she said eventually. "Sorry."

Instead of some sarcastic remark, a laugh, or smirk, he simply replied, "I will walk you back then."

They spent most of the journey in silence. Emma was grateful that her headache seemed to exclude further conversation, though she sensed the silence was also due to Darius's distracted mood.

When they reached Alistair's quiet street, Emma turned to face him. "Okay, well—"

Darius stepped forward, grabbing her and bringing his lips forcefully to hers. The smell of his strong cologne intensified, and she could taste his last cigarette. In her surprise and embarrassment, she was frozen for a moment, her mouth remaining motionless against his. Then she tried to pull away. "I can't—" she said, attempting to step back and feeling the wall behind her.

"Why not?" He stared at her, his face inches from hers, his eyes narrowed accusingly. She tried to think quickly of a reason that would be the least offensive.

"You're too young for me," she said.

He laughed and let go of her roughly. "I'm young? You're young," he said. Something sinister was once again lurking beneath his expression. "Compared to you, I'm old and wise."

Emma said nothing in response.

"I know Julian is not your brother," he said, leaning back in toward her. "And I know Lena came to your place last night without me. What did you tell her?"

She pressed her back against the wall, closing her eyes. "We had dinner, Darius. That's all."

"I don't trust you," he hissed directly into her ear. "I don't trust either of you."

She felt him step back and turn away as her heart thudded against her sternum. When she reopened her eyes, he was walking away.

"I don't trust you, either," she said. "I know you're on conditional release from prison. Lena told us. She also told me you only want us to give her money to rent an apartment so you can keep the money for yourself."

Darius's slight flinch of surprise was not missed by Emma. She felt emboldened, like she'd finally managed to land a blow on a difficult target. He turned back to face her, attempting to conceal his surprise by laughing scornfully at her.

"I followed you," she continued, taking another swing. "You aren't the only one capable of intimidation tactics."

Darius laughed again, taking a few steps toward her. "And what did you find?"

She hovered before her next admission, trying to assess whether she should reveal any more. "I saw you force a woman into a car—you kidnapped her."

His expression darkened. "You think this is smart of you, but it's not."

"Why did you do that to her? Who is she?"

He continued to stare at her for a moment before he eventually spoke. "Sometimes people deserve what happens to them because they do bad things to others."

Emma stared back at him, saying nothing in response.

"You should be more careful, Emma."

"Is that a threat?"

"It doesn't need to be." He shrugged, turning away once more.

"You don't scare me," she lied, calling after him. Despite her claim, she felt a sinking sense of dread.

Without turning back or giving any indication that he'd heard her, he kept walking.

# CHAPTER TWENTY-FOUR

Julian ran under the dappled light of the trees in the National Garden, completing the last stretch of his route. His posture was straight, his breath labored but consistent. He hadn't felt this good on a run since they'd left London months before. He felt so good that he decided to attempt to keep his pace all the way back to the apartment. There was an inexplicable sense of peace within him, as if Lena's decision to come to London with them had reduced and solidified his options, which until that moment had been scattered so widely in the unknown that he could not arrange them into any semblance of order. He imagined emerging from this situation many months down the track, having successfully executed an outcome in which he could have both fatherhood and Emma. He saw Emma holding his and Lena's baby, soothing and singing softly to it. He saw them united by the responsibility to care for it, but still free to hand that care over to Lena occasionally. The optimistic vision strengthened Julian, energizing and directing him once more. He was reminded of his firmly held belief that if he could identify clearly what he wanted, he could will it into existence.

Even Darius could not dampen Julian's resolve. Emma had returned to the apartment the day before and told Julian about Darius's intimidation tactic of following her to the Acropolis, his snide comments, his attempt to kiss her, and his threats. Hearing it all triggered something in Julian, something that should have felt like anger but instead took the form of disgust and pity and burgeoning satisfaction. The plan that they had formed gave them the ultimate power; they were leaving. Darius's attempts to exert control over them would be futile once they were gone.

The logistics of the agreement were finalized. They would return to London with Lena in a few days, after Lena had collected her passport from her parents' house. For the first time, he allowed himself to feel a small buzz of excitement at the prospect. He'd observed Emma's relief at Lena's acceptance of the plan, but if she felt any excitement, she'd been reserved about it. It was complicated for them both, but for her in a very different way. He understood that. Still, he recalled that there had been a time while Emma was pregnant when they'd both been excited. While sitting on the couch, her head in his lap, they'd discussed which attributes they hoped the child would inherit from each other. She'd diligently researched prenatal vitamins and declined the usual pink-covered pregnancy books with their platitudes and incessant *mama*-ing in favor of the *Oxford Handbook of Obstetrics and Gynaecology*. She'd even come home from work one day having bought, unprompted, a tiny pair of knitted baby socks. That version of Emma had existed and, therefore, could exist again.

They would live once more in anticipation of its arrival,

and their life would be anchored by it. He imagined Lena arriving at their cottage to drop off their child; perhaps another child—one entirely their own who had Emma's sienna hair—would be running down the path in excitement to greet their older half-sibling. He was sure it could all work out.

Julian followed these comforting thoughts, and before long, he arrived once more at the entrance of their street. He slowed to a walk, allowing his breath to level and pulling his shirt up to mop the sweat from his brow. When he let go of his shirt, his line of vision settled on three men standing across the road from Alistair's apartment building. Immediately, he recognized Darius. The other two Julian remembered from Darius's apartment; one was leaning against a wall in the shade and scrolling on his phone, and the other was smoking a cigarette. He approached with trepidation, slowing his pace and attempting to find a way that he might slip by them unnoticed. He contemplated turning and abandoning his return to the apartment altogether, waiting it out in a café until they left, but before he could turn around Darius saw him and held up a hand in greeting.

"Julian," he called out. He was smiling in his usual way, his eyes narrowed and amused.

"Darius," Julian replied, approaching them. The man who was on his phone put it away and came to stand by Darius. Julian's stomach lurched with foreboding.

"Have you been running?" Darius asked.

"Yes."

"Good," he said. "Very healthy."

The conversation was polite and bland, but Darius's eyes twitched with the effort of remaining composed. Employing the last of his hope, Julian attempted to bring the strange encounter to an end: "Okay, well, I have to be—"

The sudden crash of a hard object against the side of Julian's head wiped the rest of the sentence away. He staggered, bringing a hand up to his ear, which was now ringing violently in alarm.

"*Jesus Christ,*" he heard himself slur in a voice that sounded unlike his. His glasses had been knocked from his face. He dropped to his knees looking around at the blurry ground in search of them, but before he could locate them he was forced back to his feet and restrained.

"Listen to me," Darius hissed at him. His angry, sneering, slightly blurry face seemed to float in front of Julian. "Don't ever try to take my sister away from me again."

Julian groaned, attempting weakly to pull away.

"Trying to take her away from me—*her family*—" He was now pacing in front of Julian, speaking in fragments and shaking his head in disgust, as if he were speaking to himself. A blow connected with Julian's stomach and he doubled over, coughing and gasping. Somewhere far away, he registered the sound of Darius saying something to the other men. Then Darius's shoes appeared once again in his vision of the ground before him.

"Lena is not going anywhere," Darius said. "From now on, you will speak to me only. You will give me the money, and I will decide when you can see the baby. You will stay away from her." Darius slapped him lightly on the cheek. "Do you understand?"

"Yes," Julian replied, hoping that the right answer would secure his release. Instead, another heavy blow landed on the side of his head and the arms that held him up let go. He staggered momentarily, before the ground appeared to rise up to catch him.

.  .  .

When Julian came to, he found himself sitting on the foot-path. His body had been arranged somewhat thoughtfully against a wall in the shade, with his glasses placed in his lap. A woman with dark gray hair was crouched before him. Her face was grave and concerned.

"*My god.*" She spoke in some kind of American accent. "Are you okay?"

Julian coughed and felt his head throb hard in response, the pain vibrating through his whole body. He returned his glasses to his face and slowly began to stand.

"Whoa, careful now," the woman said, standing and holding a hand out in offering.

The ground swayed, and Julian placed a hand on the wall to support himself through another throb of pain.

"I'm okay," he said. "I'm okay."

"What happened to you?" the woman asked.

"I was mugged," he lied.

"Oh my god. Okay—stay there." She fumbled in her woven bag. "I'll call the police. Stay right there."

"No, please—I'm fine." Julian took a few tentative steps away from her.

"I really think—" She now held her phone in her hand.

"This is my apartment." Julian pointed. Ignoring another plea, he slunk slowly away across the street like a wounded animal.

In the elevator, he rested against the wall and tried to calm his breathing before beginning to tentatively explore his head with his fingertips. He could feel a slickness that indicated a small amount of blood.

Inside the apartment, he found Emma in the kitchen. She saw him and immediately rushed to him. "What's wrong?"

she asked, her wide eyes moving quickly around his face and body. "What happened?"

"It was Darius and his friends. They attacked me," he explained, allowing Emma to lead him down the hallway to the couch.

"You're bleeding!" she cried.

He reached the couch and sat down heavily.

Emma moved to look closer at him. "Do you feel okay? Should we go to the hospital?"

He shook his head, causing it to throb again, though the pain seemed to be receding slowly.

"You have a cut on the side of your head."

The mention of his head reminded him that he'd taken a hard punch to the stomach, too. He pressed a hand against his ribs and winced. Emma left the room, returning with some tissues, which she began to carefully hold against his head.

"Why did they do this?"

Julian tried to recall what Darius had said to him. "He knows Lena is planning to come to London with us. He's evidently quite angry."

Emma's face creased with concern. "She told him about it?"

"I don't know," he answered. "I mean, she must have."

He pulled his phone out of his pocket and saw that it was still on Do Not Disturb. Lena had tried to call him three times. He called her back, and she answered immediately.

"Lena, what the *fuck* is going on? Why does Darius know—"

"Julian?" she said, her voice thick with tears. Her distress caught him off guard.

"Lena? Are you okay?"

"No!" she cried. "I need to get out of here."

"Where are you?"

Emma, sensing a shift in the tone of the phone call, questioned him with her eyes. He pulled the phone from his ear and put it on speaker.

"I'm at home—I need to leave now—Darius is angry." Her speech was coming out in panicked, fragmented gasps. "He's trying to stop me from leaving—I need to leave."

"Where is he?"

"I don't know. He's not here right now."

"Okay—"

"Can we go tonight?" she pleaded. "*Please.* I have to get away from him—it's not safe."

Julian and Emma looked at each other.

"What is he going to do?" Julian asked. "Will he hurt you?"

"I don't know," she sobbed.

"Okay. Come here," Julian said firmly. "Come to the apartment. We'll buy flights and we'll leave tonight."

"Okay." Lena sniffed, the plan already working to calm her.

"Don't worry about your things, just bring your passport. We can replace anything else. Let's just get you somewhere safe. Then we can figure out what to do next."

"Okay."

"Lena, be careful."

"Okay." She hung up.

"Oh my god," Emma said, covering her mouth with one hand.

"We need to pack," Julian said.

Emma stood and began collecting any of their belongings that were in reach, taking all that she could hold in her arms to the bedroom.

"There's a flight at ten past five," Julian called out to her as she pulled their backpacks out of the wardrobe.

"Okay," she called back. She thought of Darius, of the violent version she'd watched attack that woman on the street. She imagined him attacking Julian. She'd been with him only yesterday. Had he intended at some point to hurt her, too? She recalled how brazenly she'd taunted him; how, in return, he had only warned her and left.

Julian was collecting the clothes they had left to dry on the balcony when the intercom buzzed.

"I'll let her in," Emma called out to him from the bedroom, dropping the shoes she was holding.

When she opened the door, Lena stood with her arms crossed; her eyes were puffy and red, and her mascara was smudged.

"Come in," Emma said. "Are you okay?"

She didn't move. Instead, her face arranged itself in an indiscernible expression, some blend of fear or apprehension combined with something Emma was confused to realize looked like guilt. It was then that Darius stepped into view.

"Hello." He smirked, his expression manic. "I'd like to speak to Julian."

Before Emma could process his sudden appearance, he'd pushed past her. Her eyes then fell on Lena, who looked back at her with a pinched expression.

"He followed me. I didn't know," she explained frantically. "He forced me to let him in."

Emma spun away from Lena and called out to Julian.

# CHAPTER TWENTY-FIVE

From the balcony, Julian heard Emma call to him. He turned in time to see Darius crossing the living room with Emma following him, her face stricken and panicked.

"Hello again, friend," Darius said, arriving on the balcony with a monstrous smile on his face.

Julian stepped back warily. "What are you doing here?"

"What am *I* doing here?" Darius replied, laughing, before wiping his face clean of expression. "I'm here to talk to you. I think you know why."

"I see you didn't bring your friends this time."

Darius's eyes narrowed.

"Leave him alone!" Lena cried, arriving on the balcony behind Emma. The intensity of her plea seemed to indicate the continuation of an argument that had started before they'd arrived.

Darius ignored her and took a step toward Julian. "I told you to stay away from my sister, and you ignored me." Veins had risen to the surface of his forehead. "And then I hear that, not only have you disobeyed me, but you are now planning to leave with her tonight."

Julian's instinct was to somehow smother the impending explosion to protect Emma and Lena. "Darius . . ." he entreated.

Ignoring him, Darius launched himself at Emma, slamming his forearm around her neck and dragging her back to him. He pulled a blade out of his pocket and held the point against Emma's stomach. She screamed in surprise, the blade preventing her from fighting back.

Julian's first reaction to the sudden escalation was to notice its absurdity: Darius suddenly wielding a knife and threatening to hurt Emma; Emma's scream—a sound he'd never heard before.

He remained motionless with shock while Lena rushed forward, begging Darius to let go of Emma. Darius yelled at Lena in Greek—whatever threat he'd made working to keep her back. She began to sob in frustration.

"Let go of her," Julian finally said, surprised by the calmness with which he issued the demand. Fear and the knife kept Emma still and silent, though Julian could see her chest rising and falling rapidly.

"No, not until you understand." Darius's eyes were feral-looking. His lips were curled into a snarl. "You will give us the fifty thousand now, and then you will never speak to Lena again."

"That's impossible," Julian said. "I can't just give you a sum of money like that. I can't just transfer it or withdraw it from the bank, not without procedure and questioning—"

"I think if you care about her"—he jerked his forearm around Emma's neck—"you will find a way to give it to us."

The "us" was confusing. Julian looked at Lena, attempting to assess whose side she was on. She was staring at Darius, possibly refusing to meet Julian's eyes.

He turned to Darius. "The bank won't just give me that kind of cash—"

Darius groaned in irritation.

"Darius, think about this," Julian then said, calming his voice down and speaking slowly. "What are you actually planning to do here? I can't give you the money right now. It's going to take time to get it to you. You can't stand there holding a knife to Emma and wait."

Darius said nothing. He seemed suddenly unsure of himself. Julian looked at Emma; she was staring back at him with wide eyes. He saw an opportunity to talk Darius down. It was a risk, but given his other option—attempting to physically restrain Darius—was far riskier, it was worth a shot.

"I don't think you mean to hurt her." Julian held a hand out as if to soothe a wild animal. He moved and spoke slowly. "You'll end up back in prison for a long time if you do that. There must be another way to sort this out."

"I think you are lying," Darius said. "Give me whatever money you have—watches, jewelry—then I will let her go, and we will leave."

"We don't just carry cash, I told you. We don't have any jewelry."

Julian held up his hands to show his bare fingers and wrists. Darius looked down over Emma's shoulder at her hands—she wore only a simple gold ring on her left index finger.

"It's worth nothing," she hissed.

"Lena," Julian appealed to her, "you need to help me explain that I can't do what he's asking."

Lena began to plead, "Let her go! I'm going with them, and you can't stop me."

Darius closed his eyes in frustration. "I told you not to speak to her," he said, his face tightening in anger once again.

Julian wondered if he'd made a mistake in calling his bluff.

Emma registered that the pressure of the tip of the blade against her had eased slightly. Sensing an opportunity that might not arise again, she moved toward the blade, feeling the bite of the point as it pressed into her skin, and swung her elbow back blindly. It connected with the side of Darius's head with surprising force. She launched herself away just as Lena threw herself at Darius, attacking his back with her fists and yelling frantically in unintelligible Greek. Darius, distracted by the sudden flurry of Lena's fists, didn't see Julian lunge at him. He grabbed Darius's knife-wielding arm and yanked it away, the jolt knocking the knife from his grip and causing it to clatter down on the ground. Emma ran to the knife, grabbing it and launching it through the balcony door and into the apartment, far away from their reach.

"Go inside!" Julian shouted to Emma, wincing from his earlier injuries.

She ignored him, instead watching as Darius attempted to release himself from Julian's smother.

"You don't care about me!" Lena shrieked at Darius. "You're selfish! You only care about yourself!"

Julian stepped to the side of Darius and continued to hold him by the neck of his shirt while Darius groaned and attempted to escape his grip. With only the weight of his body against Julian's, he had far less control. Julian pushed Darius to the ground, pinning him down while Darius squirmed and cursed. Perhaps realizing that his efforts were futile, he stopped and began to grin at Julian.

"You are a weak man," he spat. "You have been given everything and now you think you can take whatever you want. It makes you weak."

Julian dropped his forearm to Darius's throat and pressed down. Quickly, Darius's face turned red, veins contending for space across the surface of his forehead.

"You're choking him," Emma said, but the words reflected off Julian's impassive, remote expression. He continued to press down, his face inches from Darius's, who was starting to turn purple.

"He's choking," Emma repeated, more desperately. "Julian, *stop*."

She crouched down, getting into Julian's line of sight. He stared at Darius with an unseeing intensity. Darius's own eyes rolled around as he tried to breathe.

"Julian, you're going to kill him. Stop!" she shouted.

Julian met Emma's eyes. Shaken from his trance, he released his grip on Darius. He stood up and stepped back, leaving Darius coughing on the floor.

"You would let him try to kill me?" Darius asked Lena. His voice strained. "You would stand there and do nothing after everything I have done to protect you?"

Lena said nothing, her eyes red and wet with tears.

"You should know"—he was now talking to Julian as he slowly began to stand—"it was Lena's idea to do all of this, to threaten you for money. She was planning to trick you and take your money. Only now, she has another plan. Now she's decided to go with you instead."

"That's not true," Lena retorted bitterly. Furious tears rolled down her cheeks. "It was all your idea."

"She's lying." Darius shook his head. "How do you think I know about your little plan? She told me all about it. You can't trust her."

"*You're* lying," Lena cried.

Darius glared at her, his eyes narrowing. "You should probably know this too," he said without taking his eyes off Lena. "The baby is not yours."

Lena released a scream of frustration. "That's not true! He's making things up!"

Darius turned to Julian and addressed him. "The real father is a boy her age."

An image of the young man in the alleyway flashed into Emma's mind. She saw him hooking a finger under the cuff of Lena's denim shorts.

"She knew he would not be much help." Darius shrugged. "He has no money. His family are poor. So she decided to tell you it was yours. She hoped that after the baby was born, you would no longer ask for a test."

Lena was stunned into momentary speechlessness, either by Darius's divulging of the truth or by the diabolical detail of his lie. Emma looked at Julian; the declaration had wiped the expression from his face.

"Is this true?" he asked Lena. "There's no point in lying to us. I told you we're going to do a paternity test as soon as we can."

Defeat arrived on Lena's face, darkening it like a shadow. She remained silent.

"So when you told me there was nobody else who could be the father," Julian continued coldly, "when you *slapped* me because you were offended by even the insinuation—you were lying?"

"*Please*. Don't listen to him. I need to get away from here," she pleaded, finding her voice once again. "You told me you would take me with you."

Julian shook his head, ignoring her. "What exactly were you planning to do when I found out that the baby is not mine?"

Darius laughed. "She was hoping by then you would have already given her the money."

Lena turned to Darius. "You're ruining everything!" she screamed. "You're lying because you're jealous that I could have a good life without you, and you would be here alone." She launched forward, swinging her fists and attempting to hit him.

Darius laughed, grabbing her arms and restraining them easily. "How quickly you forget that I spent my whole life protecting you."

Lena continued to cry. "You just want me to be stuck here with you. You're pathetic. You're lonely and sad, and I hate you. I *hate* you!"

He stopped laughing and stared at her as she struggled against his strength, his face twisting with hurt. In a quick movement, he shoved her away from him. She stumbled, caught off guard by the sudden shift of her weight. Failing to regain her balance, she fell backward, landing hard against the railing of the balcony, which gave out instantly under her weight. There was no scream; she only gasped in surprise as she disappeared over the edge.

The moment seemed to stretch, though it could only have been a few brief seconds. The three of them stood in shocked silence and stared at the broken railing. Then she landed. The dull, sickening sound of her body making impact with the ground echoed back up to them. Darius let out a strangled, panicked yell. Calling out her name, he rushed to the edge.

When he turned back, his eyes were unfocused in distress. He fled past Emma and Julian through the apartment and out the front door.

Emma and Julian remained where they were, rigid with shock.

"She fell," Julian stated as if processing aloud what had just happened. He stepped toward the edge and looked over, immediately recoiling from what he saw and stepping backward. He placed a hand over his mouth.

"Oh my god," he said, his face tight and pale.

Unconsciously, Emma began to follow him toward the edge, intending somewhere in the back of her mind to see what he had. Julian crossed the balcony to restrain her.

"Don't look," he said, holding her against him.

They heard Darius downstairs release a sound, like a howl, something made inhuman by shock and pain. It echoed up to them as Julian continued to hold Emma, his arms wrapped around her shoulders while her arms hung limply by her sides. She remained speechless.

"She's dead. We need to call the police," Julian said eventually, releasing her and stepping back into the living room. Scared that if she was left alone on the balcony, she might be overcome by an urge to look over the edge, Emma followed him in.

"We need to make sure all our stuff is packed," he said, his voice strangely detached. He was checking that their passports were with their bags. "When we go to the station, we're going to take everything with us."

Emma watched him, unable to bring herself to move. "Are you okay?" he asked. "You're bleeding."

Looking down, she lifted her shirt to reveal a small, superficial wound. Julian brought out his phone, tapping and then holding it to his ear.

"Hello? Sorry, I only speak English. Yes," he said. "A woman has fallen from a balcony. She's died—"

Emma walked away from him and into the bathroom to find some tissues or a bandage. Instead, she was snared by the sight of her own expressionless face in the mirror. It looked back at her, cold and impersonal, as if it did not belong to her. An unexpected wave of nausea hit, cresting instantly. She pitched forward and vomited into the sink.

# CHAPTER TWENTY-SIX

Julian was sleeping. Once the plane had taken off and the rattling settled into a deep hum, he'd simply placed his head against the back of his seat and left Emma behind. She watched him, tracing her eyes along his profile, from chin to forehead and back. He hadn't even bothered to switch off the light above him. It shone directly onto his face, casting shadows that settled deep into his frown lines. Her eyes lingered once more on his mouth, on the small downturn at the corner of his lips.

After Julian called the police, Emma heard him talking to Desi on speakerphone. She'd advised them to gather their bags and passports and wait for the police to arrive at the apartment. She then got off the phone to contact a colleague of hers who would be able to help. A little while later, two officers arrived at the door. They walked through the apartment, opening the balcony door and letting the sound of voices, sirens, and beeping horns in. The street below the balcony was now cordoned off, and traffic was backing up in the surrounding narrow one-way streets. One of the officers explained to them that Darius had fled on foot when the police arrived. A search was being conducted to locate him. Emma and Julian were then escorted down through the lobby to the street, where another two officers were waiting with a car to take them to the nearest station.

In a small, windowless room, Desi's colleague negotiated—via phone call from their chambers—for Emma and Julian to return to London once their statements had been taken. They then recounted the events of their entire time in Athens, explaining how they met Lena, how they came to have a relationship with her and the announcement of her pregnancy, before moving on to Darius's threatening presence and his attempts to extort them. With the context in place, they gave their statements of the events of the day as specifically as they could.

After about an hour, a message was passed on to them that Darius had been found and arrested a couple of streets away, and the knife had been collected from the apartment as evidence.

With Darius in custody, it became apparent that the police were unhappy with the passive nature of the events. They pressed Emma and Julian, asking over and over: *Was she pushed on purpose?* Perhaps hoping that they could paint Darius's intent differently. One of the officers disclosed to them—maybe with the idea of encouraging them to shift their view of the events—that Darius's probation officer had not been able to make contact with him for over a week.

After their statements were completed and photos were taken of the small laceration Emma had on her stomach, and of the bruising and cuts on Julian, they were given styrofoam cups of instant coffee and left to wait for what seemed like hours while the police and Desi's colleague further negotiated the details of Emma and Julian's return to London that evening. In the end, they were approved to leave provided they met with an officer upon arrival to confirm their details and remained contactable.

It was evening when a taxi finally drove them to the airport. The scenery passed them as a blur of tunnels and freeways—the dark shape of the hills rose and loomed around them. At the airport, they entered the banal chaos of the check-in queue and were accepted into the shuffling crowd with indifference. Emma was unable to comprehend that they were unmarked. She felt sure that even a cursory glance at them would reveal their bizarre circumstances, their proximity to tragedy, and incite stares or whispers. Instead, eyes slid over them, distracted by the more pressing desire to drop off bags, receive boarding passes, and successfully make it through security with belongings intact. At their gate, they found a corner where they were alone and waited once again. They were unable to leave each other's side. They stared at the floor, occasionally drawn back to whispering repetitious statements like, "Oh god, the moment she fell," which then sparked yet another recount from each of their perspectives, even though the material was long ago exhausted. The idea that they would ever recover from what they'd seen, that they would ever be able to talk about something else, was impossible to believe. They boarded the plane in a dazed silence.

Now that Julian was asleep, the noise of Emma's thoughts had begun to fill the silence. But her thoughts were not the company she wished to keep, none less so than the small feeling of relief that had begun to make its presence felt. It was not an unfamiliar feeling; she recognized it as the same layered, complicated relief she felt after the miscarriage, a guilty sense of freedom that she respectfully concealed out of sight and visited only privately.

She looked at Julian again and wondered whether, if she was honest with him, she would find he felt the same. Would that be any consolation? Or would their guilt, reflected in each other, only exacerbate the feeling? Emma knew that Julian's eyes were shut too tightly, too forcefully to truly resemble sleep. His left eyelid practically twitched under the force. He had chosen to retreat, and Emma wondered then what private thoughts he felt the need to conceal.

Julian had closed his eyes to simply take a moment to himself, but as time stretched, the undemanding quiet was hard to leave. Alone, he could explore his thoughts freely, feeling the full shape of them with only his own judgments to answer to. The price he paid for his privacy was that he was assailed by the image of Lena's body on the concrete. She'd landed face down, and mercifully, he'd had the foresight to look away before too much detail was absorbed. Still, his brain analyzed the image and grasped for meaning to explain the incongruity. Rather than fight the process, he allowed it in the hope that he would desensitize to the image faster if he didn't recoil from it. Already, he felt the roiling, sick feeling in his stomach settling; the torrents of cold dread that surged through him were losing their strength. He tried to direct his attention from the past to the future, to dream in the way that always made him feel in control. He saw London, their flat, and his desk, but he could not place himself back there. Instead, he found comfort in his visions of the cottage. It was warmly lit by a fire, with Emma smiling at him from a rocking chair as she nursed their child—only her face was slightly blurred. The more he tried to imagine her there, the more the image of her obscured. He knew why: he was willing her into the image, knowing that she did not belong there. Realizing he couldn't hide in the future either, Julian returned to the present.

Emma was still watching him when he eventually stirred, his eyes flickering first and then slowly opening. She returned her eyes to the screen on the back of the seat in front of her, attempting to blink back the rising tide of tears caught in the bottom rim of her eyelids. She found relief in the fact that each second that passed carried them further and further away from Athens, but when she considered their arrival back in London, the return to their apartment, the halting of momentum, dread rose in her once more. Part of her wished that they could remain suspended in the air forever, then they would never have to return to their lives and reconcile with what had happened. They would never need to come to terms with what share of responsibility was theirs—what share was hers. They would not have to stand face-to-face, look into each other's eyes, and decide where they would go from here. A tear fell from her cheek into her lap. Julian reached his hand out and took hold of hers, stroking it with his thumb for a moment before giving it a firm squeeze, their shared custom, a wordless reminder that they were allies against the common enemy of the journey. She waited a moment, swallowing as another tear dripped from her chin into her lap. Then, without taking her eyes from the screen in front of her, she squeezed his hand back.

# CHAPTER TWENTY-SEVEN

ONE YEAR LATER

Julian checked the time, his index finger tapping impatiently on the back of his phone. He'd expected that she would be late, but his forecasting had only compounded his impatience so that he felt it long before she was even late. He slid his phone into his back pocket and looked around. Regent's Park at lunchtime midweek in the middle of summer was busy. He stood to the side of the broad gravel track, out of the way of the runners, students, tourists, and pacing office workers—like a stick caught and suspended against the ebbing flow of a river. When a woman nearby vacated the end of a bench, he crossed the path quickly toward it.

As he sat, he thought of his and Emma's first date. He could see her sitting next to him on the bench in the park so clearly, the pale, freckled skin around her eyes crinkling as she laughed, the clear green of her irises in the sunlight. He could recall how strongly he was drawn to her, to all the angles she revealed of herself—like her sad but sweet cynicism and the way that disposition didn't preclude her from a strong sense of humor. He was shocked by how quickly his feelings for her had grown over the course of that short date. When they said goodbye, he'd been so sure.

For a moment, Julian imagined time folding like a piece of paper so that he both stood where he was while his past self met with past Emma for the first time on that bench in another part of London. He was happy with the notion, happy to leave those past versions of him and Emma there laughing and sharing their lunch break. He was content with the idea that that scene could be repeating itself infinitely, even as the present carried them in another direction further and further away from that moment.

Emma checked the time on her phone, dragging her teeth across her bottom lip apprehensively. She was not yet late, but the threat loomed, creeping toward her with each second the train sat still. It had stopped in a tunnel minutes ago, and since then, she'd stared at her own darkened reflection. The image held her likeness—her shoulders lifted with anxiety, her brow furrowed—yet it had the flatness of a photo, allowing her to view herself with detached curiosity.

Despite the lengthening delay, all the passengers sat still, refusing to break character, perhaps believing that if they held up their side of the bargain, the train would have no choice but to hold up its own. Their faces were slack with boredom; some had their eyes closed, preferring to walk their thoughts across the clear stages of their own minds, while others scrolled on their phones. She would like to be bored like them, to rid her chest of anxiety and replace it with nothing, to sit back and be carried along like an infant in a pram, content knowing that she would arrive wherever she was going whenever she

got there. Instead, her heart thudded with a strange strength
that felt as if it rocked through her whole body.

When the train suddenly jolted forward once more, Emma
sighed with relief. They quickly reached speed again, the windows and doors in the carriage rattling loudly. Emma stood
and took a place next to the door, her leg jigging with contained animation. The platform arrived, and the train crawled
along it, coming to a slow, drawn-out stop. The doors opened
with a thrust of air, and she stepped out against the current
into the ceramic bowl of the underground, dragging her small
suitcase behind her.


Julian heard her before he saw her. He turned in the direction
of her voice. She was half-running, her cheeks flushed with the
look of someone who was racing the clock. At the sight of her
effort, he forgave her instantly for making him wait.

"Hey, you," she said, arriving and hugging him. "Sorry I'm
late—such a nightmare getting out of the office today."

"It's fine, really."

They pulled apart, and Desi held him by the shoulders,
smiling. "I feel like I haven't seen you in months!"

"It's only been three weeks." He laughed, turning away
from her to begin walking.

"Wait," she stalled. "Before we start walking, I'm desperate for a coffee."

He waited outside the tiny café nearby while she went in.
Before him, beyond the gravel track, tourists and office workers, zealously protecting the purity of their lunch breaks,
adorned the field like lily pads on a calm pond. Had he still
lived in London, he might have found himself drawn to the
green expanse in front of him and to the charm of the sun on

his skin, but nowadays he got more than his fill. Only yesterday, he'd spent hours, blissful uncounted hours, building trellises and planting runner beans. The day before that, he'd actually fallen asleep beneath a tree, like a character in a whimsical children's novel. Each time he returned to London, he waited to feel some longing for the place, some wish to be absorbed into the hum of energy, of commerce and progress, of the feeling that he was only moments away from realizing his full potential, but those feelings never came.

"Right, let's go," Desi said, returning.

As they walked, Desi spoke about the case she was currently working on. It had recently taken a complicated turn after the wife of her client had fled to Dubai with their two small children before a prohibited-steps order could be put in place. Her client was bereft and now set on vengeance, leaving her to manage not only the proceedings but tense emotions.

"Actually, I don't really want to talk about it." She sighed, wrinkling her face unhappily and giving Julian a glimpse into the stress that had recently begun to turn her hair gray in great streaks. She knocked her shoulder playfully into his. "I want to talk about you. How is country life treating you?"

"It's nice," Julian said, thinking of his cottage and its overgrown gardens. "I'm slowly sorting it all out."

"That's wonderful!" She beamed at him. "Oh, that's so great!"

The exaggerated positivity in her voice bordered on condescension as though she were laboring intensely to manage his mood and keep the conversation buoyant and light. He eyed her suspiciously, and her expression turned sheepish.

"What?" she asked.

"You're being"—he looked ahead—"overly chipper. Strange."

"Have you spoken to Emma lately?" she asked, ignoring him.

"Not for a month or so," he admitted. They'd exchanged messages briefly just to check in on each other. "She's doing well. Her journalism stuff is going well—"

"Will you send her a message today?" Desi ventured carefully. "Seeing as it was a year ago today that you . . . left Athens."

"Maybe. I don't know."

"Julie," she said flatly.

"Believe me, we've discussed it plenty." He thought back to all of the hours they'd spent dissecting events, the reassurances repeated like mantras in the dark when they found themselves awake and stuck viewing it all on a loop again. When they'd arrived at Heathrow, they were taken off the plane first and then to the nearest police station to give their statement again. After that, they were free to go home. He recalled when they entered the flat and found everything exactly as they'd left it, which should have been a comfort but instead made the place feel like it belonged to some other couple, some past version of themselves that no longer existed. When they went to bed that night, they reached for each other, their bodies moving urgently in the dark with an intensity that seemed to surprise them both. The event carried a tone of consummation as if they were new to each other. In a way, they were.

The act was not repeated for weeks because, after that, the paralysis took hold. They gave themselves grace to process, grieve, and adjust in their own ways. Julian began going to a particular coffee shop, where the woman serving the customers reminded him of Lena. He would order his coffee and catch glimpses of her, imagining that it was Lena herself—alive, healthy, happy. Watching her gave him a strange sense of peace. Then one morning she was no longer there. When she didn't return, he assumed she must have moved on to another job.

Sometimes, when he let himself fill with gratitude at the way the sun fell on him through the trees or at the way his breath filled and emptied his lungs as he ran, he thought of Lena and Darius and felt a searing shame and guilt. He would never know if he'd been the father of her unborn child; he would never know if Darius was lying in a desperate attempt to prevent Lena from leaving him behind. But he did know that had he and Emma never stepped into their lives, Lena would still be alive. How could it be possible that he could be here experiencing life like this right now, that he and Emma could have escaped so easily back into a life that appeared entirely unchanged? For months, he remained haunted, waking some nights with a pounding heart from visions of Lena falling, Emma falling, himself falling.

Emma pitched more articles to her editor. Soon, she was regularly offered assignments: smaller, manageable articles she could write while she worked on her more ambitious essay and narrative pitches. Julian didn't return to his paper. Instead, he took on a teaching role, finding an uncomplicated sense of accomplishment every time he was able to repackage and deliver a concept in such a way that the students' eyes lit up with comprehension. Hours and hours slipped by productively. Their work was their only source of momentum. In contrast, their relationship had entered a holding pattern. The issue was that to move forward together, they would need to move in the same direction. Julian, under the privacy of the duvet, scrolled through real estate websites for acreages, cottages, something with multiple bedrooms for guests—for potential future children. Emma traveled—weekend trips to

European cities to follow a story, interview someone, or write a review for the arts editor she'd started working closely with. She went to Edinburgh, then Rome, then somewhere else, then Rome again, coming and going under the guise of obligation and feigning regret at the distance it kept creating between them. But Julian knew that she must have pitched the idea in the first place or at least offered her availability. They were waiting, he supposed, for some external circumstance to deal the fatal blow, to finally waste the last of their spirit. Eventually, the end came in an undramatic way: with quiet tears and grim acceptance, they spoke and held each other on the couch for hours. Then Emma simply packed a bag and left.

"There isn't anything left to be said between us," Julian concluded. "And you know, maybe she doesn't even want to be reminded of—"

"I just don't understand!" Desi burst out, startling Julian so that all his thoughts fled like birds from a tree. He understood immediately that they'd arrived at the specific point that Desi had been working her way toward: his and Emma's separation.

"I thought you would've got back together by now!" she cried. "You've been through so much together! How did this happen?"

"It's actually pretty simple. We wanted different things, and we couldn't reconcile it."

From the corner of his eye, he could see Desi looking at him with a mournful expression on her face, as if she disapproved of his answer but had no power to change it. It was so easy for her to view them from the outside and lament the fact that they didn't get back together. He didn't fault her for it; he'd do the exact same thing if she and Camilla ever parted ways.

"It's just . . . sometimes I worry about you all alone in your cottage," she admitted. "You're not a solitary person, Julian."

"*Julian?*" He laughed. "You must really be worried."

She frowned at him again.

He stopped walking and turned to her. "If you keep looking at me like I have a terminal illness, I'm going to get straight back on the train."

"No, no, don't do that." She grabbed him by the arm.

"What if I told you that I'm genuinely, truly enjoying my life? Would you even believe me?" He shook his arm free of her claw-like grip. "Because I am. I'm slowly restoring the cottage. I find teaching rewarding. I'm happy."

"I would believe you—I *do* believe you—"

"Well, then, stop worrying about me, or Emma for that matter. We're okay, both of us." He thought of the last weeks of their relationship: the stalemate of cold silence. "We're better, even."

Desi said nothing.

Julian hovered over a decision before making up his mind. "And I'm not entirely alone," he said. "I've met someone."

Desi's face lit up. "Really?"

"Her name's Lydia. She lives in the village. She's an artist—landscapes. She's excellent, actually."

"That's great! How did you two meet?"

"She has a gallery in the village. I saw her art first—in the window. Then I went inside, and that's when I saw her."

Desi's phone began to ring, and she pulled it out of her pocket. "Shit, sorry," she murmured, making an apologetic face at Julian as she answered and wandered away from him. "Yes? No. No. No."

He stood for a moment, looking out in the direction of

Primrose Hill, thinking of Lydia laughing and clomping around in his garden wearing a pair of his boots. Then, another image of her delivering coffee to him in bed wearing nothing. He lingered there.

"They need me back at the office." Desi sighed, returning to his side and sliding her phone away. "Oh, but I want to hear all about her!" she whined. "Why don't you stay with us tonight? In the guest room? Camilla would be so excited. You could get the train back tomorrow. *Please.*"

Julian laughed. "Okay, okay."

"Great." She hugged him. "Just head over whenever. Go through the gate. Camilla will be in the greenhouse." She was already walking backward away from him. "I'll be there at seven. But if you want to go now, Camilla will make you tea. Tell her about Lydia." She wriggled her eyebrows suggestively before turning away. "Bye," she called behind her. He watched her walk away, her phone pressed back against her ear.

He laughed affectionately at the vision of her, people parting around him as they passed. Then he turned and walked on.


After stowing her suitcase overhead, Emma placed her notebook, novel, and phone on the table in front of her and slid into her seat, releasing a sigh. She'd made it, but, given that the train was already preparing to leave St. Pancras, only just. She imagined explaining to the arts editor that she'd missed her train to Paris and, as a result, would miss the appointment that she'd taken ridiculous lengths to secure. She would not be exclusively interviewing Agathe, the ninety-two-year-old fifth-generation shoemaker whose signature boot design had been copied without her permission, reproduced in a factory, and had revived single-handedly the sales of a celebrity's fashion house that had recently—until now—failed to catch the interest of the public for nearly four seasons in a row.

It was Emma's decision to stop at the sandwich shop that she hadn't accounted for. She pulled the sandwich out of her handbag and set it on the table before her. Pickle and cheese. A symbolic selection, but only partially, seeing as it objectively remained her favorite. As she'd rushed to buy it and then dashed off to departures, she hadn't even had time to consider the meaning. Looking at it now as the train tentatively began to move, she thought of Julian, then of Athens, then of Lena. All morning, she'd pushed down the knowledge that it had happened exactly a year ago, but she knew the moment she sat still, it would return. Few circumstances encouraged deep pondering more than a train ride that extended for many empty and expansive hours.

She stopped fiddling with the packaging of the sandwich and picked up her phone, scrolling back to find the message thread between her and Julian. They'd last exchanged messages a month ago. Briefly and politely, he'd congratulated her on the new feature she had written, and she'd congratulated him on the progress of his cottage. *Thanks, Em x* was the last message. She'd taken the opportunity to gracefully end the conversation there.

She typed out a message.

*It felt weird not to message you today,* she began. *Although it feels weird to message you too. I didn't know whether to acknowledge what today represented. I don't know whether we have some responsibility to each other in that way. I suppose that's up to us. How do you feel about it?*

She contemplated how to continue the message, trying to

determine whether she even needed to send it. At times, as they'd attempted unsuccessfully to return to their lives in London, Emma had wanted to discuss Lena and Darius and all the many decisions that had led to the accident, but she knew Julian felt the weight of reliving it more acutely than she did, and so she began to defer to him. To avoid ambushing him, she stopped instigating conversations about it altogether. Besides Desi and Alistair, they told none of their friends or family. Even Alistair received an abridged version that left out the details of Lena's pregnancy. Emma couldn't stand to imagine the story spilling forth and being altered, exaggerated, as it spread. The thought of someone she didn't know gasping over their wine and small plates as the story was retold made her feel sick. This decision meant they only had each other to talk to, and when, over time, Emma began to feel that Julian no longer wished to discuss it at all, the experience became like a rock fastened to her ankle: something she must drag into the future with her.

In the first weeks upon their return to London, Emma had experienced a sudden racing heartbeat or, occasionally, a strong palpitation as if her heart were tumbling down from her rib cage. She knew these physical symptoms originated from the guilt and shame she was repressing to shield Julian. In her desperation to release her thoughts, she'd met with Desi in a café near Desi's office. Although it was not her intention, Emma immediately began to cry, confessing her darkest feeling: that she felt responsible for Lena's death. Desi had received the outburst gamely, her lips pulling into a tight frown as she stroked Emma's hand.

"It was an accident," she kept repeating. "Nobody's fault."

"No, Desi," Emma eventually cried. "I don't want to be

absolved—I want to be punished. I need to be punished so I can start to move on."

Desi was out of her depth then, her face furrowed with unease, and Emma realized that nobody available to her was likely to understand her feelings. They were even less likely to provide her with the means for atonement she was looking for.

After that point, she buried herself in deadlines and sought penance by severing herself from Julian's affection. He was hurt and confused, she knew, but she was undeserving of his love, undeserving even of the arguments he would attempt to make to challenge her belief.

Was there any point in bringing it up again now, a year later, and forcing the memories upon him? Hadn't they agreed time and time again, when they were still together and still hoping to work through it all, that they needed to stop trying to find meaning in Lena's death? It would never make sense.

Maybe it would be better for them both if she didn't re-open the conversation. Maybe she was right that he wouldn't want to be reminded now. He hadn't messaged her after all, and that was a sign that he didn't want to talk about it.

They rarely spoke to each other now. The last time she saw him was a couple of months after they finally separated when he'd invited her over to collect the last of her things from his flat. He'd just sold it and was moving into a limestone cottage on an acreage in Oxfordshire, a process that had taken a couple of months and so had given him time to grow accustomed to the reality that he was leaving his London home. She, however, was blindsided by the sight of the hollowed-out flat. It was entirely stripped of evidence they'd ever lived there. Sunlight, now undeflected by their furniture, cast complete and solid shapes on the floors. She stood bewildered in the empty living room, unprepared for the abject feeling of failure that overcame her. At that moment, she wondered if they'd really meant it when they attempted to return to each other across the chasm between their diverging paths. Had they *truly* exhausted the option of finding some habitable midway place? When faced with the erasure of their life together—the reality that their love for each other had left no mark on the physical world—it seemed like a cruel and unjust end. Perhaps a compromise had simply been left undiscovered. She felt this despite knowing that there was no middle ground between parenthood and a childless future. She'd become emotional then, tears surging in her eyes. It was Julian's turn to stand bewildered. She didn't tell him she was mourning their relationship all over again nearly four months after it had ended. She was embarrassed by the thought of him reading into it some deep regret, some desire to reconnect, when that wasn't what she wanted. She kept apologizing while he found her some tissues. He didn't know what to say. They hugged for a moment. Then she collected her things, made up some pressing appointment, and left.

Soon, Emma's train emerged out of the dark London tunnels, crossed the marshes of the Thames, and was submerged once again before it reached the contrasting brightness of North Kent. She put her phone back down on the table and looked out of the window. Though the scenery was shifting from industrial to green, the view was nothing special. She only took it in because she knew that it would soon transition into darkness as they passed through the Channel Tunnel. Emma looked at the sky—blue today, optimistic and expansive. It was only as she thought back to how she felt after leaving the flat for the last time, as she climbed onto the bus, teary and clutching her box of belongings, that she realized she no longer carried the heaviness. She didn't need to message Julian because he didn't need her to. They no longer needed anything from each other except perhaps the occasional wave from across the expanse. She picked up her phone and deleted the message. She would wave another day.

# ACKNOWLEDGMENTS

I would like to thank Clio Seraphim, Leila Tejani, Genevieve Buzo, Alex Craig, Pippa Masson, Andrianna deLone, and everyone at The Dial Press, Random House, Allen & Unwin, Curtis Brown Australia, and Creative Artists Agency who has helped to guide this book along. Special mention to the hardworking copyeditors who make every draft immeasurably better. I've been so fortunate to work alongside so many wonderful people on this journey so far.

Thank you to early readers who provided wisdom and encouragement: Benjamin Stevenson, Chloe Elisabeth Wilson, Andrianna deLone, and Pippa Masson.

The fierce advocacy of booksellers and readers left a lasting impact on me when I published my debut novel, *Search History*. I'm so grateful for every single mention and recommendation— thank you, thank you, thank you.

Teddy, thank you for keeping me company through the

final months of editing this book (and thanks for occasionally giving me a kick—literally—to remind me of the bigger picture).

Chris, every book begins and ends with you—I'm very lucky.

# ABOUT THE AUTHOR

AMY TAYLOR is a writer based in Melbourne (Naarm). Her debut novel, *Search History,* was published in 2023.

Instagram: @amy_ester_

*Books Driven by the Heart*

## Sign up for our newsletter and find more you'll love:

**thedialpress.com**

@THEDIALPRESS

@THEDIALPRESS

Penguin Random House collects and processes your
personal information. See our Notice at Collection
and Privacy Policy at prh.com/notice.